LET ME SEE IT

LET ME SEE IT

STORIES

James Magruder

TRIQUARTERLY BOOKS
NORTHWESTERN UNIVERSITY PRESS
EVANSTON, ILLINOIS

TriQuarterly Books
Northwestern University Press
www.nupress.northwestern.edu

The following stories have appeared, sometimes in different form, in the following
publications: "Prologue" in *Mary*; "Tenochtitlán" in *Subtropics* and *New Stories from the
Midwest*; "Use Your Head" in *Bloom* and www.reduxlitjournal.com; "Treasure Map" in the
anthology *Boy Crazy*; "Elliott Biddler's Vie Bohème" (as "Matthew Aiken's Vie Bohème")
in *New England Review*; "Hootchie Mamas" (as "Roadhouse Dollies") in *The Harrington Gay
Men's Fiction Quarterly*; "You've Really Learned How" in *The Gettysburg Review*; "Buccellati"
in *Bloom*; "Elbow and Legs" in *The Normal School*; and "Let Me See It" (as "Very Lambert
Strether") in *Subtropics*.

Printed in the United States of America

10   9   8   7   6   5   4   3   2   1

Library of Congress Cataloging-in-Publication Data

Magruder, James, 1960– author.
    Let me see it : stories / James Magruder.
      pages cm
    ISBN 978-0-8101-5244-1 (pbk. : alk. paper)
    I. Title.
    PS3613.A3473L48 2014
    813.6—dc23
                                2013046188

for Steve Bolton,
who heard every word

CONTENTS

Prologue   1

Tenochtitlán   3

Use Your Head   23

Treasure Map   39

Elliott Biddler's Vie Bohème   51

Hootchie Mamas   67

You've Really Learned How   87

Mistress of the Revels   111

Buccellati   129

Elbow and Legs   149

Let Me See It   165

Acknowledgments   191

LET ME SEE IT

PROLOGUE

2008

Tom Amelio's aunt Ruth has begun sending him small stuffed animals, the promotional tie-in kind thrown last minute into bags of fast food. This past Christmas, she sent him three animals and a knife. It was an eight-inch folding blade that commemorated the Battle of Fredericksburg, with a medallion in relief of Robert E. Lee glued into the butt of the handle. His aunt, Tom knew, had grown up in Fredericksburg in a white clapboard house that had served as a Confederate hospital after the battle. As a child, she was told stories about ghosts and names written in blood in the attic of the old house fronting the Rappahannock River.

Aunt Ruth doesn't wrap the stuffed animals. They arrive safe in their plastic pouches, but the Christmas knife came wrapped in an empty box of biscuit mix. The lid was Scotch-taped shut and the crinkled piece of block-printed gift paper was clearly a reuse. The knife zipped out of a black leatherette crescent. Dangling from the end of the zipper was a small tag shaped like an animal pelt and stamped with a gold-leafed guarantee of authenticity. General Lee's portrait was painted in gray, pink, and black enamel.

Tom doesn't believe in past lives, or rather, he hasn't read up enough on the subject to take anything but a neutral position, but his first cousin Elliott Biddler, the last time Tom saw him, in Paris, had said that he had always supposed, for laughs, that he had to have been one of Belle

Watling's girls in *Gone with the Wind*. Elliott said he had been hot his entire life for white southern men: old, young, lumpy, wiry, gay, straight, the Boo Radleys and the Rhett Butlers and every bubba in between. He loved how generations of unmongrelized Scots-Irish blood showed in their bony faces, in their long arms, square fingernails, lank hair, and deep-set eyes. Moreover, they were polite, they knew how to have a good time, and let us never forget the molasses drawl and their access to authentic idiom. Elliott confessed that southern men made him hot because he found something sexy about sleeping with the direct descendants of the doomed boys in gray.

Tom is not southern, and is hardly a Biddler, as far as that goes. In 1954 his mother, Janet Mary Biddler, married Alphonse Amelio, a Korean War vet who became a butcher. The Biddler side turns up in the wedding album, unsmilingly so, but people wore more sober faces for photos then. There was no overt rift; Tom's mother had married down, down and out. The Amelios stayed put on the Kansas side of Kansas City, while Aunt Ruth and Uncle Henry and the three cousins seemed to move every other year. Gypsy feet, Tom's father would sigh, transcribing another new return address from his in-laws' Christmas card envelope. He thought cousins should know their cousins.

If, in his thank-you note, Tom were to ask his aunt Ruth, whom he's met only a handful of times, why she had sent him a lobster, a bunny, a turtle, and a Robert E. Lee knife for Christmas, he imagines her saying that he ought to take more of an interest in where he came from. He knows her gifts are meant for her son Elliott, long gone. Tom expects Elliott would have had a field day parsing preconscious motives on his mother's part—a bent for southern men, Ruth might be warning Tom, could kill him in the end too.

Tom is forty-eight years old, with his own mother to parse. He does not want to make a funny story about how his aunt sent him a knife and three stuffed animals for Christmas. Tom doesn't make funny stories. That was Elliott's job.

TENOCHTITLÁN

ELLIOTT

1971

After getting an A+ for my "Western United States" salt map, eleven colored states covering three square feet of plywood, I wanted to make a historical building out of sugar cubes. But Miss Vojta said we had to work in pairs for the next project, and I was odd man out in the pack of five I ran with. Brian and Doug and Kurt and Pat didn't take social studies seriously.

I moped about this to my mother, who was making pepper steak. She wiggled the meat slugs she took from the lake of flour on the counter and leaned back when they hit the oil in the skillet. The velvet bow nesting in her upswept hair, plus the ball of black panty hose sitting in front of her purse on the telephone desk, meant she had a date. She was rushing dinner, and it was her evening purse, so I guessed it was an older man driving out from downtown Chicago. Somebody Mrs. Shestak knew, probably.

My mother reached over the stove for more flour, then, eyeing the dusty canister and her dress, hesitated. "What about Lisa Montalbano? She's no dummy."

"She's a girl," I said, appalled by her stupidity.

I moved in for the rescue. I swung a little cupful of flour in a wide arc around her back and slowly tipped it out onto the waxed paper. A trickle of watery blood from the package of meat was snaking into the flour like a bend of the Colorado River on my salt map.

My mother tilted her head toward the window over the sink, and her beads slid under the pucker of her satin collar. "Donnie Keller's in your class, isn't he?"

"I guess."

"What do you mean, 'you guess'? He is or he isn't, Elliott."

The Kellers lived behind us, and two houses to the left. I looked through the stained-glass mushroom ornament hanging in the kitchen window. There was a stand of old trees separating the back lots, but since it was winter, I was able to pick out the Kellers' deck through the branches. Mr. Keller hadn't brought in their barbecue kettle, and there was a car tire propped against the built-in deck bench.

My mother pushed the rotating corner cabinet with her foot and plucked off a bottle of soy sauce as it spun by. The cabinet was one of my favorite things about this house, where we had lasted almost two years.

I said I didn't like pepper steak.

"It's your brother's favorite."

My brother, Frank, was playing hockey on the subdivision pond. I wanted to hear "It's one of your father's favorites," as if saying it, plus the gingery fragrance spiraling through the vents in the lid of the electric skillet, could draw him home from his bachelor pad in Oak Brook, where he joked that the stewardesses lay thick as thieves around the indoor pool.

"Am I going to get to meet him?" I asked.

It would be too dark out to spy on her date from my bedroom window as he clicked up the flagstone steps. Frank didn't seem to care who rang the doorbell for my mother on Friday and Saturday nights. My sister, Tracy, was too little to understand the finer details of our parents' trial separation.

"Not until the third date, Elbow," she said, making dinner hiss as she added the pepper strips. "If there is one," she added.

I opened the silverware drawer to start on the table. My father's new forks had three tines, not four. His plates and glasses were square, the kind astronauts and *Love, American Style* characters used. The furniture in his apartment was bright and modern, not colonial. I pictured him rolling on the shaggy sheepskin rug in the living room with stewardesses flown up from the pool. Stationed behind his leather reading chair was a tall, curving floor lamp with seven separate light bulbs on their own stems. Their hot starburst eyes pointed the way to the Age of Aquarius and away from us.

The next morning, instead of cutting through the backyards, I walked the long way around to the Kellers'. The good cartoons were still on, so the streets were deserted. The mailboxes at the ends of the driveways had dropped their tongues to wait for lunch from the postman. It was January, and the cold pinched my earlobes. I'd swiped Frank's wool Green Bay Packers hat in case Donnie cared about sports.

He opened the door. Donnie Keller was the brown of gingersnaps, because his mother was Mexican. For that same reason he didn't have friends, but he did pay attention in class. One time I'd finished a multiplication speed drill, turned over my paper, and looked up to see that Donnie had finished ahead of me.

It was easier for both of us to pretend that my visit wasn't a surprise.

"Elliott," he said, hopping on the tile in his bare feet. "Come in."

At the sight of me, his little sister, Silvia, who had lost the race to the door, hung back in an archway sucking her thumb. She had no pajama bottoms on. I heard the blur of rapid channel switching. Donnie yelled to his other sister, Regina, to change it back to *Jonny Quest*. He ran into the living room—the wrong place for a television—and they started arguing in Spanish. That was strange enough; even more surprising was that no parent shushed them from the top of the stairs when the knob came off the TV and Regina started screaming. The rule was, dads slept in on Saturdays, and no waking them up.

The only other piece of furniture in the living room was a bare-legged yellow sofa heaped with stacks of Hot Wheels track. Regina, halfway through a frozen waffle, had been watching TV on a green plastic bag spilling white foam peanuts. A jagged section of waffle was sticking to a comic book on the floor. My mother wouldn't have known what to tackle first.

Donnie showed me the rest of the downstairs. The Kellers' four-bedroom Ginger Creek house was as big as anybody's, but it was so empty of things, our voices echoed as we followed the dirty foot trails in the tan, wall-to-wall carpet. The windows, smeary with fingerprints, had no shades or curtains. Towels, sweaters, and pants tangled up in balls, and orphaned socks were dropped all over the house, like markers to missing chairs, tables, love seats, buffets, and credenzas. I began worrying that the Kellers slept in piles of rags or, worse, wood shavings like my hamster, Jethro. My mother was proud of her decorations, the crewel kit Liberty Bell and Flag House wall hangings, the wooden grenadiers and painted plaster drummer boys that traveled with us from house to house, but the Keller walls were empty. A pair of candlesticks and three clay pots on the den mantel were the only knickknacks on the whole first floor.

We found Mrs. Keller in the basement, grinding corn in a stone bowl. The dryer boomed behind her, keeping time with the knock of her pestle dripping with golden slush. Darker than Donnie, with thick eyebrows, she looked like a picture in my geography workbook. He introduced us, and she bent to cup my face in her hands; her shiny black hair parted around her arms like a pair of curtains. She had a firm belly, and her nipples bumped out under her T-shirt like chewed gum wads. She said something in Spanish, and Donnie said, "English, Mamá." Still smiling, she pressed her fingertips into her lips. I couldn't guess her secret, unless maybe Mr. Keller was asleep in the crawl space behind the utility sink.

Regina and Silvia were watching a girl cartoon, so we went up to Donnie's room. His bed had a racing-car spread, and there was a map of Latin America hanging over his desk. I brought up the social studies project and explained sugar cube houses. I had been leaning toward the Governor's Mansion in colonial Williamsburg, the symmetry and stateliness of which had impressed me in an issue of *Smithsonian*, but since it was his room, I let Donnie go first. Clapping his hands, he said that we should build the Templo Mayor de Tenochtitlán.

"Show me," I said, buzzed by the twisty sounds in the words. Donnie ran down the hall for something, and I took the opportunity to shuck my sweater. I'd noticed that their dining room thermostat stood at eighty, fourteen degrees higher than the setting at our house.

He came back with the *T* volume of the *World Book*.

"That's our encyclopedia," I said, like it had flown over the trees between our yards and into his hands. "Where did you get that?"

"My parents' bedroom."

An encyclopedia in a bedroom—like a waffle on the floor. Our *World Book* was kept in a den cabinet, so that we could all get at it for homework.

The Aztecs had built the Templo Mayor, or Great Pyramid, of Tenochtitlán. It wasn't smooth like an Egyptian pyramid; it was a double trapezoid with jagged stairs going up like crocodile teeth, or the edge of a saw. Donnie said that it wasn't a tomb, like for the pharaohs. The Aztecs used their pyramid to get the sun to rise every morning, feeding their gods dripping human hearts in front of a miniature temple on top. They put the hearts in the Jaguar Bowl. Donnie pronounced it "Yah-gwar" until I made him spell it out.

What with the Jaguar Bowl and the *tzompantli*, or "skull rack," decorations on the sacrificial platform, Tenochtitlán was another A+ project for sure. We could spray paint the pyramid yellow. For the temple roof we could glue milk straws to cardboard. We could make trees out of brown pipe cleaners and Easter basket grass, and I could press my skull ring into modeling clay for the *tzompantli*. The first practical step would be to swipe a board from behind the construction trailer down the street. But first Donnie taught me how to pronounce "Tenochtitlán," then "Tehuantepec," "Quetzalcóatl," and "Huitzilopochtli." By the time I had to go home, we had tied sweaters around our waists for warrior skirts and had made a little dance out of the names, chanting in circles around his room with flat arm movements and profile heads.

No, his dad wasn't asleep, I explained to my mother, who was doing bills at the telephone desk. She had a thousand questions, starting with the handmade tortillas we ate for lunch. In her universe, tacos were corn shells that came in a kit with spice packets, so she didn't believe me when I insisted that Mrs. Keller's were fresh and floppy.

"Was there a car in the garage?" she asked.

"We didn't go in the garage."

"You went everywhere else."

"I hate cars."

She always forgot this. Brian and Doug and Kurt and Pat covered their notebooks with STP decals and drawings of giant mag wheels. They spent their allowances on the latest Hot Wheels and their free time building hot rod models. I stuck to monsters. Of the four essential monsters, my order of preference went: Dracula, the Wolf Man, Frankenstein, the Mummy. Dracula was best because he could talk and fly. Slow and silent, with only one usable arm, the Mummy was stupid. I kept my painted Dracula model on my nightstand next to my lamp and watched his phosphorescent head and hands glow in the dark after lights-out. Donnie's favorite, he said, was the Wolf Man. That made sense, because he was brown too.

Without saying so—she didn't have to—my mother was trying to find out whether Mr. and Mrs. Keller had split up. Divorces were happening all around the Ginger Creek subdivision in 1971 and Mrs. Shestak, who wore psychedelic minidresses and frosted her hair, kept track. My father had left us eight months ago, right after my tonsils came out. The tonsils part I remember because I had woken up in the middle of the night with a sore throat and heard my mother shouting, "Go to her then, just go to her!" I sipped ginger ale on my nightstand and listened to Jethro race in his wheel. Before I fell back asleep, I had decided that "her" meant my grandmother in Pittsburgh, but that same weekend, when Frank, bawling like I'd never seen, asked my father why he was leaving us, I stared at the black hockey puck on my brother's bedspread like it was the button to push for the Name of Her.

Now my father had a mustache and a Capricorn medallion, and he came every Saturday from Oak Brook and took us out in shifts, first Tracy for a hamburger and an ice cream sundae, then Frank and me for pizza. I'd pick off the oily pepperoni discs and line them up to drain on my napkin.

"Did Donnie say what his father does for a living?"

"No," I lied, bored with the conversation. Mr. Keller was a journalist. Donnie had shown me an article about sharks in a science magazine with the name Warner Keller in cursive under the title. "I don't even know what he looks like."

"He's a good-looking man," said my mother.

That was a strange comment. "How would you know?" I asked.

"I met them at a party when they moved in." She paused to tear a check from the book. "His eyes are ice blue. He looks very white. But that's probably because she's so dark."

I remembered the tiny, feathered hairs edging the sides of Mrs. Keller's forehead. She'd put her elbows on the table and eaten four soft tacos with us.

"She's not *black*, Mom. She's just Mexican." I stomped off toward my room.

"I know perfectly well what she is, Elbow."

"Don't call me that." The short version of my grandmother's nickname for me, Elliott le Beau, the Handsome Prince of Somewhere French, was Elbow. We called my brother Legs, because of all the sports he played. He and I didn't get along one bit.

"And take something from the steps if you're going up."

This she said ten times a day. Flush to the staircase spokes was an endless inventory of school papers, doll clothes, crayons, clean laundry, and bathroom supplies. Just like I did with my father's stewardess jokes, I ignored my mother when she said she wanted a rancher for her next house. If he didn't come back—they were only separated—we'd have to move again, this time to someplace so small I'd have to share a bedroom with Frank, which would be a disaster. Ginger Creek was an expensive subdivision, and divorced kids disappeared every summer.

From the hallway I remembered to ask about her date. I heard a rubber band snap around a stack of envelopes. "Older than Moses," she said.

I jumped to the fourth step on the stairs. I loved that she told me things like this. Sometimes she called me "my little listener." I liked that better than Elbow.

"What's his name?"

"Davis. He owns a catamaran," she said.

I asked her what that was.

"Look it up," she said, knowing I would.

Young and mod in white lace-up boots and midi skirts, and Swedish like the tanning secret, Miss Vojta was the best fifth grade teacher to have at Bel Air Elementary. In conference at her desk, she suggested an easier sugar cube project, but Donnie's excitement, his suave repetitions of "Tenochtitlán," won her over, too. I nodded whenever she looked my way; I think she was counting on me to make it happen. From the corner of my eye, I saw Pat smirking with Doug.

My good grades made my spot in the pecking order shaky, but I couldn't just ignore Donnie in the coatroom after the bell rang for morning recess. He timed his question about where to buy glue so we'd still be talking as we approached the four-square court.

Pat, in A square, was mashing the ball against his hip. Donnie got in front of me in line without being invited to play. He had nothing to lose, even if I did; Pat, oddly, didn't make a federal case out of it, just stamped a heel on the asphalt and pulverized the squiggles of dried mud that fell from his treads.

Working together, Pat and Doug knocked Kurt out of B square. Donnie stepped into D. He turned out to be good and eliminated Doug and Brian almost immediately. Our white hands turned red and purple in the cold, but Donnie's, weaving at the end of windbreaker sleeves short in the wrists, were brown and limber. He was excellent at fake-outs. Some girls, noticing the change in the lineup, even came to watch.

Donnie avoided knocking Pat out until the glory of A square got too hard to resist. It made sense that Pat, when he lost, would decide to bounce the ball off Donnie's head and start the Frito Bandito song. By the time Mr. Arnold pulled them apart, Donnie had a split lip and Pat had pushed things further by calling him a Mexican, making it sound dirtier than any swear word.

My turn came at lunch. My mother had packed egg salad that day, easy to jump on. Pat made fun of its fart smell and made me throw it in the trash. It would be a tough climb out of the hole, and Pat, by keeping silent himself, let Kurt and Brian and Doug know that laughing at my television commercial imitations, at my "I vant to suck your blood" routine, and all the other methods I'd devised to make and keep friends in all the schools I'd passed through since kindergarten, was out of the question.

I stared at the folded paper triangle passing from Doug to Kurt, their index fingers and pinkies spread at the edge of the table as goalposts.

Leaving the table before the bell rang could mean permanent expulsion, and even though I was runt of the litter, I'd worked hard for my spot.

Pat suddenly shut the lid to his lunch box. "Hey, Biddler," he said. "What was the name of that thing you're going to make with Frito Bandito?"

"Tenochtitlán," I replied, slurring the syllables to show I didn't care. Donnie, still in his windbreaker, was sitting all by himself at one of the fourth grade tables.

"It's a temple for human sacrifices," I added, thinking gore might interest him. "The Aztecs cut out their victims' hearts and burned them in a bowl."

Pat shook the crumbs out of a box of pretzel sticks onto his tongue, then sucked his cheeks. Doug and Kurt kept flicking the paper football back and forth. "Ten-knock-titties," Pat finally said.

They all laughed, itching to repeat it, while I slid a foot onto Pat's tight-rope. If I played it wrong, I might be rewarded with a terrible, enduring nickname.

"That's right," I said, agreeing to everything. "Ten-knock-titties."

My mother closed the pocket doors to the living room, but I could still hear her in there with Mrs. Shestak. The pocket doors were another cool feature of the Ginger Creek house; I would pretend I was a butler and say things to my sister like "Shall we go into the drawing room?" Tracy was out with my father. To kill time until he came for Frank and me, I'd gotten on my knees in the den and started finger-combing the tassels on the oval floor rug. When I'd worked my way to the sliding glass door, I pushed the curtain open and looked for lights on at the Kellers'. I pictured Donnie sitting cross-legged in their empty dining room, watching our board dry. We had hauled it from the construction pile and hosed the dirt off the day before. We put it in the exact center of the room, under the chandelier. Then we stacked ten boxes of sugar cubes into a 4-3-2-1 pyramid. Two bottles of glue and two jars of green tempera paint for the grass stood guard in the corners.

"A sack of corn in the pantry, Helen," my mother was saying to Mrs. Shestak. "And next to nothing in the cabinets. He's been gone three weeks, and she says he hasn't called since last Tuesday." Mrs. Shestak had come over because, after a run to the grocery store for the cubes, my mother had gone with me into the Keller house.

"Booze?"

"None anywhere. I checked."

Mrs. Shestak murmured something I couldn't hear. From the location of her voice, I guessed she was sunk into the new love seat. My mother had only recently revealed to me that the supersoft blue-and-cream love seat was another ploy to keep my father interested in his family. New furniture made less sense to me than the Christmas we got skis, which we used twice, or our cocker spaniel, Duffy, who still needed housebreaking. Frank and my mother scrapped all the time about the piddle papers in the basement. I sided with her, because Frank had definitely reneged on his promise to walk Duffy twice a day.

"I did, and she told me he wouldn't *let* them go to church. That was the only time she cried."

"Mexicans are very Catholic," said Mrs. Shestak. "Can't she go when he's out of town, find a priest to help?"

"I told you they don't have a car."

They started murmuring again. I crept back to the pocket doors and pressed my ear against the wood. I heard my mother flick the lamp on the marble-top credenza. Dusk had settled in, so she'd be drawing the sheers after that, another homing signal for her wandering husband.

"Oh my god, Ruth," Mrs. Shestak said loudly. "Drugs."

"Helen! You don't know that."

"An American journalist brings his family up here from Mexico because of the police—he disappears all the time, the money comes and goes—and it's not drugs?"

I rolled back onto the rug. In the Age of Aquarius, drugs, like stewardesses, were on every adult mind. A high school nurse had made a special trip to Bel Air Elementary to show the fourth, fifth, and sixth graders a marijuana movie. I'd spent a couple of recesses imitating the pot freak-outs for laughs, and then we all forgot about it.

I loosened the laces on my good shoes. Even though it was just pizza, my mother had made me put on a dress shirt. I didn't mind. My father's car came up the driveway, and I stuffed my thumbs in my ears for show. It killed me that he rang the doorbell to his own house.

We were Catholic too, so Mrs. Shestak assigned the Kellers to us. That Sunday, my sister, my mother, and I, plus Donnie, Regina, Silvia, and Mrs. Keller, piled into our station wagon and went to St. Elizabeth's. Frank had spent the night with my father in Oak Brook after a Blackhawks game and would lord it over me later.

The Keller girls shivered in their frilly dresses, so starched they poofed up like white octopus heads when they sat in the pew. Mrs. Keller's bizarrely long veil and big, glittering rings seemed to lend her devotional superpowers. She shook her clasped hands over each shoulder like a prizefighter as she prayed loudly in Spanish, bowing her head lower than anybody's, the swings of her arms gigantic as she crossed herself and thumped her heart. During the "peace be with you" greeting—the absolute worst moment in Mass—she clutched me and kissed me through her veil. Donnie, on the far side of my mother, reached behind her skirt to squeeze my hand in peace. "They're very free with themselves," I could imagine my mother saying to Mrs. Shestak.

Tenochtitlán presented an initial engineering problem. Using solid layers of cubes would waste time and materials, but the whole thing would collapse if there was no interior support as we built upward. I thought that crafting a set of graduated cardboard boxes to put inside the walls—a smaller pyramid inside the notched, exterior steps—might make it more stable. Donnie didn't understand the kind of light cardboard I meant, so I asked him whether his dad wore white shirts to work.

He took me into his parents' bedroom. The wood floor was cool on my bare feet, and there was a smell of incense, fainter than at the Chess King, where Frank bought his bell-bottoms. When my eyes got used to the dark, I discovered the missing furniture. A row of four bureaus blocked the windows. Two carved chests sat on top of them, with books stuck under the legs at the uneven places. The rest of the books, dozens of them, were stacked from the chests to the ceiling. Armchairs and ottomans lined the wall on both sides of the bed. A tier of coffee tables covered with arrangements of urns, quartz figurines, and painted clay birds clung to the opposite wall like a giant wedding altar. It was like the picture of the Chamber of the Pharaohs in the *World Book*.

"We got robbed a lot in Mexico City," whispered Donnie. The puff of his breath on my neck made me feel like an explorer, or like Jonny Quest on a dangerous mission with Hadji.

The bed glowed like a clearing in a jungle. Floating to the floor from a ring in the ceiling was a lace tent. The spread and the bed skirt were embroidered with twisting green vines and blue and red flowers. The head-board was scrolled iron; its center pointed up to a silver sunburst mirror. Yellow velvet bolsters, like rolls of butterscotch candy, guarded two rows of snow-white pillows. There were red and blue candles on the nightstands.

"How do you get in?" I breathed.

Donnie parted the curtains at the foot of the bed and waited.

I took a step toward the entrance, half expecting the flock of painted birds to swoop in ahead of me. Donnie's brown arms seemed to drink in the lace as it fluttered against them. I saw a white body and a brown body clasped together, rolling on the flowers in the center.

"Cardboard," I said suddenly.

All well and good that the Kellers had bureaus and knickknacks, but my mother said that you can't eat coffee tables. So it came to pass, after a few weeks, that the price of admission to see the jungle bed, a trip I now needed to take every time I went over to Donnie's, was a bag of groceries left for me at the bottom of the stairs. The first time I was instructed to tell Mrs. Keller that they were pantry holdovers that shouldn't go to waste. True enough—the tins of smoked oysters and vienna sausages, the dusty cans of succotash and boxes of popover mix, had been with us for at least two houses. But then my mother started sending over hot dogs, blocks of cheese, oatmeal packets, lunch meat, cans of kidney beans and peaches and frozen orange juice, and finally, when Aurora Keller's fourth pregnancy was confirmed, boxes of powdered milk. Real milk, she tried to explain to me, would be charity.

Donnie hated these offerings. I think he pretended I was leaving a book bag in the kitchen chair and wouldn't acknowledge my presence until I was kneeling beside him next to Tenochtitlán in the dining room. He hummed, eyes closed, over the sound of his mother in the kitchen loudly blessing mine, La Santa Ruth of Ginger Creek, as she put away the groceries. One day in the cafeteria, he caught my eye from his solo spot at the fourth grade table and set aside his bologna and cheese sandwich. We weren't friends at school, but I liked to track where he was.

Our pyramid began its ascent. Donnie would dot glue on twenty cubes and hand them to me one by one. I'd lay them out. He didn't wear underpants. Whenever he leaned way over to shake the last cubes from a sugar box, I'd sneak looks at the start of his crack. Then we would switch, or cut more strips from Mr. Keller's shirt cardboard. When our necks got sore, we'd have whip fights with pieces of Hot Wheels track. Then we'd lie back and discuss the temple decorations for the top—would we make our warriors out of clay, or would we substitute red plastic Indians from the hobby shop? One day Donnie surprised me with a small copper disk, one of his mother's earrings. He said that if we painted the concave side with red nail polish and glued in some cinnamon Red Hots as hearts, we'd have the perfect Jaguar Bowl.

We were finishing the left staircase on the pyramid one night when the front door opened and the house caught fire with Mr. Keller's greeting. Donnie got to him first. He leaped and locked his legs around his father's waist, then kissed him right on the mouth. His squealing sisters pulled their father to the floor by his arms. Mr. Keller was happy to let them cover him with fists and legs and feet. His wife patiently waited between his two suitcases.

I flattened against a wall. Friends left when dads came home, but I couldn't slip out. Adjusting to their thermostat, I had taken to dropping my own ball of socks, sweater, and school shirt just beyond the dining room archway.

Before he could greet his wife, Mr. Keller had spotted El Templo Mayor. He got up on his hands and knees. Silvia swiveled onto his back for a short ride to the pyramid.

"Who's this?" he asked, noticing me at last.

"That's my friend Elliott," said Donnie.

"Hello, Elliott."

I nodded, unable to speak. Like my mother said, Mr. Keller was good-looking. He had bright blue eyes, like the picture of a timber wolf I'd cut out of *Ranger Rick* and put on my bulletin board. His hair was so blond, his head glowed pink underneath. His chin was split like a white apricot, and he had a small gap between his front teeth.

"We're making Tenochtitlán out of sugar cubes," Donnie said.

"So I see," said Mr. Keller. They had the same dimples. "Very cool."

"I have to go home," I stammered.

While I fumbled with my socks, Mr. Keller told us that the Pyramid of Huitzilopochtli had originally sat on an island in the middle of Lake Texcoco, and that the city, called the Venice of the New World, had been destroyed in the Spanish Conquest of 1521. I snuck a look at Mrs. Keller. Her hair switched back and forth behind her head while she braided it. The foot trail in the carpet in front of her was a stream, muddy but easy to cross.

I put my coat on. Donnie was wriggling on the floor on his back, the way Duffy did. His shirt had ridden up; the hollow of his navel was like the end of a cinnamon stick.

"Tomorrow, tell Miss Vojta that I'm sick," he said. "Right, Dad?"

Mr. Keller, steering me to the door with his hand on my shoulder, laughed.

"Elliott! Elliott! Tell her I have a bad sore throat."

As we passed Mrs. Keller, I heard a sharp intake of breath. Before the front door closed, I thought I heard them come together with a moan. Maybe a house didn't need so much furniture.

"What does Helen think?"

"Don't call her that, honey. Call her Mrs. Shestak."

"What does *she* think?"

"She thinks I owe Davis another chance, because it wasn't his party."

"Okay then, give him one," I said loudly, so she could hear from the walk-in closet. I took her detachable rhinestone shoe buckles from their place on the first tier in her jewelry box. I put them over my eyebrows and leaned into the vanity mirror. It looked stupid.

My mother was dressing for date number four with Davis, the tax attorney who lived on the twenty-third floor of Lake Point Towers, an address that made him rich enough to get another chance, no matter how old and crusty he might be. This time I was permitted to say hello. I'd already filled a little crystal bowl with cashews and set out the scotch for their drinks. I'd also plumped the cushions on the love seat and drawn the pocket doors for privacy.

I had done my research. A catamaran is a twin-hulled sailboat the two parts of which are connected by a deck. I checked for one at the hobby shop where I bought monster model kits, but they only carried battleships and the *Niña*, *Pinta*, and *Santa María*. My mother had been explaining to me that someone had passed her a funny-smelling cigarette at the party Davis had taken her to on date number three. "Marijuana. Also known as pot, reefer, cannabis, and mary jane," I had said, as if I were zipping through the blanks on a health quiz.

"Okay, Elliott, that's enough. Whatever those people were smoking, I told Davis we had to leave. He wasn't too happy about it, I can tell you that."

Now she stepped from the closet in her sleeveless turquoise dress with the silver braiding around the hem. I tucked the shoe buckles back in their velvet nest.

"How do I look?"

"Pretty," I said. "Sexy," I added. "Sexy" was another Age of Aquarius word everyone was using. "Pretty sexy."

"Don't be funny. You're ten years old, almost eleven."

She sat down at the vanity and combed two hooks of hair forward in front of her ears. Then she sprayed them in place. They were lady sideburns, but not half as blond as Mr. Keller's. It was unfair that Donnie had gotten to stay home from school three days that week.

"Have you talked to Mrs. Keller?"

"I did, sweetie."

"He'll be back," I said. I knew it was wrong for me to be happy, secretly, that Mr. Keller was gone again. He'd left Friday morning, flown away at sunrise.

"Hmmm."

"He's on assignment," I said, using Donnie's words in a superior tone.

She took her seat at the vanity and considered this for a moment.

"Honey, Malaysia isn't like your dad taking a trip to St. Louis. Mr. Keller paid the bills and left money for an obstetrician. I told her I could get her to an appointment."

I ran over to the tall bureau and yanked open my father's empty sweater drawer. I started pulling out old pieces of dry cleaner tissue and crumpling them in balls.

"What's wrong, Elliott?"

"Does he get one more chance?" I had promised to stop pestering her about whether my father was coming back, but sometimes I couldn't help myself. Getting straight As, locking my legs around his waist, kissing him on the mouth wouldn't keep him. It was all up to her, not me, didn't she know that?

My tissue missiles were weak and clumsy, not the intended effect, so Little Listener stood by the window and listened to her think in the vanity mirror, watched and listened to her think about finally pushing the button for the Name of Her. She tipped her perfume bottle over once. The stopper came out with its tiny glass squeak. She dotted a wrist, then rubbed it against the other. Her scent attended to, she now could speak.

"Your father doesn't want another chance."

"Yeah," I said, caving quickly, too quickly, always on her side. "I know."

I flopped onto the bed and buried my face into the spread. Like everything in the house, it was colonial style; its thousands of white nubs formed a giant eagle. I knew from experience that if I lay there long enough, the nubs would make little welts on my face. I shrugged her hand off my back, listened to her feet puff into her high heels. Eventually I rolled over. No matter how sexy my mother made herself, three kids were a liability, so I'd better not look like I had the measles when I asked Davis bright questions about catamarans.

Mr. Keller had left money for winter coats, too, so after another dramatic Mass at St. Elizabeth's, my mother took Aurora and the girls shopping at Monkey Ward's.

Donnie and I had the house to ourselves. Sunday cartoons were the worst, and more Tenochtitlán seemed too ordinary, so we got on the floor in his parents' room and flipped through a guide to Arctic mammals. I stopped to point out a cross-section picture of seal fur. Donnie wouldn't tell my mother why he didn't want a warm coat, but now he said to me, in a small and careful voice, that his yellow windbreaker helped him pretend he was still in Mexico City with his old friends.

"What were their names?" I asked, surprised and then ashamed. Here I had endured four moves, four different schools, but it hadn't occurred to me, not even once, that Donnie had had a whole life, in another language, before Chicago.

He picked at a strip of laminate on one of the dressers. "Daniel, Antonio, Jaime, and Juan."

I placed him there, the smiling center of a different pack of five, in a blindingly hot and sunny school yard. Behind the gingersnap boys, at the edge of the jungle, was a row of mothers grinding corn. The fathers were higher up, with feathered headdresses, cutting out hearts. I set the book down.

"Did you used to play four-square?"

"No," he snorted, "not that stupid game you and your friends play."

We had never mentioned the fight with Pat Norton.

"It is stupid," I said, my face watching the book again. "What did you play in Mexico?"

He stood up, so I did too. I shivered at the cold on my feet.

"Monsters," he said, looking at me funny. I didn't believe him and said so, but I giggled when he growled through his bared bottom teeth and made Wolf Man claws with his hands.

"They're not my friends," I said. "I mean, not really. Not anymore."

He tried to hide his smile. He took a step toward me. I made the sign of the cross, even though that only stopped Dracula.

"We liked swimming best of all," he said.

"Swimming," I said. My throat felt scratchy. I took a step onto a new tightrope. "Did you wear bathing suits? To swim in?"

Donnie shook his head no. He lifted his hands and growled again. I swung my right arm in front of my face like I was drawing a cape.

"I vant to suck your blood" was the last thing I said. Very soon we were in the silent center of his parents' bed, tipping back and forth inside a white pyramid of lace. When our mothers and sisters came back from Yorktown Plaza, we were in the living room, sneaking looks and sort of watching a Zorro movie.

It was already dark out when I got home, but I pulled down the shades in my bedroom anyway. I blew gently on Jethro, curled in the corner of his cage. He woke up, and I fed him two treats, which he put in his cheeks for later. Then I showed him the silver bracelet Donnie had given me. I tapped it against the bars until he came over and sniffed it with the little black bead of his nose. The bracelet was a silver cuff, etched with a line of jaguars walking single file down the middle.

I stripped to my underwear, put on the bracelet, tied a sweater around my waist, and snaked around my bed doing our Tenochtitlán dance. My cue to stop would be the slap of Frank's hockey stick coming up the driveway.

The next time I went over Mr. Keller opened the door. His head gleamed in the porch light as he leaned down to see who I might be.

"Elliott, right?" he said. "Come inside." His tie was loose, and his shirt was wrinkled. His hair poked up too; clearly Donnie and the girls had just pulled him down to the floor by way of greeting, as they had the last time he'd come home.

"Uh—I can come back tomorrow. If you're eating dinner."

"Aurora's still cooking, but that's all right, Elliott. We can set a place for you." Mr. Keller's voice was friendly, like the host of an afternoon cartoon show.

"I already ate. Salisbury steak."

"I see. Well, come in anyway."

Donnie came around his father as I was wiping my feet on the towel in the foyer. His face fell at the sight of what was balanced against my hip. Mr. Keller noticed too. "What do you have there?" he asked.

"What?"

"In the bag. More bricks for El Templo Mayor?"

"Oh no, Mr. Keller, that part is just about done. We're almost ready to spray paint."

"I saw. It's impressive. I'm glad Donnie has a friend like you." He turned to link us together, but Donnie had vanished.

"Me too. I can come back tomorrow."

"No, take your coat off. The family likes it hot in here."

I wanted to smile, but I guess I was upset to see him. I told Mr. Keller that, no, I preferred the cold, the same lie I'd given crusty old Davis McGill in our living room. I'd also told Davis that I loved hockey and snowmobiling and wanted to learn how to chop wood. He had a camp in northern Michigan for ice fishing and winter sports.

It was a mistake to let Mr. Keller hold the bag of groceries while I stuffed my gloves in my pockets. He pulled out a box of macaroni and cheese. And another. And a bag of navy beans. When he got to the package of hot dogs, he shouted "Aurora!" and I saw a vein split the middle of his forehead. He gripped the bag like the neck of a cat and took off for the kitchen.

It got fast and furious immediately. Donnie's parents sounded like the late-night Spanish commercials on channel 26, turned up to a deafening volume. Pans and cabinets slammed and crashed, and the girls started to cry. It was definitely time to go, but I had one last thing to give.

I crept into the dining room. My parka weighed a hundred pounds in the heat. Donnie, sitting on his heels, head bent, was a block of stone. He wouldn't look up. So I tapped the flat altar atop the pyramid with my left index finger, then pointed it to my closed right hand.

I turned it over and let him see the gift in my palm: a circle of colored scarabs set in a gold pin, swiped from the tangle in the bottom of my mother's jewelry box. I had selected this piece because it was beautiful, and because the tiny hash marks on the scarab wings reminded me of the streaks of paint on the cheeks of the Aztec warriors in the A–B volume of the *World Book*.

His fingertips touched mine. I wanted to tell him that I had been sleeping with the jaguar bracelet. I wanted to tell him that I had decided to stop wearing underpants and that I was going to save up money for a trip to Mexico City.

Mr. Keller's head popped through the doorway. Our hands flew apart. He said something loud and long at his son.

Donnie, his eyes glistening, answered in Spanish. "*Caridad*," he said softly.

"Say it in English, and say it louder, so Elliott can understand."

Donnie's hand, jerking a little, was closed around the pin. "Charity."

"That's right, charity. *Caridad* means charity!"

I looked up and said it was my mother's idea. Donnie's father was unrecognizable. The rage in his face could have set his straw hair on fire. His wolf eyes shifted, then fixed on the pyramid until they seemed to cross. Then he was back in the kitchen, yelling, in English now, that my mother and the Ginger Creek Salvation Army could all fuck themselves; he knew how to provide for his family.

A drawer pulled open, then there were scraping metal sounds. Donnie's mother started wailing again; Regina and Silvia were weeping. Donnie's head drooped lower and lower; his T-shirt had pulled out of his dungarees. I wanted to cover the skin with my hand, let my palm protect the three bumps of his backbone.

"You tell your mother to stay out of our business."

Mr. Keller had returned, balancing something shiny in his hands. I scooted backward on my butt as soon as I saw the flowered oven mitts. I knew it was water, but it felt to me like a tidal wave of boiling blood poured from the cooking pot Mr. Keller held over the Great Pyramid of Tenochtitlán.

Our project bubbled away into a lake of sugar and sodden shirt cardboard. The dent from the pot was the first decoration to grace the Kellers' dining room wall, and my mother said it was a miracle I escaped with nothing more than a wet ski jacket.

Donnie never came back to Miss Vojta's class. The Kellers disappeared a week later, in mid-March. What was left of El Templo Mayor—a piece of plywood streaked with green tempera paint—I found in a pile of junk on their back deck. Their house sold at the beginning of April. My father let us finish the school year at least.

USE YOUR HEAD

TOM

1978

Tom Amelio, legs wedged into the chute of space under his bedroom desk, was trying to write his first condolence note. He was eighteen, too young to have devised a cluster of dignified, repeatable sentences with which to express sorrow.

July 20, 1978

Dear Mr. and Mrs. Hills,

I am so sorry

It was shocking to hear

He scribbled Hitler mustaches over the false starts. The sound of the pen on paper reassured him that work had begun. He flicked his old Tensor lamp on and off. He wanted to finish a rough draft before his hands began sweating under its heat. He was working with notebook paper first, just as he did for English essays. To his left was a slim box of the special black-bordered paper that *Funeral Customs the World Over* had mentioned. He had had to go to three card stores in downtown Overland Park to find it.

Jeff Hills had swerved off Metcalf Avenue and into a tree going eighty in the middle of the previous day. A group of girls from Shawnee North had parsed the shocking event at Zip'z, the make-your-own sundae franchise where Tom worked. The local paper had yet to cover the accident, but eighty miles an hour was their agreed-upon detail. Tom noticed too that the recollection of Jeff's glossy, shoulder-length hair had brought them close to tears, as if death were especially senseless in the case of blond boys. The girls didn't know that he had known Jeff too, and long before they had, back when Jeff had sported a bowl cut and freckles. He offered them free soft-serve as a distraction from their grief and from his own confused feelings. Jeff Hills was the first person he knew who had died, and the box of stationery didn't carry instructions for what to say, or how to say it.

Jeff and I were at Hocker Grove Junior High together

You moved away in the summer of 1975

I still live on Hedley Drive, where you used to live

"Used to live" was horrible. Tom set down his pen and carried his work through the dark house to the edge of the den. His parents' faces glowed blue-yellow in the reflected light of *Barney Miller.*

"Mom? Pop?" His mother stopped crunching ice, so he went on. "Should I write 'Principal and Mrs. Hills' or 'Mr. and Mrs. Hills'?"

Questions of protocol, he knew, confounded them. When the second store didn't have mourning paper, his mother had raced the engine and told him to go back in, buy a card, and be done with it.

" 'Principal Hills' is respectful," said his father.

"But he wasn't the principal of *my* high school," Tom countered. Debate had been one of his extracurricular activities.

His father released the handle on the recliner, and his feet touched ground. "Good point, son. I'm sure 'Mister Hills' is okay, too."

"Call him Clifton," said his mother, in her "la-de-dah" accent. "Or Clifford. Which was it?"

"Janet," said his father.

"Always strutting around in a jacket and tie, like he was the prince of Hedley Drive."

"He's a principal, Mom," said Tom. "What else is he supposed to wear?"

"The couple of times I met *her*, she seemed unhappy. Pretty little thing."

"Well, she must be miserable now, because her son is dead," Tom snapped. "And she only had the one."

"Don't be smart," said his mother. "And take the clothes out of the dryer if you have nothing better to do."

"I *was* doing this." Tom crumpled the sheet of notebook paper and aimed it at the Chiefs wastebasket by the plate glass window.

"You could call him what you called him when they still lived in the neighborhood," said his father.

Tom couldn't remember what they had called Mr. Hills. His position as principal at Shawnee Mission North made him a hands-off dad—a car turning, then a peripheral garage door going up while they played touch football in the front yard. All of the boys would stand at attention until he'd gone inside, though Jeff sometimes gave him a weird, mocking salute. The Hills family had moved to a better subdivision the summer after freshman year, and Jeff switched from Shawnee West to his father's school. Tom remembered Mrs. Hills—Sally—better. She worked at the Olathe Public Library, and she was, as his mother remembered, pretty.

"It's nice that you're doing this," his father said. "It's not necessary, kid like you."

"I know," Tom replied. He bit a fingernail and wondered, impolitely, if Sally Hills were wearing her black nightgown at that very moment, black a useful emblem for mourning her son and seducing her husband at the same time. It was the kind of polluted thought Jeff himself would have put into words if he were still alive and they were still friends.

His father was standing now, trying to read Tom's mood. He flexed one heavy, marble leg, then the other. "I'm getting some ice cream," he said. "You want any?"

Having ice cream with Alphonse would mean discussing Jeff Hills in the kitchen. It was too soon for that. Tom shook his head.

"You get too much of that anyway, am I right?"

"You are right, Daddy-O," said Tom, slipping away. Pausing in the hot sleeve of the hallway, he heard his father say to the icebox, "Jeff Hills had one heck of an imagination. Be sure to tell his folks that."

Making a batch of sugar syrups the next day at Zip'z, Tom pondered Jeff Hills's imagination. Upon learning of Tom's free ride to Purdue, his boss, a Yugoslavian refugee named Iulian Bogetich, had made Tom "junior manager" of the parlor, which meant he opened the store three mornings a week for an extra seventy cents an hour. Tom enjoyed testing his strength by hoisting five-gallon barrels of milk product with one hand onto his shoulder and into the machine, but replenishing the syrups was quite another thing. It required titrating jug after jug of viscous sugar water with eyedroppers of chemical flavorings. Peanut butter and bubble gum smelled the worst.

Thinking back to seventh grade at Hocker Grove, Tom remembered the original, pre-druggie Jeff. How they'd first met—pickup street hockey? the school bus? whipping dirt clods at the ponies in the horse farm?—was less clear to him than the floor plan and furnishings in Jeff's house up the street. The Amelios had a dinky rancher with no shade, but the Hillses' Dutch colonial, framed by a pair of impressive birches, had two full floors covered with old intricate rugs. They had Chinese trinkets, and drawings on the walls with tiny numbers penciled in their bottom corners, and the living room furniture went together without having to match.

Ten minutes after their first soda and chips, Jeff had shucked his clothes in the upstairs hallway and dived onto the double bed in the guest room. "I like to feel free," he announced. Tom had two older brothers, so Jeff naked didn't seem as big a deal as the walls of books in Mr. Hills's study and the freestanding Formica island in the kitchen.

Tom ripped open and dumped ten-pound bags of confectioners' sugar into the giant syrup drum next to the standing freezer.

Dear Mr. and Mrs. Hills,

   *I remember how in seventh grade Jeff would call up after school
while you were still at work and tell me about a new way he'd
thought of to whack off. I sat in your kitchen in your elegant home,
twirling in the yellow space-age chairs, waiting for the timer to ding.
Then Jeff would take a hot orange out of the oven, stick his dick into
the hole he'd cut into it, and squeeze. He said it felt amazing.*

Tom's penis was already too big for oranges. Jeff's was small, like a baby
lamb chop, the leg bone pointing up, the scrotum just one mouthful of
meat. It had pretty much stayed that way through freshman year, the last
semester he and Tom had had the same gym period.

Dear Mr. Hills,

   *I remember watching Jeff whack off with a handful of your menthol
shaving cream. I tried it at home with my Pop's. Boy, that really stung!*
                              Sincerely,
                              Thomas A. Amelio

Tom sprayed hot water into the drum. Neither one of them could ejacu-
late at that point, but Jeff had said they should get a head start on puberty.
Wanting an audience more than a co-conspirator, he hadn't seemed to
mind that Tom wouldn't attempt his brainstorms in front of him.

Dear Mrs. Hills,

   *I'm going to miss Jeff. I remember one time he pulled some hair
out of your hairbrush, smoothed it into a pad, and then Scotch-taped
it onto his pubic bone. He said Mr. Hills called it a "merkin." For
a boy with terrible grades, he had a fine vocabulary. He did like to
read. He must have gotten that from you.*

Then Jeff had put on his mother's long blonde wig and round sunglasses to complete what he called his Playboy Bunny look. He sashayed

to the front living room window, threw open the sheers, tucked his penis between his legs, and rocked his hips like a hula girl for all of Hedley Drive to see. Tom's ginger ale came out his nose, it was so hilarious. Jeff claimed he gave the mailman a more elaborate show on the days he stayed home sick—there was time enough then to stuff a bra and put on his mother's black baby-doll nightgown and her sanitary napkin belt.

> You may not know this, Mrs. Hills, but Jeff wanted you to wear tampons instead of pads. He dared me once to shoplift a box of them at the Walgreens.

Tom grew a little careless with his work: the stream of starter syrup caught the sides of several jugs. The minute he turned his back, ants would mount a parade to meet the drips. Squatting with a Handi Wipe, he accidentally dropped the mixing ladle into the wet mop bucket, as if Jeff's ghost had jostled his elbow to reassert his historic ability to make clean things dirty.

Dry toppings were next. Tom dished coconut flakes, M&M's, Rice Krispies, chocolate chips, jimmies, raisins, almond slivers, peanuts, and mini marshmallows into clear-topped containers. He couldn't get over the amount of junk people would pile onto a dish of ice cream just because it was free. They'd sprinkle corn chips and bacon bits, if he set them out. Pepperoni. Parsley sprigs. Eggs. At least one kid puked every other day.

> Dear Mr. and Mrs. Hills,
> I didn't believe Jeff when he told me he had once put an egg in his ass, because I thought it would break. It occurs to me now that he meant a peeled, hard-boiled egg.

Their division happened during Halloween season freshman year. After pushing the neck of a speckled gourd up his butt, Jeff had gone to hunt down his mother's hand mirror while Tom stayed frozen in the swivel chair, staring at the intersecting rings of corn oil on the Formica island.

A car coasting down Hedley had spooked him into action. He capped the Mazola bottle, shoved it back in the cabinet, and then reshuffled the

LET ME SEE IT

gourds in the holiday centerpiece. He called out to Jeff that he had to go and ran into the cold, his shirtsleeve, blotted with oil, sticking to his forearm.

Dicks were one thing; ass stuff was queer, beyond witness or encouragement, so Tom had ignored Jeff's subsequent invitations to hang out. Jeff made friends with Randy Cooper, a neighborhood burnout, and that was that. By Thanksgiving weekend Jeff had scored his first nickel bag and Tom, until then a completely indifferent student, had caught up in geometry, biology, and social studies. He became a grind, joined the wrestling squad, paid attention, applied himself, and never looked back. When the Hillses moved to Cedar Creek the following summer, he decided that he missed their house, quiet and composed, more than he did Jeff and his sex stunts.

One time junior year, at a tournament at Shawnee North, Tom had spotted Jeff lounging in the stands, surrounded by friends. His hair was nearly as long now as his mother's famous wig, and he had his arm around a pretty girl in a pom-pom uniform. The stoner and the socialite—Jeff had obviously lost none of his bad-boy charm. Standing in his singlet, lumpy with strength, Tom sunk his shoe into the soft wrestling mat and knew that he was more respected than liked.

He was too young for regrets, yet mourning Jeff that day in the ice cream parlor—if smutty recollections between serving customers can be called mourning—allowed Tom to see that he already possessed a history. To realize that, even at eighteen, his life could have gone in a very different direction was reassuring. But then his father, who was head butcher at the Kroger's in the same strip mall as Zip'z, came in on his lunch break and floated the notion that Jeff Hills had chosen death the way Tom had picked Purdue.

"Why do you think he did it?" was his first question after sitting down with his pizza slices. Tom gave him a root beer and change. Alphonse—"Al," for short, embroidered in blue on his apron—never took freebies.

"Did what?" replied Tom.

"Drank himself to death."

"Pop! It was an accident." Tom had no supporting evidence for his statement; there was still nothing in the papers about what had happened.

His father sucked his teeth in disbelief. Sunshine lit the hairs on the bridge of his nose. Iulian Bogetich, whose shaved head and tinted aviator glasses made him look like Kojak, had hair there too. If hairs ever dared to sprout on his nose, Tom would tweeze them, every single day if necessary.

"You can't drink yourself to death at our age," said Tom. "We studied cirrhosis in health class."

"Use your head, Tom. You don't run into a tree at three in the afternoon unless you're drunk off your ass. Or worse."

"They haven't ruled out engine failure."

Alphonse laughed, then pushed a green pepper tail into his mouth. "If you was doing eighty in the Dodge, you bet it would fail."

"Nobody knows how fast he was going."

"You said eighty."

"I was only repeating what I heard."

Discussing his long-ago semi-friend with the most concrete thinker he knew, and a butcher to boot, was leading Tom toward the body. Was Jeff Hills cooling on a slab, or lying in a drawer? Was he strung upside down to drain, like the sides of beef in Alphonse's meat locker? What *was* left of him? What were his remains? Had parts of his brain sieved on impact through his nostrils and eye sockets, spattering the bark, or had it gone the other way, a branch poled through his ears, long hair and leaves ratted in a green and gold wreath? Thoughts of Jeff compounded with a tree made him think of that Ovid story they'd read in Enriched Senior English.

"His parents spoiled him rotten. Poor kid."

"*Poor?* Get real, Pop."

"You know what I mean."

"Jeff was happy-go-lucky. He was an—"

Tom was about to say "exhibitionist," but that would send the wrong message, and besides, he knew Alphonse didn't like ten-dollar words flung his way.

What he wanted to tell his father was that in late June, not three weeks ago, Jeff had come into Zip'z with the munchies and, after offering his hand to Tom over the counter, had sat at that same table. He said he had heard through the grapevine about Tom's graduation speech, and now he wanted to hear it, or at least the gist of it, or at least—and here Jeff had adopted the shaky voice of an old lady English teacher—"the topic sentence." Blushing to think that Jeff might have come just to see him, Tom had changed the subject to whether it was true you could get high on hits from the whipped cream canister.

"You can cry if you want to," said Alphonse.

That his father knew how he was feeling, sometimes before he did, terrified Tom. "What are you talking about, Pop?" he said, loudly. "I don't cry."

"Maybe so, but it's okay to."

"I didn't know him, not anymore. We had nothing in common."

"That can make it harder."

Just before leaving that night, Jeff had held out a grimy baggie of 'shrooms. A graduation gift, Tom supposed; fortunately, a family of four's timely entrance kept him from having to refuse or accept the offer. That was the last time he saw Jeff alive.

Tom curled his father's paper plate around the cast-off crusts. "You want a sundae, Pop? You can make it in a Tigers cap."

This was a new Zip'z promotion. Customers could make their own sundaes in a hard plastic cap of their favorite pro baseball team. In Overland Park, a suburb conceived as an escape across state lines from the bad schools and racial perils of Kansas City, the Cardinals outsold the Royals three to one.

His father smacked his belly and said that soft-serve tasted like lipstick. He stood and held his arms away from his body. Tom went to retie his apron.

"I'd love you, son, even if you'd gone bad. You know that."

"I know, Pop," Tom answered quickly from behind. Too quickly, because then Alphonse turned and caught him in a mortifying bear hug.

"Your mother, too."

"Right," said Tom, breathing through his mouth.

"I'm gonna miss you in the fall, you know that?"

"I know that."

Gone bad—like meat, or fruit, or cream—Tom thought after Alphonse had left. But he hadn't turned out badly, so maybe it was an easy thing for his father to say. And on the other hand, if it didn't matter that he'd done well, why had Tom bothered to become the pride of the guidance counselors, debate team co-captain, and third in Kansas wrestling for his weight class? When their schedules matched, father and son walked home together, and Alphonse would shoot down every hint Tom made about how expensive Purdue was going to be, even on scholarship. He had heard from his mother that his cousin Elliott was starting Cornell in the fall. She seemed to relish the idea of her brother Henry going into hock over that.

Two more days passed before a death notice appeared in the *Sun* below Jeff's pouty yearbook photo. He looked like a Beach Boy, free and fun and foxy, the Shawnee North girls said on another round of sad speculation. Tom, wiping down their table afterward, thought how Jeff would have been great for business. Nobody could snow or sweet-talk better than Jeff Hills on a jag. He would have made Zip'z a teen hangout.

Tom had completed and returned his housing form, but the condolence note still flummoxed him. He stared at his hands, andirons baking under the Tensor lamp. The eloquent phrase from the obituary, "in lieu of flowers," dammed up his thoughts. The more he remembered Jeff, his wily SAT vocabulary antonym wiggling in the window of a Dutch colonial, the less he felt he could express sorrow or dispense comfort to Mr. and Mrs. Hills. Flowers would have been perfect.

"Just write what you feel," said his mother, pausing in his doorway to roll her eyes at the snowdrift of paper wads in his wastebasket.

She really didn't get it. "I don't know what I feel," he said to the wall in front of him.

"Then take a break and go clean the grill. Your brothers are coming for dinner."

Dan was a Culligan Man, and Dave sold Magnavox. Tom didn't relish an evening of their put-downs. Neither one of them understood his need to be the first Amelio whose given name you had to guess at, because it wasn't stitched onto a shirt pocket.

His mother was exasperated, but for once she had a useful suggestion. "You know there are books for this. Check out Emily Post, for God's sake."

"It has to be original."

She uncrossed her arms and, still hugging the doorway, said, "You think sorrow is original to you, Tom?"

Before he could manage a response to this curious question, his mother was making a blasting, nasal sound, a prolonged, undulant cry more piercing than a whistle. It seemed to rattle the rancher and made the hair stand out on his neck.

Never in his life had she produced such a noise.

"Keening," she said when it was over, with more than a trace of a smile.

She'd scared him, and they both knew it. She moved on before he could turn away from her again.

In his high school library, where he tutored summer algebra on his non-Zip'z mornings, Tom went back to *Funeral Customs the World Over* and learned that keening, a communal practice in Ireland and many Mediterranean cultures, was both an expression of sorrow and a profession. Since sorrow came more easily to some, old women could get paid to wail the way his mother had. They could do it for you; the best keeners could keep it up for days.

He wound up ignoring Emily Post. Instead he scanned three examples in *Correspondence Made Easy* and dropped it into the book return before he could memorize whole sentences—another scholastic talent that had helped him ace written exams and craft crushing rebuttals in debate tournaments.

When he couldn't locate a word in any of the dictionaries on the shelves, Mrs. Wilderman was happy to lead him to *The Compact Edition of the Oxford English Dictionary* in her office. She handed him the oblong magnifying glass and closed the door behind her.

In volume 1, A–O, on page 1775, column 4, final definition: "Merkin, counterfeit hair for women's privy parts."

Tom curled his arms around the heavy blue slab and let its weight draw him down until his cheek lay flat on the conference table. The secret, small-print specialization of "merkin," so ancient and tiny you needed a magnifying glass to find it, made Tom's career decoding trigonometric identities and trade tariffs and the laws of noble gases seem like a swill at a giant, common trough. Jeff Hills had been a body *and* a book, a dirty one maybe, slim with wide margins, but one whose secrets had been removed from the collection. Death was a loss of knowledge in the shelf of the world.

That thought was worth writing down.

He straightened up and blotted the dictionary with a sleeve, just in case, and replaced the glass in its little drawer.

Out of habit Tom checked his locker, emptied now for a month. That he expected to remember its combination until the day he died suddenly seemed an impossible burden. Before closing the door, he practically begged the coat hook to tell him whom it would have hurt had he eaten even a crumb of a graduation 'shroom. Jeff's last words, said with a wicked shake of the baggie, were, "C'mon, Tommy. For Hedley Drive and auld lang syne."

Leaving school, he deliberately ducked the cases flanking the principal's office. "Thomas A. Amelio 1978" was etched on a plaque and two silver cups. Jeffrey Hills's permanent record was unsigned graffiti, seeds and burnt matches, heated oranges and a sweet, peaceful reek.

Several nights later, Tom was waiting out the end of his shift. When the bell tinkled by the door, he thought it would be Iulian, coming to close after payroll. Instead, a tall man in tennis shorts and a green cotton sweater greeted him by name.

"Um . . . hello, sir," said Tom, puzzled. Grownups never ate ice cream alone.

The man shifted a brown grocery bag from one arm to the other, took a few steps in, and extended his hand. He was handsome in a tired way. His hair, cut over the ears, was a mix of blond and gray.

"It's Mr. Hills, Tom," the man finally said.

Tom started to blush. "I'm sorry." They shook hands, and then he gestured vaguely at Mr. Hills's summer attire. "I didn't recognize you."

"No real reason you should, Tom," said Mr. Hills. "People don't recognize other people out of their habitual contexts. When I was just starting out, I taught history. The first few summers, to make ends meet, I sold encyclopedias door to door."

"Really?" He couldn't picture Mr. Hills as a salesman.

"When my students answered the door, and it did happen, I would estimate that fully two-thirds of them didn't recognize me. They could only see me in the protective coloration of a jacket and tie and a piece of chalk in my hand."

"How about the other third?"

Mr. Hills, as if expecting the question from the alert pupils, smiled. "They'd scream."

Tom, not knowing whether this was a joke, stalled by wiping the counter.

"Your father told me you were working here," said Mr. Hills.

"You talked to my father?" Tom, first in his class, was nonetheless alarmed at the thought of any principal chatting up Alphonse.

"I was just at the Kroger's." Mr. Hills set his bag down. A carton of eggs was tilting on top. Tom had to agree about context, since it seemed weird for a principal to buy groceries. Then he remembered what had happened—Mr. Hills had to be out shopping for his wife.

"How is Mrs. Hills? Is she . . ."

"She's doing remarkably well. Thank you for asking."

Mr. Hills pinched the bridge of his slender, hairless nose. His watch was loaded with extras.

"I'm really—" Tom started.

Mr. Hills folded his hands and let them hover above his waist, the way Alphonse did to say grace. "Your note was a comfort to her," said Mr. Hills. "It was a comfort to both of us. You have a way with words, Tom."

Even dressed for tennis, Mr. Hills conformed to Tom's image of what his professors would be like at Purdue. Polished and accommodating, tempered with strictness.

"And a natural ease of expression," continued Mr. Hills, as if he were introducing Tom at an awards banquet. "Your commencement speech was one of the best I've encountered, and I've heard and read a lot of them."

Tom was too amazed to play it cool. "You read my speech, Mr. Hills? How could—"

"You wrote and submitted it beforehand, did you not?" Tom nodded. "Well, when a pupil does something outstanding, principals can be like proud parents with bragging rights. We circulate major achievements amongst ourselves, on mimeo."

Tom didn't know what to say. Mr. Hills began moving down the toppings bar. As he spoke, he peered at the labels and lifted lids in order to grasp the fantastical concept of the make-your-own sundae.

"I found your observation about how, after four years spent striving to self-differentiate into jocks and socialites and brains and band fags and stoners, how all of your classmates looked *exactly* alike in their caps and gowns, particularly astute."

"I guess that was my major point," said Tom, rattled to hear Mr. Hills use the proper slang for their cliques. "We're not really all that different underneath."

"Correct, Tom. We all start from the same place. Everyone loves to hear an old truth in a new way." Mr. Hills slapped a lid shut. "I gave your speech to Jeff to read."

"You did? Really?"

"Now whether he read it or not . . ." Mr. Hills blew out a long breath and ran a hand through his hair.

Tom wanted to ask if he remembered what exact day that had been. Had Jeff read the speech and then come to see him at Zip'z? Or had he been too zonked to read and decided to just come over to hear the gist of it? Had he died knowing the gist of it?

Dusk had settled in now; the vast parking lot was filling with flashlight taggers. Tom remembered playing it with Jeff in the horse farm behind their subdivision, their beams joyously crossing and bouncing off the fence posts and white feed buckets. He went by "Tommy" back then.

With his shift over in twenty minutes, he would have preferred not to have to reclean the soft-serve machine, but he asked his visitor whether he might like a sundae.

Mr. Hills rubbed his stomach. Tom calculated that he was probably the age of an actual Beach Boy, all grown up. "I've been stuffed with casseroles for days."

"On the house, Mr. Hills." For Hedley Drive and auld lang syne.

"Very well."

"Chocolate, vanilla, or swirl?"

"What is 'swirl'?"

"Chocolate and vanilla."

"Vanilla's my meat and drink."

"We have a baseball cap promotion, Mr. Hills. I can put your ice cream in your favorite team's cap."

Some kids on bikes whizzed under the lights in front of the store. At the end of the toppings bar, Mr. Hills was jiggling his hand in the left pocket of his shorts, counting change.

"I'll take the Cardinals. No, make it the Phillies. I grew up outside of Philadelphia."

"I think I knew that," fibbed Tom, turning to the shelf behind the soda machine. He grabbed the Phillies stack and pried off the top cap. He'd let Iulian know it was time to order more Cardinals and Twins. He turned back, and Mr. Hills was somehow right there, directly across.

"It's funny, Thomas," he said softly. "Or rather, it's a wretched thing, but how I sometimes wished, watching you mature, that you could have been my boy. Your mind. Your character. Your . . . physique."

Mr. Hills's eyes were shining with something that wasn't tears. The sentiment, the whispered second syllable of Tom's given name, the point of Mr. Hills's tongue touching his top front teeth—Tom realized that Mr. Hills's hand wasn't counting change. Jeff had been a leftie, too.

Mr. Hills's voice grew quieter still. "I'm going to need to use the facilities before I enjoy my confection."

Unable to speak, Tom nodded to the back of the store.

The bathroom door closed, but he didn't hear it lock.

The cold of the lever on the soft-serve machine steadied his hand until the solid white tip of the ice cream showed itself. Tom would not have been surprised to watch the end of a peeled, hard-boiled egg emerge from the star-shaped metal die.

He set the filled cap down; then, to regulate his ragged breathing, quickly crouched behind the counter on all fours, as he sometimes did before stepping onto the wrestling mat or even before making a rebuttal in a debate final.

Though not nearly as obscure as "merkin," Mr. Hills's use of the word "confection" ratified an innocent sentence in the second paragraph of Tom's final draft of the condolence note:

> *I feel certain that many of Jeff's finest qualities–his sense of humor, his sociability, and above all, his imagination–came directly from you.*

Tom stood and tried to use his head. He moved to the open storeroom. The back door was padlocked, but the wall phone stood above the utility sink in case he might need to call Kroger's.

The noise inside him, shrill and burning, he recognized as keening. He was suddenly keening with feelings, feelings that jumped straight to facts, with no time in between. He saw Jeff's body, his limbs detaching and falling like fiery logs across the hood of a car. Part of Tom grieved for him, grieved for a boy who should have had a dark-haired father like Alphonse to keep him from harm, but the greater part of him was terrified. Not of Mr. Hills, the power of whose imagination had driven his son to suicide, but of the pent-up force thundering between his own legs.

The keening grew louder, burned brighter. Jeff Hills was safe in the ground now; the gist of Tom Amelio, a typed speech on four sheets of mimeo, was inches from a different flame. Until Principal Hills, a tree so strong that his son couldn't destroy him, not even going eighty, reappeared to make his dessert, Tom flipped lids on the toppings bar and stirred fresh circles in his syrups.

LET ME SEE IT

TREASURE MAP

TOM

1979

When Tom Amelio came home one day from class, there was a folded piece of paper under his door. He picked it up and read a handwritten message at the top of the sheet:

> Confidential. This is for a psych project on attitudes toward male homosexuality. Please return to S. Pollock, Harrison 5418.

The questionnaire was typed, mimeographed, scientific.

> Using a scale of one (most repugnant) to ten (most pleasurable), please mark your personal response to the following twelve activities.
>
> 1. Touching a man.
> 2. Putting an arm around a man.
> 3. Holding hands with a man.
> 4. Kissing a man.
> 5. Touching a man's penis.
> 6. . . .

*

Next morning, Tom was in love for the first time. It was the spring of his freshman year, and he had decided to be in love with the boy across the hallway on the basis of his responses to a questionnaire slipped under the door by a psych student in their dorm, last name Pollock, that neither of them knew. Whether Boyd's answers, neutral fives, sixes, and one seven that he let Tom skim with disbelieving eyes, were from hypothetical projection or practical experience, Tom would never care to discover. Tom, with his nines and tens, made a vow never to mention the questionnaire. It was buried forty fathoms deep, in the twelfth century, behind ten castle walls, with black-hooded marksmen at every postern and vats of smoking oil for backup. Tom immediately suppressed Boyd's neutral fives, sixes, and one seven to focus solely on the side of the fence Boyd had dropped over. His was an easy hitch of one leg, then the other. Tom's felt like a giddy, scarlet vault.

For several days he remained unwilling to believe. He regarded Boyd, rather than looked at him. His Person, not his Answers, devastated him now, and there stretched before them weeks of dreamy, springtime callowness. Boyd had left Tom to guess, suppose, surmise, left him to become the maker and the knower of roads. What burned in Tom was not lust, but inquiry. It was the getting behind Boyd's eyes, the slipping into his form and features, the sifting of his habits, convictions, false fronts, family. He—Boyd McIlhenny—Tom allowed himself to say his full name—became the ontology of observation. Tom smiled to use this word, dropped casually in history section by his T.A. Boyd became the nature and relation of his being. Boyd gave him words. Boyd was a university of words, a list of wonders who made wonders in Tom, wonders to be tested on.

Boyd was waking in the morning knowing where his eyes would go. He was a constant stop, a putting down of the foot, no matter where Tom might be, to acknowledge him walking elsewhere. Tom placed Boyd into the rhythm of his walk: in the instance of falling between feet, he thought Boyd, he breathed Boyd in, he thanked Boyd for Boyd, Boyd ineluctably there, before he dropped the other foot, completed the Boyd stride, and breathed him out.

He placed Boyd consciously in his breathing so as not to lose him during those moments when he turned up in person, unaware that he could take

Tom's breath away. Boyd was about not losing breath and balance, because on certain days, with the magnolia buds popping like gumdrops on their branches, Tom, fizzy with feeling, thought something might pop from him in front of thirty thousand coeds. The fizz, the geyser, was all, endlessly renewing, endlessly slaking.

*

Tom was especially grateful for the progress of Western Civilization After Luther, for it met two mornings a week, so early that it became his duty to dress in the dawn and cross to Boyd's door at a quarter to seven. Boyd, the fairest of Irishmen, would poke his head out and let Tom, the Italian troll on scholarship, know that he could retreat to his room and complete his toilette, whence he would find him at a quarter after in front of the elevator, whence they would proceed to breakfast together. Boyd was whence, and where, and whither. While he brushed his teeth, Tom listened to Boyd shower, happy to share the verdigris reach of Poseidon's fingers through the pipes.

In line behind him, Tom ordered whatever Boyd ordered, not much, and Tom was in training for love anyway, an egg, some orange juice, toast held out on tongs by a bleary hairnet. Tom would leave his crusts behind, a detail calculated, as were all things done before Boyd, to demonstrate that nothing was of significance. Crusts? Tom was not that hungry, the calories were in the crust, Boyd and Tom were having themselves a breakfast with their morning.

Tom ate quickly to have time to get Boyd his coffee. He wouldn't walk for it; he'd bowleg it to the beverage bank like it was a chuck wagon in the Oklahoma Territory. Though truthfully from Kansas, Tom was Oklahoma on these mornings, loping on his lonesome. That motion connected to a lax sideward throw of the legs, which gave him room to lasso two cups with one hand from the rack and let them dangle, roped dogies on his fingers, middle and index, until he was good and ready to set them both, still laced inside his grasp, under the spout, which he palmed with his free hand. While the coffee poured, Tom would keep shaking his legs to communicate the message that his sleepy stems were still waking up, but oh how virtuous to have early classes, and oh how good this java was going to taste; he and his pardner, breakfast-having range riders, were going to drink it up, the Drink That Won the West, good to the last drop.

Their coffee orders diverged; Tom would drop the body language, sorry that Boyd preferred half-and-half. It meant Tom couldn't pour it in and stir with the same spoon he used for his milk. Tom, undeserving of half-and-half, would pull two bullets from the crock and let the water drip from their plastic ridges. To know how his beloved took his coffee, and to act upon the knowledge, was the Pike's Peak of breakfast.

After breakfast, the steep pitch of Slater Hill allowed no lope. Tom trailed behind to Western Civ, a packhorse forever in Boyd's wake. It seemed elaborately careless the way Boyd went to class, a pen in his back pocket, an undersized notebook gripped by one corner like a checkbook. Tom would ponder the insouciance of Boyd's beat-up boat shoes and sockless feet, jealous of those who knew him when the shoes were new.

Approaching Heavilon Hall, Tom would be irked anew that civilization post-Reformation was taught in a hideous modern structure. In the converging funnel of students, he would pull abreast of Boyd, wishing to shield him from these assassins in the Forum. They would move through the bottleneck of the door, then climb the empty stadium of Heavilon 201 to claim their seats in the first row of the second landing. Here at last was room for Tom to stretch his legs, another portrait of nonchalance, and time enough, fifty minutes, to study Boyd's knee, a pale Irish isle bordered by a tear in his jeans. Tom was right-handed; Boyd was left-handed, so their hands scribbled side by side, Boyd's handwriting open and square, Tom's a crabbed and secret servant's scrawl.

*

Late one chilly morning, holding off indoors, Tom and Boyd were lying atop a grassy hillock or knoll or mound or butte, somewhat counterfeit as nature went, since the student union hummed across the path. The wind was high and brisk; they leaned into each other when it blew down their careless necks.

They were stretched out, feet to head, facing each other. Both leaned back on their elbows. What were they talking about, were they even talking? Tom watched Boyd's long, tapering hands dust blades of grass between thumb and forefinger as he talked. Tom rubbed the earth in ten places with the blocky balls of his fingertips. Ten tulips would grow there overnight, red as the daubs on his windswept knuckles. Tom's fingernails were square, Boyd's were oval. Nail shapes were inherited traits, thought Tom, wanting to meet Mr. and Mrs. McIlhenny. His own parents, Alphonse and Janet, were suddenly dead for a ducat, drowned at sea, burnt in a brush fire, held for a ransom beyond his means. All of Boyd was all he had.

A gust hit and Tom turned on his side toward Boyd. Before he could recover his place from this breach of boy conduct, Boyd clamped his calf and plucked a beetle from the back of Tom's trouser leg, his hand electric through the cloth. Tom heaved himself upward. A beetle, said Boyd. Tom hemmed something, abba dabba honeymoon, yabba dabba doo, the sun was in my eyes. The bug raced through Boyd's fingers. His hand was there, *had been* there. Tom caught his breath. I am not afraid of insects, he said. Boyd seemed to find this formality funny and he flung the thing away.

*

Oiled at noon on the Mall, arranged on a pair of bedsheets, Tom and Boyd and Rhoda were blocks away from their dorm and hundreds of miles away from their homes in Overland Park, Evansville, and Great Neck, which they'd been describing, eyes closed by the sun, jet-fueled by coconut oil. Rhoda anchored their center; her one-piece so matched the yellow sheets that Tom and Boyd seemed to be lying on her magnificent train, footmen to the queen of the Hawaiian Long Island. Boyd had gone more native than Tom. His chest was turning cinnamon. Rhoda spoke while Tom spread her red-lemon locks, coarse as unstrung rope, into a sunburst around her head. His care liquefied her voice. The heat and siren call of summer soon cast a spell.

Attentive to his mistress, Tom bade her turn over, then creamed her back with unguent. She sighed that Boyd and Tom had to fly east for a visit. Boyd looked at Tom through sleepy lids and agreed indeed they must. Tom's heart pulled his hand to his chest; his T-shirt would forever bear this oily imprint. Rhoda said they could stay in her brother Ronnie's room, both of them; Ronnie was going to dental school. Boyd asked whether the room was blue, and she giggled. Tom asked whether it was blue like the Amazon, and she slept.

Tom and Boyd settled back to roast, conjoined in her munificence. After ten minutes, Boyd sat up and said hey. Cooled by the shade he cast, Tom looked over. It is blue like the Amazon, Boyd said. He grinned, and his teeth were all Tom saw, pearl and spice; what Boyd possessed was what the explorers set sail for; he'd spun the astrolabe inside Tom, who set a fresh course until the sun slipped below the pillowcase.

*

Tom was having his hair cut. For the first time since grade school, his ears would show. The shape of his head would reveal itself through this haircut. Who he was before the fact of Boyd tumbled down the barber's sheet in smudgy cinders. Tom was going to be a new country.

At dinner he tried again, as he had at Easter, when he wore the bow tie, to inscribe happenstance into a Kansan sense of timing. He said this haircut was a summer haircut.

It did not wash.

A tormentor asked whether there was an autumn haircut for the harvest moon.

A naysayer said his ears were boomerangs.

A philistine said his head was shaped like a half-peeled banana.

A yahoo wondered whether his mother got to keep the forceps.

Two down the table and across Boyd fed. Tom did not always sit beside him. Sometimes he loved the air between them. Between mouthfuls, Tom heard Boyd say he thought his haircut looked great.

Very Fire Island said Rhoda.

That island Tom couldn't place. He'd not heard of it.

Finish your cobbler, said Boyd. He pulled at an ear and smiled. He meant Tom's ear. Tom was not a new country. Tom was his protectorate.

*

One day Boyd brought Tom to Revival House, a secondhand clothing store in College Town. Sheila Scholl, whose purview was turbans and tea dresses and Tangee and tuberoses, saved merchandise for Boyd, shaped his taste, sold him surplus. From her dais, she watched the big parade down Salisbury Street. Hey babe, she asked Boyd, where you been keeping? She took up Tom's hand while Boyd made the introductions.

Everything amused them. The trash barrel of crinolines, the rat's nest of wedgies in the trunk, the chintz dressing curtain, the ash on Sheila's cigarette heading for the rhumba in her bosom, the teeth of the hound in the Prince of Wales jacket she'd slipped on Boyd.

He stood before a full-length mirror. Nice broad shoulders, Sheila S. rasped, saluting his form in the way Tom denied himself.

She picked a bowling shirt for Tom, turquoise rayon with a rooster. In said shirt he stood, felt her tug the sleeve. He liked the checked trousers Boyd had put on. Sinatra pants, she called them, take them off, your pal should have them. Boyd demurred. She insisted he take them off, they fit Tom's rooster, take them off. She had one hand at Boyd's waist, one hand on Tom's.

Sheila S. insisted on immodesty. Boyd dropped his trousers. Tom dropped his and stepped out of them. The rhumba coiled around his legs. Her garnets rolled across her throat as she sang a song to Tom's blue boxers. Only gentlemen wore boxers, she pronounced. Then, amidst the frippery of the years, she tilted and looked at Tom. Through her boogie-woogie cloud cover, Sheila sent a message with canny lizard eyes. Nice match, she said, putting Tom and Boyd together like a suit.

Benediction received, Tom went crimson. What gold escaped his eyes that this bawd could pan?

*

Tom and Boyd and Dave and Billy went for a run one Saturday afternoon. Dave had been a miler in high school and paced them toward the Wabash. Tom liked the sound of his feet on the ground as their four-boy tattoo invaded the streets. Neighborhoods knuckled to their message. He very much liked the locomotive ease with which he removed his T-shirt in full stride. He tied it around his waist as he accelerated over the river, which rushed to meet them. He felt nearly naked, a Roman torso hung above the water. The air took his jubilant dew. His hair, in truth too short to stream behind him, did its best. He pulled ahead of Boyd, whose gym shorts the green the fade of spearmint Tom liked best of all.

Dave was surprised to find Tom two strides back. He pointed left, then sprinted forward. Everything went green as Tom sucked air down Stadium Avenue; they were form, they were velocity, they were saving Greece from the Persians, they would do this every other morning. The four of them burst through a parking lot, shot through a funnel like blades of grass into a lawn mower bag.

Tom squatted on the pavement, panting. Dave shook his legs backward like a colt. Tom knee-bent his face into his shirt at his waist. Boyd placed his hand between Tom's shoulders to keep from falling over. They would shower after in adjacent stalls. Tom would never let him fall.

*

On the eve of St. Hilary of Arles, Tom and Boyd visited a cemetery. They slipped about the tombstones until a soused and wobbly Boyd stopped to lie atop a crypt. The stars would steady him, he said. He fell quickly to sleep. Tom sat astride a cenotaph, his ankles pressed in the web of his hands. He looked to the clear, ringing heavens. He watched over his sleeping lord, would wake him when the time felt right. Tom was not a gargoyle. He had never felt so happy.

*

Six of them played hearts in Dave's room, hunched over the cards like gangsters. Boyd wove in, passed a flask, flopped back on Dave's bed and

LET ME SEE IT

cut his forehead on a metal post. He declared blood, then bolted. Even before Tom got up, the other boys had turned back to the game. They knew the invisible rope would yank Tom from the room, so he moved even faster. That way no one else could gauge its length.

Boyd made good time in the dark, but Tom located him in the trefoil recesses of the War Memorial, slumped against a column as if struck by lightning. The dream of Tom's days—Boyd's hand in his—was nothing like his dreams as he cleaned the bloodied fingers with his handkerchief. Ten minutes before he had been playing hearts; now he nursed his true love's forehead. There was a foreign palm open on his leg, a saint's relic to be tucked into his pocket, the names of the dead cold against his back, and a flask gleaming on the cobblestones. The provident juxtapositions of life overwhelmed him.

Tom marched Boyd to the roach coach to settle him with food. He was making change when Boyd bolted again. This time he couldn't find him. Heading up the back stairs to the dorm, he heard a *psst.*

Boyd was inside a spreading forsythia. Tom gave him his food through the leaves, then crossed his arms. Come in, said Boyd. Tom scooted under the canopy, where the crouched and aboriginal Boyd told him that Rhoda had rebuffed his pass and was the reason for this drunk. Tom seized the flask, poured out the contents, and burst from the Boyd fort, the edges of his nurse's cape tearing on the branches.

The corridor was quiet. At the end of the hallway, uncertain of his footing, Tom stared at the forsythia from the window until it caught fire.

Boyd surprised him from behind. The light, he said, hurt his eyes. Tom dared to bring a chair and pillow from his room. He stood on the chair to remove the globe from the lamp. It tipped, and dried insects fluttered like rice puffs down his arms. He loosened the hot bulbs until they expired. His fingertips pulsed with heat. Tom touched them to the carpet. Five irises would grow there overnight. Their shoots would stipple Boyd's eyelids in his sleep. The boys murmured on. They would sleep in the hallway between their opposing thresholds. The last thing they saw was milky light from the moon.

*

Tom was in the Earth and Atmospheric Library. It was Friday night, but he wasn't playing hearts; he was doing research in the map room. He might have found his major. This Tom owed to Boyd, who had planted him in the stream of what had been and was and what was still to come, made of him a scholar of surroundings.

Far away a generator blew in a shower of sparks. The campus blacked out utterly. Tom rushed the doors. The charts on the timbered table rustled in the wind he made.

He ran west. Sirens had started up. The buildings on the Mall stood like frosted cakes in a dark refrigerator. As he approached Slater Hill, he heard a roar from below. He descended into a well of shouts, noisemakers, breaking glass, bouncing balls, catcalls, and imprecise oaths. He heard a constant thwack: claques of women were traveling the courtyards, novitiates with pocketbooks and sandals. They were comparison-shopping the abbeys, and the men, moving in pairs, were randy troubadours.

From upper chambers buckets of water and fire extinguishers were deployed. Pilgrims were droning, Candles, candles, who has candles, I need candles, have you candles? The student union was bedlam. Peasants pushed dead pinball machines just for the noise, pool balls cracked on the floor, knights were fencing with the cues. Harry's Pub was an angry rout, flushed with the odor of spilled ale.

A signal flare catapulted to hurrahs just as Tom reached his dorm. He took the stairs. Their corridor was empty, for all had joined the feast of fools. He didn't know what to do, so he listened from a ledge. Contingents cursed on the rooftops. Rumors escalated. Rape in the dining hall, the candy counter torn apart, free butts for all, six sophomores electrocuted in the outage.

With so much color in the darkness, Tom waited for the Goths. His ancestors had died on nights like this, without the North Star to guide them or a piece of the True Cross to mark their graves. He found himself praying for trade winds. He took Boyd's handkerchief from his pocket, wet the relic with his tears, steeped, wallowed, sank in his blood.

Hands grabbed him. Boyd asked him where he'd been, he couldn't find him, he was worried, he'd been hunting all over for him. You were? said

Tom, pole-axed with joy. He grew wings and flew up to witness the roiling kermis from a safer spot on the canvas. On high, nearer to the frame, he caroled to himself, Boyd had gone hunting for me.

His love grew five, ten, a hundredfold.

Down below, his eyes were bright and his lips bit shut.

*

They crept out of the forest single file and spotted the totems in the park. Some were ascendant. Some stretched out. Some hunkered in the hard-packed ground. It was close to dawn. Their concrete forms contained all the darkness in the landscape. The freshmen drank in their solemnity. They had to circle slowly through their configuration; any gaudy movement or ungentle comment could cause them to roll over and crush them.

By silent decree, Dave, who had led them here, got first survey. He entered the map. The shadows swallowed him. When he reappeared yards away, his head glowed, lit by distant klieg rays from the planetary research station.

The rest of them, a scatter, a constellation of boys, were free to test the crannies and footholds of the totems. Tom was their sextant, measuring the altitude of their celestial selves. Charles was already fifteen feet above them, scooting up and down a giant, cantilevered pencil box. Billy perched at the left tip of a mounted, cement wedge of cantaloupe rind facing the sky. Boyd inched up the other tip. They stood with an ocean between them. On a signal, they ran down the center and crossed. From Tom's vantage, this maneuver seemed to make the sculpture tilt, and recover, tilt, and recover.

Tom had yet to plant his flag. He thought he'd like to climb a tower crested by a lip with a pulpit through its center. It looked like a pushpin securing a flyaway note. From the ground he imagined that he might lie securely in its compass and see all this world, between dark and dawn, earth and sky, forest and field, all of these states at once, and calmly.

Boyd gave Tom a boost at the bottom, told him where to place his hands. Tom found his footing and began to climb the tower. The seamed concrete pushed sharp against his skin. He reached the lip and knelt. He didn't have time to read the transitions he'd imagined down below because, with a feeling close to dread, Tom with velvet ears and periscope eyes and millipede skin, sensed Boyd making his ascent. He was climbing to Tom, rising past fives, sixes, and one seven.

Tom peered over the rim. He saw the crown of Boyd's curls. He was conscious, acutely conscious of a new vista, the man he knew by heart arriving headfirst from the lap of the earth. His short breaths chuffed. Tom closed his eyes.

Boyd had been right. The lip did have room enough for two. The pulpit divided their hips. Its shape resembled, now that it contained them both, a stigma in a calyx on a forty-foot stem.

They lay feet to feet, head to head. Beyond Tom's left elbow and Boyd's right elbow all space dropped away. The rope was coiled inside their boat. They were curled in the sky, towed instead by the rope of time. Tom turned his head. Boyd turned his head. They looked. They saw.

Tom pressed down all his fingers.

Flowers wouldn't grow in stone.

They were the flower.

All else was stone.

.

ELLIOTT BIDDLER'S VIE BOHÈME
ELLIOTT

1981

Another twenty centimes pinged into the giant clamshell. Elliott bookmarked his Zola and slid down the bedspread into a seated sulk on the rug. There were so many ways to blow Paris, he thought, as he eavesdropped on his roommate, Bruce, in the front hall telephoning yet another actual French person. This one, Martine, needed less convincing than Béa or Poucette or Gaby to meet up later near the Boulevard Raspail for an impromptu confabulation.

Bruce was expert at threading his speech with casual, idiomatic connectives, the *eh biens*, the *tout à faits*, the *m'écoutes* that mark the native speaker and are impossible to pick up in a language lab, whereas Elliott still sometimes forgot to say "Comment?" instead of a surly-sounding "Quoi?" when he needed something repeated, which was more often than he cared to admit. Bruce used mealtimes with their host parents, Giselle and Roger Sirjean, as language practice, chattering away about the pretty flowers or stern newscaster or remarkable laundry soap on the television screen while Elliott traced the J.C. embroidered on his napkin, as if the spirit of Jesus Christ, or Jean-Christophe, the black sheep Sirjean, could furnish him with the one withering phrase to silence them all, plus the television.

Bruce Teakel, the most fluent of the one hundred and seventeen students spending their junior year in Paris on the Sweet Briar program, owed his linguistic prowess to God and the war in Indochina. After the fall of Saigon, several loads of boat people had wound up in Asheville, North Carolina. As prayer leader for the youth ministry of his father's church, Bruce had taught the refugees English, strengthening his French and becoming fluent in Vietnamese along the way. Elliott Biddler, on the other hand, despite five years of French before he began Cornell, had been unable to test out of the language requirement. Forced to begin at the intermediate level, he discovered he enjoyed acquiring a new set of tools. To take but one example, he delighted in grasping the difference between the relative pronouns *ce que* and *ce qui* and deploying them in sentences of his own. Second semester, he kept up with grammar and conversation and added a freshman seminar on Camus, Sartre, and Sarraute.

In the fall of his sophomore year, on the same day that the American hostages were taken in Iran, his father had died of a heart attack. "Je suis le fils dont le père est mort"–Elliott had written this in his French notebook the next morning as he prepared to reschedule an accounting exam. Whether the odd nominative predicate in "I am a son whose father has died" was a way for Elliott to manage his grief is open to debate, but it nevertheless locked into his brain for all time the use of *dont* as a more elegant choice for "whose" than *de qui* or *duquel*.

Three days after the funeral in Cincinnati, Elliott changed his major from economics to French literature. English would have been the obvious choice, but Elliott could be perverse, and so French it was. Now, five months into his year in the City of Light, Elliott's language skills put him somewhere in the lowest third of the 1980–81 Sweet Briar College cohort. Required now to *live* in French, he discovered that its reduced vocabulary and constrictive syntax had stripped him of nuance. Every day he woke up knowing that he would make mistakes. There were few occasions for *dont* at the Sirjeans. Madame and Monsieur called him Elli, an appropriate reduction, he thought. He was Ellie Mae Clampett on *The Beverly Hillbillies*, another American rube out of her depth.

"Bon ben, Martine, à ce soir," Bruce said, ringing off. The slangy elongation of her name—"Martín-*uh*"–made Elliott want to tip the bottle of black ink on the desk table between their beds. Not content with French and Vietnamese, Bruce was now taking Chinese at the Paris III campus. When he wasn't out cultivating that most elusive of creatures, the actual French friend, he spent his evenings filling grid-paper notebooks with columns of brushstroke characters. Elliott sat across from him, silently processing his bile in postcards and tissue-thin aerogrammes. The number of his correspondents, which grew to include former high school teachers, distant relatives, and even his little stepbrothers, Duane and Matt, stood at fifty-three.

Elliott pulled his duck boots from under the stereo console and slipped them on. He would leave before Bruce had a chance to ask him if he were free that night. Tagging along was not something Elliott Biddler did. He tucked a sweater into the waist of his overalls and reattached the straps to the bib. Going for his coat, he caught the reflection of Bruce's Bible in the mirrored closet door rather than look at the angry red knots on his face. Then he circled the salon and liberated a piece of marzipan from a box next to Madame's thumb-worn pile of royalty magazines.

They could eat all they liked for breakfast and dinner, but snacks weren't part of their contract. Bruce and Elliott were Giselle Sirjean's second pair of *bébés américains,* and her disappointment in them was clear. How short they fell of Doug (pronounced "Doog") and Leslie, the lumberjacks of '79–'80 who, in her accounts, were virtual Hemingways, always returning at dawn reeking of women or drink. When Giselle had made them soup, she would stand a spoon upright in the tureen and dare it to fall. Those were the soups, she'd say, to satisfy Doog and Leslie's hungers. Bruce, one hundred and twelve pounds and prone to chills, couldn't be fattened up, and Elliott resisted pleasing her with his appetite almost on principle.

"Où vas-tu, Elliott?" Bruce frowned, still seated in the telephone chair in the hall. They spoke only French to one other, a high commandment of the Sweet Briar program that Elliott would never, in his pride, break. Bruce had blundered early on by correcting Elliott's grammar; now there was little they shared besides a desk and a towel rack.

Elliott defiantly chewed the marzipan lime he had taken. Never mind the house rules or its conceivable hazard to his skin, so smooth and tranquil back home. Not only had Paris effaced his personality, it had seeded a crop of cysts across his jaw and cheeks, raging, inexpressible sentences that hurt to the touch and resisted pharmaceutical treatment. His face was bumpy as a hand grenade. Giselle thought that his acne was a delayed reaction to his father's death. Elliott didn't have the French to tell her that she was full of shit. She'd once halved a turnip and bid him to blot his *boutons* with its curative liquor.

"Je m'en vais," he replied, after a dramatic swallow. He swept out of the apartment, confident that Bruce would remove the telltale paper sleeve from the candy box.

Had they elected to converse in English, the young men, so different in temperament, would have found themselves agreeing on at least one point. The Sirjeans were vulgar people. Not in the sense of lewd or indecent, but in the sense of common. Unlike many in the Sweet Briar program, neither Bruce nor Elliott came from wealth, but certain niceties prevailed in their homes. The Teakels and the Biddlers didn't watch television during dinner or use the toilet with the door open or have screaming fights about their children in front of guests and boarders. Chez Sirjean shenanigans were a running feature in Elliott's foreign correspondence.

Elliott was not without friends. Ninety-six of the one hundred and seventeen students on the Sweet Briar program were women, and many, as bewildered and mistranslated as he was, welcomed his company. On another Saturday, he might have met Julia and Sheri and Carolyn for *un crème* and a slice of the Louvre, but that particular day, having been outdone by Bruce's clamshell treasury of glittering gamines, he crossed the Marais for a trip to the Centre Pompidou instead. He registered the damp, septic smell of old bricks under the north arcade of the Place des Vosges, but little else. Pausing on the Rue de Turenne, he looked in every direction before drawing aside the orange rubber curtain of a passport photo booth.

The third shot today was particularly hopeless, so ghastly it brought a smile to his lips. He was able to devise its legend instantly. Setting his foot on the adjustable stool, he took out a pen and, using his knee as a desk, wrote on the back of the strip: "Quasimodo Boards the Treblinka Express."

From a distance, Elliott fancied the Centre Pompidou, with its tangle of exterior duct systems in kindergarten yellow and red and blue, a color transparency in a medical dictionary—it was like a cross-sectioned cube of his seething, purulent skin. Closer up, it looked the way he felt: raw and childish, a cultural mistake. He flashed his ID to the attendant, and the escalator carried him to the third-floor library. After brief consideration, he chose a copy of *Winesburg, Ohio* and sat down to read at the corner of a long table.

Discovering American literature was another way to blow Paris, but it couldn't be helped. By January, the Pompidou library had become a refuge for Elliott, a bibliographic taking of the waters midway between the Sirjeans in the eleventh arrondissement and the suite of Sweet Briar classrooms in the fifth. Like a sweeping stretch of Boulevard Haussmann, the bindings on the books in the American lit aisle were uniformly gray, with white-windowed titles, but between the covers were baseball diamonds and truck depots and town meetings and juke joints and wheat harvests and the legible transgressions of legible persons. Unable to disappear into drama or poetry, Elliott spent soothing afternoons on near-canonical shorter fictions like *Ethan Frome, The Ballad of the Sad Café, Lucy Gayheart, Billy Budd, Of Mice and Men, The Awakening,* and—unavoidably—*Daisy Miller.*

Elliott was able that day to overlook Sherwood Anderson's stylistic debt to Gertrude Stein, whose painstaking lexical salads he associated with his own word-by-word transactions among the French. He had been to many an Illinois county fair and could station himself more quickly in Winesburg's kitchen alleys than, for example, on one of Melville's convoluted quarterdecks. These people I know, he thought to himself as he looked up in a pause between stories.

Two tables away, a man was staring at him. Elliott flushed and resumed his reading, but was soon sneaking looks up after every page, then every paragraph. Minutes went by, sentences started and stopped over and over. Patrons sauntered past, brushing the table with long, limp scarves, but the gaze held. Eventually the fixity of his purpose must have struck the stranger as absurd, because he grinned at Elliott obliquely, then smiled outright.

Fleeing his only sanctuary would leave him to the streets, so Elliott held tight to his corner of Huck's raft, as it were. The *dragueurs* that the Sweet Briar staff had warned them against, the army of charmers infesting the American Express office and a thousand other locations, were assumed to be solely interested in women, a situation that left him without tools for outwitting his arousal. Straight boys go to England their junior year; gay boys, and the unsure, go to France. Stateside, Elliott had dabbled both ways, but so far in Paris he'd felt too ugly and miserable to put himself out in any direction.

The stranger wasn't oily or unkempt or Algerian. His sandy, neatly dressed hair was combed straight back. The tops of his ears were delicately pointed, like elf shoes, and the convex curves of his face were the opposite of sinister. A college education was a given, or why would he be cruising a library? His eyes were gray or blue or green, at any rate *not* brown, a final safety feature for the American *faux-naïf* in Oshkosh overalls and duck boots from Maine.

Alpine, Elliott thought. Wood. Chocolate and cheese. Clocks.

He gave into a smile at last, whereupon the stranger stood and supported Elliott's assessment by being taller than most Gauls, a fir tree who brushed the shelves with clean, fresh branches as he slipped into the stacks. Covering his erection with *Winesburg, Ohio*, Elliott went to replace it on the shelf next to *Go Tell It on the Mountain*. He loitered in this Main Street tagged with his sorrows. He pitched his ears for snowshoes rounding the corner. The voice, he knew, would be as clean and clear as a Swiss train whistle.

The next morning Bruce was drawing Chinese characters in a shaft of light liturgical in its intensity as Elliott pretend-slept on his stomach in a swirl of emerald satin bedclothes. Their tiny room held two beds. Elliott manned the giant Second Empire barge, which gleamed like a pagan altar, while Bruce had the Murphy bed. He was slender enough to recede into the wall with the mattress, should the force of one of Giselle and Roger's nocturnal rows break through the plaster and drive its way into their chamber. They were to switch sleeping stations on the first of February.

Elliott was waiting Bruce out—difficult to do when every stroke of the pen felt like a stab to his very full bladder.

How was it possible that Elliott Biddler, twenty years old, in *Paris*, for God's sake, had forgotten *sex*? Had anything ever been more exciting than Gérard Dupont popping the side button of his overalls and reaching inside with his paw? No belt, no button, no zipper, no prep, it was something near to rape, in the best possible way. Had anything ever been more authentically romantic than Gérard Dupont's liquid good-bye on his stairway landing in the Left Bank—"On se reverra quand?"

Too jazzed to be embarrassed about his French, Elliott had had to make Gérard repeat it, more slowly each time, until he could piece together a literal translation: "One. Will see. Each other. Again. When?"

"À bientôt," he'd answered at last. He had touched two fingers to the pointed peak of Gérard's left ear. Then Elliott had made the sign of the telephone—he wanted the Sirjeans' phone to ring for *him*, over and over, until the chestnut trees bloomed in the boulevards. He'd come in at four thirty in the morning, happy to have the cabbie keep the change, happy to pull a Doog and Leslie.

Elliott turned onto his back and let Bruce see that his eyes were open.

The scratching stopped.

"Et alors, où étais-tu?" said Bruce, failing to muffle an accusatory tone.

Elliott sensed that his roommate had not given up on the wish to know him, suspected that he was even kept close in his prayers, but so little had passed between them, or ever would, that he flirted with telling him the truth. He had been rutting for hours with his first older man in a seventeenth-century walk-up in Saint-Germain-des-Prés. *That* conversation, however, would tax his French and kill the high, so he fibbed, in the plural: "Chez des amis."

It was a bit of a dare—would Bruce ask the rude and doubting "*Which* friends?"

Bruce bit his lip and finished a column of characters while Elliott traced his hand over a lion-footed naiad on the mahogany bow. According to Giselle, the barge had been the site of Jean-Christophe's teenage debauches with every slut in the neighborhood.

"Tu t'es bien amusé?"

Elliott threw aside the covers and breathed in the smell of sex on himself. "Oui," he said. "Beaucoup beaucoup."

Several weeks later Bruce was captaining the boat bed while Elliott played courtesan on the Left Bank. Gérard Dupont's lack of a schedule signified either a lot of money or no money at all. He simply said that his time was taken up by a "project literary in nature." The pair of fountain pens anchoring the stack of pages written in Gérard's bold, ropy hand pleased Elliott to contemplate from the chair where he sipped coffee and listened to his swain wash up. Gérard wrote in the evenings, so they met afternoons, the ritual question "On se reverra quand?" popped on the fade-out clinches in a hidden courtyard off the Rue Dauphine.

They went to museums devoted to small subjects, like masonry or the history of monastic life; each of these expeditions seemed to dissolve another dulling coat of paste wax the city had pressed upon Elliott. Gérard encouraged his demands for showy kisses in unguarded rooms, and Elliott learned not to panic when Gérard crossed over velvet ropes and invited him to test pieces of brooding feudal furniture. As the junior partner in a carnal arrangement, Elliott felt no pressure to speak, so eventually he started talking, and not as language practice. Imitating Bruce would have made him too self-conscious, but listening to Gérard comment in offhand public situations was giving him the confidence to begin to drop the *ne* in negative sentences, to try the impersonal *on* instead of *je* and *nous,* and to disdain complicated classroom tenses like the past conditional. His painstaking *pour lequel* and *pour laquelle* became a quick *pourquoi.* The obligatory "Bonjour, M'dame" to merchants grew stronger, and he began to ask for things, rather than point. Twice in history class at Clignancourt, waiting for the instructor to arrive, he made general comments to other students in his section. One of them responded, words coming back, words to savor.

Such was Elliott Biddler's bohemia, no less distinctive for being small and particularly his. Under Gérard's Alpine influence, he wasn't the dumbstruck Elli staring at his dinner or the morose bookworm pitching a pup tent in the American literature aisle at the Centre Pompidou. As his French developed a more becoming slouch, he saw more of the city and less of his shoes. His new pair of skinny plaid trousers that he'd *haggled over* at an open market astonished Julia and Sheri and Carolyn, as did his command of the cake selection when he took them to a tiny *salon de thé* near the Odéon that he and Gérard liked to go to.

The sex matched the courtyard of the busy street: it was quiet, detailed. Both kept their eyes open for long stretches of it. They were worth watching, Elliott thought, loving the idea of being in the third person as he drifted to sleep against the smooth taffy of Gérard's chest.

Elliott began coming out that spring, first to his Sweet Briar chums, and then in jaunty aerogrammes that began, as often as not, with the Piaf-like "I met a man." His family, however, could wait. *Those* people, he rationalized, didn't *deserve* this piece of information—with one distant exception. From his having shown up at his father's funeral, and from the formality of his condolence letter, Elliott suspected that his first cousin Tom, now a junior at Purdue, might also be gay. Without ever having met his uncle Henry, Tom had driven to Cincinnati all by himself. In his aerogramme, Elliott (very) belatedly thanked Tom for his expression of sympathy, then wondered why their parents had been such antipathetic siblings before he slipped in blunt references to a *Paris toujours gai*. He didn't know whether Purdue, renowned for its science and engineering programs, required a foreign language, but sex, he wanted Tom to know, was the ideal way to pick one up.

One drizzly afternoon, surrounded by breathless magazine profiles of the just-affianced Lady Diana Spencer, Giselle Sirjean remarked to Elliott, who was coming out of the toilet, that his face looked "less violent."

He stopped to consider this. In his wallet was a half strip of photos taken that day in the booth on the Rue de Turenne. Gérard's goofy kiss captured in one of them hadn't left any pain on his cheekbone. He found the spot, pressed lightly, then ran his fingers in a gentle comma down his jaw.

"Je pense que vous avez raison, Madame."

She reached for the box of marzipan. "Vous en voulez?" she asked.

Elliott stepped onto her rug and selected a strawberry. They enjoyed an exchange of declarative sentences about Prince Charles's choice of a bride and the cold of Chicago winters. Then Elliott made a show of being astonished to learn that Madame had never been to the Rodin Museum, where he had spent that very afternoon. He was in the midst of telling her which metro to take and where to change when—surprise!—the notorious

Jean-Christophe, gone missing for months, let himself in with a key he wasn't supposed to have.

Mother and son went right to it. Even by Sirjean standards, this match was a doozy, lavish in outflung hands and lengthy, nonverbal gutturals rising from the throat. More gratifying still, there was Elliott to play to, an audience to be addressed at every turn. All of Jean-Christophe's girlfriends were whores. That last one, Jasmina, was a camel. He was a shiftless, half-witted bum with a bottomless thirst. Everything he had put his hand to had gone to shit. The proof of that was under his fingernails. He'd flunked out of radio announcers' school. He couldn't saw a board in half. He couldn't chop the head off a chicken. He fucked anything with tits. They could fill a nursery school with his fetuses. They were sick of bailing him out. He'd broken his father's heart. He was a plague and a scandal.

Jean-Christophe collected himself and launched an assault in the kitchen, clattering lids and pulling drawers open until Madame howled from the salon not to steal her things. Elliott might have beaten his own retreat during this brief intermission, but he wanted more of the prodigal son's hooded eyes and deep dimples. J-C needed a shave, and his finger-nails *were* dirty, but beyond that? Madame could convict him of anything but unattractiveness.

Jean-Christophe returned with a tumbler of his father's best whiskey. Giselle cut to the chase and asked him what he needed the money for—an abortionist, a loan shark, his pusher—but Jean-Christophe would not be rushed. He offered a cigarette to Elliott, who refused, then lit his own with an onyx elephant lighter.

She was a castrating bitch. She was a smothering cow. She drove away all his girlfriends. They were terrible parents. Laurent and Thierry hated them, too. They pinched pennies until they screamed. Nothing he ever did was good enough. They set him up to fail. Laurent and Thierry got everything. He got the crusts, the cores, the peelings, the parings, the leav-ings. Even Doog and Leslie had come before him. He'd spent his life beg-ging for their love. They needed to die so that his life could begin.

Eventually, mother and son were weeping on the persimmon-colored fainting couch, clasped in a heroic embrace, the photo spreads of the future king and queen of England wrinkling and tearing under their bottoms.

Jean-Christophe shook hands good-bye with Elliott. As he made his way to the hallway, a swag of greasy hair fell across his bedroom eyes. He stood at the open door, brazenly counting banknotes.

"On se reverra quand?" Elliott called out confidently, rapidly, without any preparation.

In this new context, Gérard Dupont's romantic "When will we see each other again?" became an ironic Gallic observation, an overt judgment of Jean-Christophe's slippery character and at the same time a covert acknowledgment of his personal appeal. J-C winked, pulled an imaginary arrow from his chest, scooped the change from the clamshell, and shut the door.

Madame, to Elliott's immense satisfaction, almost bust a gut laughing.

Then, one day in the middle of March, too soon for chestnut blossoms, Gérard called and asked to meet at an address in the Rue d'Assas. Elliott found him smoking a cigarette right around the corner from the Sweet Briar offices. More than hoping to be caught in the act by a passing *Américaine* of his acquaintance, he pressed his whole body against Gérard and gave him a lingering kiss on the lips, in response to which Gérard observed that it was bad form to communicate germs in front of a VD clinic.

Gérard gave an outline of the case to the stunned Elliott. Having awakened to familiar symptoms, he had gone to be tested that morning. That Elliott was presently asymptomatic did not signify much. Gonorrhea didn't always show up. And actually, he might not have contracted it; it was a mischievous bacterium. (The adjective he employed here, one Elliott would never forget, was *espiègle*.)

Gérard managed to talk Elliott into the clinic by saying that a visit to a doctor on the Sweet Briar list would go on record; the testing here was entirely anonymous, and free. He pulled Elliott down a narrow corridor and got him moved to the top of the list—something about an unmissable history tutorial at four thirty—but after finding him a seat, he proceeded to leave for a previous engagement.

The waiting room, once Elliott adjusted to the dim lighting through the glass brick windows, seemed a creation of central casting for cartoon *dragueurs*: men of every Mediterranean and African hue, their faces seamed by age, or work, or poverty, lined the walls. Turbaned men, men in coveralls, men who paid for it. Most of them silent, some bored, some scowling, and all of them brown-eyed and smoking.

Listening for his number, Elliott opened his Clairefontaine notebook. He stared at a sheet until the grid became less blurry. He found a pen and then, lacking a useful language in which to capture this singular occasion, he borrowed one of Bruce's and began to work his humiliations, one square at a time, into a column of characters composed of brushstrokes.

He drew the mouth of the receptionist, who had greeted Gérard as if a friend had merely stopped by for a beer and a blood test. He drew an army helmet—catching the French disease in Paris was the punch line to a joke more antique than the doughboys.

He invented characters for the triple cliché of feeling unclean and sinful and haplessly Puritan-American. Gérard's declaration that Elliott had better get used to this part of the lifestyle was an amoeba with a corkscrew fringe. The condescension in his tone when he'd said it took up two more squares. Left unsaid in the rush and the shock was the question of transmission. Elliott hadn't been expecting monogamy, exactly. But maybe he had been. He drew his heart. He drew his tongue. One had tricked the other. He drew a pitchfork.

On the subway he finished his column with two last figures—a lollipop and a Z. The lollipop represented the introduction of the swabbed wire a half inch into the head of his penis. The technician had jiggled it inside him for several seconds like an uncooperative car key. The Z was the Zorro shape she swished with the wire onto a plate of agar. He was told to come back immediately should he present with a discharge. Otherwise, his culture would take several days to grow.

Then came Bruce's birthday fête. Coming in near the close of the apéritifs, Elliott passed directly into their room, pulled his bed from the wall, and tucked a small white box under the mattress. As he recombed his hair in the mirrored door, he listened to Giselle curse a balky burner in the kitchen. His skin was now clearer, or cleaner, than his bloodstream. He opened the double doors onto the salon.

Bruce, having attained his majority, was explaining blue laws to his honored guest, actual French friend Martine, a delicate girl with two sleek black braids. Elliott greeted Jean-Christophe, who had turned up with a bottle of calvados and enough material for his parents to inspire a new late-night episode of Punch and Judy. Madame brought in the tureen. With a coquettish half pirouette, she presented her broad backside to Jean-Christophe. He retied her lace holiday apron. The soup, she said, transferring her toothpick from mouth to hair bun, was spring leek.

Monsieur switched on the television. François Mitterrand's presidential campaign provided a lively topic for the first course. Amidst the salvos of anti-Socialist invective from the older generation, Elliott asked Martine some personal questions and learned that she was a Vietnamese refugee, that she was sixteen, and that she and her girlfriends had met the extremely *sympa* Bruce at church. She also liked to sing and to paint in watercolors.

At the presentation of the main course, Jean-Christophe, who had offered little more than his appetite, rubbed his hands expectantly, but when she served, Giselle began with the birthday boy.

Elliott and Bruce both wondered at the ring of dense burgundy slices on the best platter. Mutton they could smell at ten paces. Steak à la Sirjean sizzled with undulant collars of fat. Other cuts of beef had a coarser grain. Pork and veal weren't that dark. Rabbit didn't slice. Horsemeat wouldn't appear on a birthday.

"Ça sent bon quand même," clucked Bruce.

"C'est du venaison," said Jean-Christophe, trying to speed things up.

"Venaison sauce poivre," said Madame.

Bruce eagerly helped himself, but Elliott was forced to put the tongs Bruce had passed him back onto the platter. "Non merci," he said.

The refusal of her venison with pepper sauce floored Madame. "Pas de venaison, Elli?"

Elliott could have said he wasn't hungry, or was allergic, or spoken like an American and declared that deer were too cute to eat. Instead he shook his head no and said, "Non merci, Madame, le gibier m'est défendu."

"Défendu?" she scoffed. "Le gibier? Pourquoi ça?"

Of the six prohibitions printed on the prescription insert, the most inexplicable was number four—no eating of game. Elliott looked to Jean-Christophe. The family *dragueur*, wetting his throat with the house red, might know why. The malty, peaty, butch ghosts of Doog and Leslie, back-slapping in the boys' bedroom, most likely did not.

"Bon ben—," began Elliott. Then he paused. Bruce looked up at the correct use of a casual connective, as did his actual French friend, Martín-*uh* Nguyen, song leader of a church youth group Bruce led near Montparnasse. Was it jealousy over a circle of pious Indochinese high schoolers, Elliott wondered, that had led him directly into the arms of his actual and infectious French friend Gérard Dupont?

Elliott Biddler wiped clean lips with his napkin and finished his statement. "—J'ai la chtouille."

Giselle dropped the platter. Slices of venison flapped up like shingles in a tornado. Jean-Christophe lost a mouthful of wine to the tablecloth. Roger and Martine scootched back from the table as if someone had vomited in their laps.

"M'écoute, qu'est-ce la chtouille?" Bruce asked in a general way.

Conscious of having struck the jackpot—Bruce not knowing a vocabulary word—Elliott answered him in English for the very first time.

"It's French for 'the clap.'"

Bruce was still confused. "The clap? What's 'the clap'?"

"Gonorrhea."

Bruce's hands flew up to his face like Indian clubs. "You mean, VD? Are you saying you have a venereal disease?"

What Bruce was imagining could not have been worse than the posters Elliott had missed on his first visit to the clinic on the Rue d'Assas. The waxy violet and crimson sores, the wet, nacreous blisters, the poxy folds, the speckled digits and crusted lips and tarry tongues—the wages of sin coating the walls were altogether legible, to say the least.

"That's right," Elliott replied.

"How in holy hell did you get gonorrhea?"

The intensity of Bruce's horror, magnified by the fresh flute of his Carolina accent, released Elliott from all shame. He shrugged and said, "I got it from my boyfriend."

"Your *what?*"

Ex-boyfriend, he thought. Elliott's test results had elicited no sympathy from Gérard—or information about how they'd come his way. Indeed, when he insinuated at a café that the route of transmission had been through Elliott, not the other way around, Elliott decided that they wouldn't be seeing each other again, ever. Unlike poor Daisy Miller, contracting Roman fever in the Colosseum, Elliott Biddler was still *bébé* enough to heed a warning. It just couldn't be helped. He had flipped a five-franc piece into his saucer and strode away from the Left Bank and all that it had given him.

"You mean, you're a homosexual?" Bruce was saying. "Five months in the same room and you didn't have the decency to tell me?"

"Why would I tell you?" Elliott said. "You're a kiss-ass Jesus freak!"

Bruce threw his napkin to the carpet and made a delicious guttural sound deep in his throat. "Well, you—you—you're—just a mopey pizza face," he said, his voice rising higher.

"Not anymore!" Elliott shouted back.

In a silence broken only by the soft urgings of a cat food commercial on the television, Elliott became aware of an uncommon attentiveness on the part of the French. Heads forward, eyes narrowed, Martine and the three Sirjeans watched and listened, studying the young men as if they were an emergency broadcast on a foreign language channel. Bruce was still angry, but Elliott started to smile.

"What do you find funny, Elliott?"

"It's just . . . you sound so different in English."

"Well, so do you."

"I do? How so?"

There was suddenly plenty for them to talk about. And as they got down to it, hammer and tongs, roommates at last, Madame Sirjean, with a sigh, began to cover Jean-Christophe's wine stain with the contents of the saltcellar.

HOOTCHIE MAMAS

ELLIOTT

1982

"Sometimes you have to spend money to make money," said my mother from the other side of the dressing room curtain. I heard her rustling in her purse. My mother navigated life with a set of four midsized Ziploc bags. "Now show me how they fit, son."

I stopped in the middle of disentangling the glossy cardboard tag from the fly in my boxers. The smooth way her sentence rolled out made me suppose that spending money to make money was a great, general truth she had been holding back until I graduated from college. That had been five days ago. When I picked her up at the county airstrip, I was astonished at how much she seemed to have aged in ten months. After years of upsweeps, bouffants, soft perms, and body waves in shades from straw to honey, years of curling iron burns on the countertops and plastic dye gloves stuck to the bottom of the powder room wastebasket, she had let the gray come in, and come down straight in a pixie. And she was wearing tan leatherette flats, nurse shoes practically. Without her hair and heels, she looked like an unusually merry old elf, or a children's librarian. When we began to fight over who would carry her three clamshell suitcases, she began to assume her traditional contours, and I was relieved to see her reapply lipstick in the passenger mirror. Soon she was tapping the car window with a tangerine fingernail, pointing at things as if they didn't have trees and birds and gas stations in Chicagoland.

I roomed with two women my senior year, and from sloth and anxiety about life after Cornell, not one of us had given a thought as to where we'd make our parents take us for graduation dinner. By March, the only restaurant accepting reservations on the big weekend was the Howard Johnson's in Slaterville Springs, so we decided to cook for our families and make a feast of our shortsightedness. I was the one with no money, and because I had only one parent to put up, my mother was going to stay in my room and spend the week after graduation seeing the sights of Ithaca, New York. Entertaining her on my turf would be stressful, I knew, but if anyone had to worry when the families convened, it would be my roommate Janine, whose mother was an alcoholic night owl with a pronounced interest in our sex lives.

One September night I had picked up the phone and a woman's voice asked if this was Elliott. I said yes it was, and she asked me what my hands smelled like. I asked who is this? and she said this is Mrs. Hagopian, what did my hands smell like right at that very moment, did they smell like my boyfriend's crotch?

I sniffed my fingers with an audible flourish. "They smell like frozen meatballs," I replied. "Patrick's crotch smells much better than that." I'd had a work-study shift that afternoon breaking up bags of meatballs in the dining hall. Then she asked if there had been lamb in the meatballs, and I said I wouldn't know, my mother never cooked lamb. This, she declared, was not to be borne. A proper *polpetto* contained beef, pork, *and* lamb.

Janine, on the alert for such calls, was by this time holding her hand out for the phone. "Mother!" she said, pulling a strand of her hair back from the receiver. We'd known each other for only two weeks, so she might also have been embarrassed for having told her mother I was gay before clearing it with me. If I got lifestyle points senior year for living with two women, Janine and Sarah got them for living with a gay boy just back from Paris. This was September 1981.

At least twice a week that year Mrs. Hagopian, the improper Bostonian, telephoned in her cups. Sarah avoided picking up after ten, but if I

LET ME SEE IT

wasn't writing a paper or over at Patrick's, I liked to spar with her. Mrs. H. would always need to know how much "activity"—in hours and orgasms— I'd been getting and, proud of how she'd passed her large breasts and sexual appetite on to her daughter, speculated on the quality of the activity Janine was getting with Conrad, the sports editor of the *Cornell Daily Sun*. Our chats could go on for more than an hour, the equivalent, by my ear, of four glasses of wine; Mrs. H. preferred Italian whites. Sometimes, declaring herself too tired, she put Tessa or Katia, her equally provocative younger daughters, on the phone. Tessa's first question to me was whether I felched.

Janine, whose role in the family was to be appalled, barked at them all. "Janine's rather like her father, dearie dear," Mrs. H. would say— "a scientist"—and we'd laugh. The whiff of collusion flattered me. It hadn't occurred to me that parents had private opinions of their children, or that one might make friends with them.

"How do they fit, Elliott?" my mother asked again. "Come out and let me see them."

I grimaced at the dressing room mirror. "I don't like them," I said. "They're boring."

"That's not the point of them," she said. "Come on out."

The pants were midnight blue twill, pleated and uncuffed. They came with their own tricolored grosgrain belt—mocha, beige, and navy—but they were a woeful, stopgap approximation of what was necessary to pull off our scheme.

"They're fifteen percent polyester," I said, rattling the curtain rings as I stepped out in front of a three-way mirror.

"That bit of polyester helps them keep their shape. I think they look nice, son. It's possible they're too short." She was frowning at my ankles. Her lips were pressed together as if they already held the pins to hem the pants. Under the light, I saw again that there was an undercoat of fine dark filaments to her gray pixie.

"I wouldn't buy them in a million years."

"Stand up straight. I can let them down a smidge."

I was trying on pants at Gaede's Menswear on the Ithaca Commons because I had a brand-new baccalaureate in French literature and no future, and Mrs. Hagopian had said she could get me a job teaching French at the Milton Academy in Massachusetts. She had told me this on the shabby porch of our apartment. The family feed was winding down; the paper plates, dripping watermelon juice, were attracting yellow jackets; the stripping of the turkey carcass was under way in the kitchen; and the fathers and uncles had cast a pall by asking us simple, terrifying questions about our plans.

Mrs. H. must have felt my heart leap at her promise of employment, for she leaned over, pressed my knee, and whispered that she was a significant donor to the Milton Academy, and they owed her. When I came up to Boston the following weekend for Janine's graduation party, she would arrange an interview for me with the Languages and Literature dean.

I had to believe her. This was now May 1982. We were in the midst of the first great postwar recession as well as the year the media announced that anyone who didn't *know* computers was forever fucked on the job market. Shipping a case of Mumm's in advance of her arrival in Ithaca, Mrs. H. had money and certainty and *Boston* behind her. One bite of my spinach ricotta pie and she had asked why I had omitted the nutmeg. Instead of admitting that the house was too cheap to buy a jar of nutmeg for a mere dash of it, I asked her how she had guessed about the nutmeg. Her husband was Armenian, she said, but she was Florentine. There was no guesswork involved. All spinach dishes were enhanced with a scintilla of nutmeg.

I waited until bedtime to tell my mother about the job lead. She had just set her jewelry on my scalloped dresser tray. Without makeup, her face was the color of sand. "God is good, son!" she cried. She raised her arms to thank Him, and I looked away from the outline of her body backlit through her nightgown by my reading lamp. She had met Jesus in a big way while I was in high school. He served as antidote and counterweight to my gruesome stepfather.

"The Hagopians are an interesting family, and such spirited, good-looking girls." All during the party Tessa and Katia, gorgeous, smirking witchlets, had asked my mother faintly mocking questions she pretended not to understand.

Janine's and Sarah's families had left town after the feast, but as I said, my mother was staying on for the week. Monday after breakfast, she placed my nice clothes on my bed and began to strategize.

My one suit was winter wool. My tweed jacket, a milky green antique, would not stretch to June. Shuffling my stock of vintage ties from shirt placket to placket, she talked fabrics: seersucker and all its shades; the merits of linen; summer-weight silks and the different grades of khaki; she invoked celebrated suits from my late father's closet, got caught on a particular madras jacket, a genuine Hickey Freeman, bleeding insouciantly over time, the one he wore to business classes in the unholy heat of a Philadelphia summer.

She wanted me to join in, face the challenge with her, but I said I didn't know who the fuck Hickey Freeman was. She brought a finger to my face, but instead of a reprimand, she crowed that a blue blazer was the answer to prayer; a blazer to match the blue of my eyes was the instrument for my ascent to paid employment.

I sat on the bed and dug my elbows into my knees as a vision of this blue blazer, vivid as a tongue of fire, led her to praise her foresight in teaching me bridge and the waltz and the fox-trot and dinging manners into me and proofreading my bread-and-butter notes through high school and cajoling an old set of golf clubs out of my uncle Gordon. Did I polish those clubs? Did my friends know I played golf? Had I sat up all night playing a penny a point? Had I regretted not joining a fraternity after all? Had I sent graduation announcements to all the Biddler uncles and cousins? I may not have gone to a private school, but here I would teach in one, imagine the preparation for life I would experience! She spent much of that afternoon turning my collars with the sewing kit she kept in one of her Ziplocs.

All that week, while traversing the wonders of Tompkins County, she didn't see God's hand upon the landscape, she saw center-vented hopsack with insignia buttons. Divining my disinterest in this Pentecostal blazer as a hedge against admitting out loud that there was no money for one, she cheerfully suggested we hit the secondhand shops. That was when I finally lost my temper and said that the Milton Academy should hire me for my scholarship, my command of spoken *idiom,* my knowledge of literature and civilization, not for my wardrobe. I flung off my sandals and stepped into Buttermilk Falls to short-circuit my seething brain. She bent down and pretended that she'd never seen a fern before. My mother and I have never been able to have it out.

I had saved Gaede's for Thursday, our last afternoon together. Upon entering, she closed her eyes and prayed for a moment by the sale table. Then she stretched her arms toward the rack of sport coats along one wall, and her body followed hard upon. She pinched and dropped the left arms of every blazer from thirty-nine short to forty-two extra long. Disappointment was swift. She announced that the material didn't justify the prices, a preemptive, face-saving maneuver, a country cousin to her "I can make that at home for two dollars" response to restaurant menus. I wanted to leave, but she would not accept defeat. She had to prove to Gaede's that we could afford nice things. "You could always use another pair of pants," she said brightly.

Now she was staring at my ankles. "I think they're a smidge too short. I can hem them, honey," she said. "I brought an iron; nobody will know the difference."

"The length is fine."

"Are you sure you don't want to find nicer shoes? My treat."

"NO! No. How many times do I have to tell you?"

"You don't have to take my head off. Sometimes you have to spend money to make money."

"You said that already."

"Your father said it all the time. Makes a lot of sense, doesn't it? You invest to make back. With the right outlay, things wind up paying for themselves—and then some."

I looked in the three-way mirror. I had made it through Cornell on turned collars, self-deprecating remarks about the poorhouse, and monthly payouts on my father's life from Social Security, but she didn't know how much further I had to go. For what felt like the millionth time that May, I fought back tears.

"Blue pants aren't *me,* Mom."

I wanted her to ask me, "Well who *are* you then?" but she just laughed at my nonsense. Every man, woman, and child in America had a decent pair of blue pants.

If I had to, I could borrow one of Patrick's blazers for the interview, but my mother didn't know that. She would be meeting him that last night in Ithaca. Our friend Weker, a religion major, was coming along as a buffer; I figured he and my mother could sit up and split Catholic hairs until dawn while I tested Patrick's commitment on the porch. I hadn't seen him for eight days. He had been spending the week with his family at their place on Lake Ontario, and I knew from wretched experience that his ability to love me was porous. In the fall he was going to Magdalen College, Oxford, to study African economic development, and I was intending to be inconsolable.

I knew, while living it, that I wouldn't need the passage of time or an alumni solicitation to conclude that Patrick Rowan Dulter was, to borrow a hackneyed promotional phrase, my "Cornell Experience." He and Weker lived in my dorm freshman year; the three of us were the self-designated lost Catholic boys, and I made a pass at him the night before I went home to Chicago for the summer—silently jerked him off, actually, while Weker snored four feet away. I spent the summer of '79 stoking forever-after fantasies as I circled a forklift around a crayon factory while Patrick water-skied and sent not even a postcard. That fall I returned to Ithaca and after weeks of plotting, I managed to corner him under his desk in his underwear one drunken night.

Clearly, Patrick wasn't ready for a *relationship*. It wasn't easy, but I weaned myself from his company. Then my father died. I changed my major and applied to go to Paris for my junior year. I hunkered down that spring with Brendan Markle, an Irish virgin in my trade theory class, taking his cherry thirty seconds after Sissy Spacek accepted her Oscar for *Coal Miner's Daughter*.

Wicked Brendan waited until I got back to Ithaca at the beginning of August to tell me that he had moved on to an actor who was playing Sir Dinaden in a local stock production of *Camelot*. I crashed at Weker's house in the woods, read Zola during the day while he fed beakers and graduated cylinders to an autoclave in the basement of Stimson Hall. At night we'd get shit-faced and listen to a recording of loon calls.

France was a trial. I spent more time the first few months writing letters home than I did soaking up *la vie Parisienne,* but after dumping the older man who gave me confidence *and* the clap, I wised up. I bought a striped knit tube top at Galeries Lafayette, borrowed a girlfriend's eye shadow, and hit the clubs.

A week into senior year, predictably I suppose, though it seemed miraculous deliverance at the time, I was drowsing on a foldout couch at Weker's when I felt a hand on my ankle, then a chest sliding onto my thighs. It was Patrick Rowan Dulter. I dragged him up to my face and forced a first kiss out of him. Too drunk to absorb my dose of spleen, he told me on the softest possible exhalation of breath that he loved me. We slept entwined that night, like two in a tomb—that's how Weker described it when he stumbled upon us in the morning. His surprise entrance I regarded as equally miraculous, inasmuch as it was now impossible for Patrick to try to conceal what was going on from our friends. Moreover, I now had kibitzers and backbenchers to assist in the ongoing project of making him mine forever.

Our final semesters at Cornell could verge on opera buffa, what with Patrick attempting to convince himself and others he was straight, starting with my roommate Sarah. We would break up, reconcile; I would throw his full beer bottles into the street; he would call Sarah to meet him secretly at the Royal Palms; I would pick a townie up at the Common Ground, the only gay bar in Tompkins County. But there were times, hours and hours at a stretch, days on end, magical hungry weeks on end, when we couldn't be peeled apart. Salt water is not to be drunk, because it can never slake. And you're a goner in the desert when you reach for that first handful of sand. Lying down with Patrick senior year was a banquet of salt water and sand. I'd never known such hunger, or such appeasement.

So that was who I thought I was. Mrs. H. knew who I was, but when I had pointed out the GAYPAC Office in the Student Union to my mother, her only comment was "That's disgusting."

"They're people too, Mom," I said.

LET ME SEE IT

She reached into her purse to scare up a piece of gum. "I know, but they're disgusting."

I had thought I was obvious. A junior year in Paris? Four semesters of modern dance? Vintage clothing? A striped tube top in with the undershirts?

She did tease some meaning from a pair of my shorts. Waiting for Patrick and Weker to show up that last night, I changed into a wifebeater and a pair of extremely skimpy cutoffs. The inseam might have been all of three inches long. If I sat the wrong way, my package could fall out either side.

"What have you got on, Elliott?" my mother asked when I emerged from the bathroom.

"Shorts and a T-shirt."

"Lord, son, you look like a hootchie mama."

I'd never heard her say something like that. "What's that?"

"What it sounds like. Slang for 'prostitute.'" She blotted her forehead with a dish towel. She had been scrubbing out every pot in the kitchen.

"Hootchie mama. Hootchie as in hootch?"

"Hootchie as in hootchie kootchie, as in cooching. You have decent things in your bureau drawer, and you choose to look like a cooch dancer."

"It's hot out."

"They're indecent."

"I'm wearing underwear."

"That's not the point. You have an Ivy League education and nice things to wear. You look like nobody loves you, son."

We both laughed at that. It was something she said when I was a little boy and my clothes didn't match. She turned back to rinse the sink one last time, confident I would go and change.

Weker came first through the door cradling a bottle of cognac. Patrick was wearing my favorite green shirt. From his overcrisp consonants, I knew he was already half lit. Patrick drank too much, but it was mature of me, I had convinced myself, to be able to distinguish the changes in his voice from two beers to four beers to a six-pack and beyond. I could also recognize his cough from two aisles over in a supermarket, select his undershirt from a laundry pile by its smell alone, make a freehand drawing of the birthmark on his right calf—that's what love was. My mother gave them both big, Christian hugs and told them they were just how she'd pictured them.

After an hour of gin rummy and icebox cake Weker cued her up by asking how she could have left the Catholic Church. She sighed and splayed her fingers on the kitchen table to secure her rostrum for the long witness to come. I scooped up the cards and announced that Patrick had to smoke on the front porch.

Stumbling with lust through Janine's room, I brushed my legs against her rib-cord spread. I thought of how Mrs. H. would get a kick out of hearing how I'd thrown my lover down and left sex spoors on her daughter's bed. I was, after all, going to be a guest of the Hagopians the next day, and I owed my hostess a fresh batch of activity.

Patrick grabbed my arm and we smacked in a wild embrace against the screen door. "I can't believe you're wearing those shorts," he groaned in my ear. "Are you trying to kill me?"

He did love me. "My mother thinks they're obscene."

"She's a trip," he panted, locking his fingers around the base of my skull.

I pushed him against the center pillar on the porch and slid a hand up his shirt to hold him off a bit. Beyond the box hedge a cloud of gnats was rioting under the security light. I considered looking for the moon and pointing it out to him, as a way to tether our magic to the starry firmament, but the pressure of his legs laced between mine made me too dizzy to hold ground.

A burst of laughter from the kitchen sped us up. I dug into his jeans and milked him in his shorts. Then I sat him on the edge of a painted wicker chair. I yanked the tiny crotch of my shorts and the pouch of my briefs to one side and pressed myself to his face. Just like a hootchie mama, I thought as I came in his mouth.

"You're going *where* this weekend?" he asked mournfully, flicking ash into the coffee can. I laughed at how much he loved me.

"Janine's graduation party. My mother's plane is at seven forty, and Janine wants to leave for Milton by ten."

"Where is she tonight?"

"At Conrad's."

"What did Mrs. Hagopian turn out to be like?"

"The plutocrat's wife. She's probably not so different from your mother—if you'd let me meet her."

"Fuck you, Elliott."

Patrick didn't like Mrs. H. on principle. Strangers who knew he sucked cock unnerved him. And I wasn't to meet Mr. and Mrs. Dulter and set them wondering with my crew cut and my questionable major. Patrick Rowan Dulter would turn out to be the best kisser and the last closet case of my life.

"She's quite elegant," I said. From her phone conversation, I had pictured Mrs. H. as a Neapolitan sexpot, but she had delicate features, a pale heart-shaped face, fine chestnut hair swept back from her head, and an expression that made me think sly things were happening around her every single moment.

"She says she can get me a job," I continued, reluctant to voice my hopes.

"Really? Doing what?"

"Teaching French at the Milton Academy. Where Janine went."

He paused to light another cigarette. He thrummed a bare foot on the floorboards. "You could do that," he said, finally.

"I'll be using my major," I said inanely, about to cry again. "Until I figure out what I really want to do."

Patrick couldn't read my desperation. Money meant nothing to him. My way had been to mock necessity, prying frozen meatballs apart with my hands to pay for my books and flourishes, but when Patrick ran out of underwear, he didn't do laundry, he bought new at the Co-op in packs of three.

"Do you want to teach?"

"Do I have a choice?"

I wanted him to say that living in Boston would mean I would be closer to England, wanted him to say that he loved Boston and would like to settle there after Oxford, wanted him to say that we would never be parted. Now I wouldn't ask to borrow his blazer. I wouldn't ask him for anything, ever.

But then he wrapped his arms around me and tucked his head beneath my chin. "When will you be back?"

"Sunday night. Are you going to be around?"

"I'll wait for you at Weker's. Call me when you get in."

We were starting up again when my mother whooped from inside. "It's getting on nine thirty, Elbow. Don't you want to call Mrs. Hagopian? Find out when your interview is?"

"No, Mom," I yelled back. "I told you a dozen times I'm not going to bug her about it! She's a woman of her word."

"I'm not saying *you* have to bring it up, honey. Call her, and let *her* bring it up."

"NO!" I felt Patrick shake with the giggles under me.

"Well, how about if I call her, thank her in advance for hosting you this weekend? I don't mind feeling her out."

"Mom, I swear I'll kill you if you get anywhere near that phone!"

"Don't be yelling for all the neighbors to hear. Now put out your smokes and come on in."

Once inside, I picked the scurf of Patrick's dried semen from the hair on my knuckles and flicked it to the center of the table, daring her to interpret this advanced clue of who I now was. Around midnight, she made pancakes. Weker helped, stirring the last of the cognac into the pan of syrup on the stove.

Speeding along Route 90 the following afternoon in Janine's station wagon, I marveled at the miles and miles of trees growing right up to the edge of the highway. I'd never been in New England. I'd grown up in suburbs with flat, treeless horizons, where nothing could be hidden, and I had it in my mind that since Massachusetts was so old, and therefore populous, and therefore built up, every inch of the state would be planted with colonial brick and saltbox homes.

Janine was tense. With her mother and sisters running the show, it was possible that no one had done the marketing, supervised the cleaners, put up the awnings, rented the tent, laid in a supply of charcoal, or gone up to Maine to fetch the lobsters.

LET ME SEE IT

"Should we have brought the champagne back with us?" I fretted, stuck on the unimaginable expense of entertaining eighty guests. Sitting in our coat closet were seven bottles of Mumm's left over from the case Mrs. H. had sent for our party.

"Coals to Newcastle," said Janine.

"Your father's around, isn't he?"

Janine sighed. "Daddy tries, but he can't keep them in line. If my mother got up this morning and decided to go whale watching, there's no one around to stop her."

A month or so into our phone calls, Mrs. H. had told me that she had married Mr. Hagopian because he had the biggest penis she'd ever seen. So I told her that the biggest penis I'd ever had belonged to Jean-Christophe Sirjean, the son of my host family in Paris, a man I'd nicknamed Tête de Prune, or Plum Head.

Janine leaned forward to get more give out of her shoulder strap. Her T-shirt was stuck to her back. "You want me to drive some?" I asked.

"No, I like driving."

"You know, I didn't think there'd be so many trees in Massachusetts."

"What?"

"I thought they'd be all cut down by now." She looked at me as if I were insane, so I changed the subject. "So Conrad really isn't coming?"

"It's a disaster to have my mother meet my boyfriends. It's like she wants us to have sex in front of her. She's impossible that way, my sisters too."

"Oh well, that's too bad," I said, a feeble response to her flash of anger.

"She approves of you, Elliott, because you're gay."

I didn't know what to say to that, so I put on my sunglasses and looked out the window, hoping to see a sign leading to Emily Dickinson's porch or the Old North Church or the world's first cotton gin, something, anything historic to steer me away from Janine's complicating observation.

We motored up the driveway. I say "motored" because that first sight of the Hagopians' house was quite the occasion. From the sunlight streaking a gray-shingled carriage house through the canopy of sixty-foot oaks to the worn embrasure under the dormer in the trunk room, I toured the structure and grounds with my mother's eyes. Most remarkable and preponderant was the fact of three full floors. Three floors, I thought, for the august Bostonians bearing three names—Oliver Wendell Holmes, William Dean Howells, Isabella Stewart Gardner, John Quincy Adams.

"Have you a name for the house?" I asked Mrs. H. in the kitchen. She was just back from marketing. I thought it a clever remark, more fitting than a gush over the Chinese Chippendale sofa damasked in cool federal yellow, the mahogany knife boxes, the passementerie drawer pulls, the dental moldings, the ceiling medallion in the dining room from which a four-tiered chandelier with teardrop crystals was suspended, hollowware heaped higgledy-piggledy in corner cabinets, the slate sink in the butler's pantry, the Palladian window over the staircase landing, the ornamental garden, the striped awnings on the windows facing south, the mudroom, the slipware, the game room, anything and everything I had only read about or observed behind velvet ropes.

"Hell no, we're Armenian wops," she snapped, holding out her arms. Janine went out to the station wagon, but I moved around the edge of the table to embrace her. Mrs. H. whooped at the sight of my hootchie mama shorts, which were riding even higher and looser now, because of the long drive and the porch activity with Patrick the night before. Tessa, who was flaking leftover salmon steak for the cats, ran a knife up the back of my thigh. I lurched against the wall and noticed that the switch plate next to the range was a flasher with an open trench coat. The light switch was his penis. Mrs. H. once said on the phone that her husband's dick was so large, the crotches of his trousers required special tailoring at the Harvard Crimson Shop.

"How are you doing, dearie? Did you survive Mother Ruth's visit?"

"Barely," I said. "She had a good time."

"Did she convert the natives?" Mrs. H. was testing me with her smile.

"Here and there."

"And she's gone back to Ohio."

"Illinois," I said. I thought about the ersatz colonial "pieces" in my mother's den and the three gold-bordered Limoges plates in sacral arrangement on a shelf in the dining room hutch. My only nice things, she'd say to guests.

Mrs. H. handed me a heavy white paper parcel. "Do you know what that is, Elliott?"

I squished it suggestively. "Meat," I leered.

"It's what Mother Ruth won't make you. Lamb."

"We're having shish kebab," said Janine, who was dumping her luggage in the mudroom. "It has to marinate for twenty hours in tomato paste and onion."

Mrs. H. slapped four more butcher's packages on the counter next to the sink, ran the tap, and began to wash her hands. The soap dish was an ashtray from the Ritz-Carlton in Florence.

"What can I do?" I asked.

"Help us make fruit cup," said Tessa.

Janine, Tessa, and Katia secured their thick hair in ponytails and began to convert bags of grapes, cherries, blueberries, strawberries, honeydews, bananas, watermelon, peaches, cantaloupe, nectarines, and two kinds of plums into a vat of fruit cup. While the sisters raced through the berries and the melons, I concentrated on pitting the cherries. Cherries don't release their stones in a consistent manner, so it was slow going. The cats wandered through and disdained their snack of salmon, having lunched on lobster claw. In the basement refrigerator was hundreds of dollars worth of lobster meat steeping in Cain's mayonnaise, a special local brand.

"The peaches are done," said Tessa. "I'm going to start the cream for my mousses."

She poured pint after pint of whipping cream into a metal bowl the size of a manhole cover while Mrs. H. kneaded the lamb chunks in the tomato paste and gleefully dripped gore from her fingers. Mr. Hagopian called in from work for the list of things to pick up from the Armenian grocery in Brookline. I knew I would have to finesse myself out of the shorts before he got home.

"What are you doing, Janine?" asked Katia suddenly.

"I'm cutting fruit."

"Your cantaloupe pieces are too large."

"What?"

"So are your watermelons. Make them smaller. Halve them," said Katia. To my ears, the Boston "a" on her "halve"—a snooty *hov*—intensified her correction.

"They are not too large." Janine held up two pieces in her hand for her mother to inspect. Mrs. H. declined to comment.

"Fruit cup should have small, uniform pieces of fruit throughout," said Katia.

"It doesn't matter how big the pieces are," Janine said, raising her voice several decibels.

"Each and every spoonful of fruit cup should have a range of different fruits in it. Your pieces upset the ratio."

"You're ridiculous! It only matters that a fruit cup has a variety of fruits, period."

"Really, Janine, the greater the surface area, the more it can macerate in the juice."

Katia's now-hushed tone—balm to a fretful child—pushed Janine over the edge. She threw down her knife. It pinged off the kitchen table.

"Listen to you talking about surface area! And ratio!" she shouted. "You'd think you knew something about math. Who gives a crap how big the fruit pieces are! I suppose you think we should cut the blueberries in half! You're all impossible!"

"Fine, Janine," said Katia. "It's your big day."

"That's right! It's my graduation party and I think the fruit can be any size it wants!"

Janine stomped through the mudroom, ripped open a screen door, and flung melon rinds onto a compost heap beyond one of the three patios.

It was a crackling standoff. Mrs. H., who had rustled up a glass of pinot grigio, fetched a refill from the bottle in the refrigerator door. Her fingers left meat tracks on the goblet. I focused on the chirr of the beaters against the bowl as Tessa kept whipping the cream. I began to worry that I might be a source of the tension, that Janine had brought me along only at the insistence of her mother, Mrs. H., who approved of me because we both liked cock, liked it and liked to talk about it, or maybe because I was funny or artistic or fashionably Frenchified, or wouldn't hit on her daughters or maybe because I was a poster boy for stylish overcompensation.

I should be back in Ithaca, I thought, spinning a web around Patrick's body, not tearing pebbles out of cherries for fruit cup. Calling it fruit *cup* was an affectation, as was a *scintilla* of nutmeg, and *local* mayonnaise, and *polpetti* made with three meats, and bread that came from one special bakery in the North End.

I couldn't bear the silence any longer. "Where I come from, it's called fruit cocktail, and it comes packed in a can of syrup," I said. "Sugar syrup," I added.

Mrs. H. seemed to think that was the funniest thing she'd ever heard. She gasped out "fruit cocktail" and "sugar syrup" several times and had to lay her breasts and elbows onto the counter for support. When she could stand back up, her white blouse was slugged with peach peels that had missed the discard bowl. Katia pointed them out with a scream and dropped into a padded rocker. Her laughter rocked the chair into two shelves of cookbooks. The sight of Mrs. H. daintily flicking peels from her breasts finally made Janine crack up.

In the general release, Tessa stopped paying attention to her task at a critical moment—the cream had just begun to turn to butter. This mistake was more hilarious than the peach peels and the sugar syrup until I saw Tessa tip the bowl over the trash can.

"Stop," I said with alarm. "Don't throw that away."

"It's spoiled," said Tessa.

"You shouldn't just throw it away."

"Why not? I'll make another batch."

"But that's wasting it."

"It's no big deal, Elliott."

"I'll eat it," I announced.

"It's inedible."

"No it's not. I love whipped cream. You just—shouldn't waste it." I held out my hands. "Let me have it."

Avoiding the pale grubs of butter flecking the bottom, I downed huge spoonfuls. It tasted delicious, and I said so, which set off another round of uncontrollable laughter. After that peaked, I held my spoon like a monkey to draw out the fun. Then I engaged in some suggestive tongue panto-mime. Then I puffed out one cheek to indicate that a man was giving me his cream—Patrick, Mr. Hagopian, Plum Head, whoever the women needed me to blow, whomever I had to cooch in order to land the job. I let some cream dribble down my chin. Then I switched utensils, digging into the cream with my index and middle fingers and sucking it off with a copulative motion.

Past satiety, finally through, I set the bowl down with a clatter and pushed out my stomach.

"Did you leave some for the cats?" said Mrs. H. to me, with her sly smile.

All that fat gave me diarrhea. For much of the night, between trips to my private bathroom, I curled up in a dormer and looked out at the moon-light shining on the white gravel pathways of the ornamental garden. This being the famous third floor, it seemed the likeliest portal in the castle for a storybook rescue, for the appearance of the Languages and Literature dean of the Milton Academy on a magic carpet or a wingèd steed with an offer of employment, but Mrs. H. had forgotten all about my interview. Janine could have told me that morning that it had been another drunken promise of her mother's, but the part of me that had known it all along couldn't afford to broadcast my hopes in the station wagon. The next day I need only enjoy a brisk tour of downtown Boston and the graduation party. I would write my mother that the Milton Academy wasn't currently hiring for the following academic year, but they would keep my impressive credentials on file.

On Sunday night, Janine dropped me off in front of our apartment house and went off to find Conrad. I ran to the phone and told Patrick to hurry on over. I counted three beers in his voice.

In the hustle to get my mother to the airport Friday morning, I'd left the ironing board up in my bedroom. I went to fold the board and noticed a small, balled-up tangle of black and blue threads hanging off its edge. I went back to retrieve my duffel. From the corner of my eye, I saw the breakfast plates and the omelet pan she had washed sitting in the rack on the kitchen counter. The plastic dishpan was tilted against the edge of the sink.

I unzipped my bag and wrenched out the twenty-six-dollar interview pants. I rolled the hems over. Under my study lamp, I recognized her careful, even stitches. Sure enough, without telling me—for suggesting it would have set me off—my mother had let the blue pants down a half inch and ironed new creases into them.

I kicked over the ironing board and began cursing her out. I jerked the ugly tricolored belt from the loops and found myself whipping the bed with it, to keep from crying. I was successful at this for a few minutes, but finally, when I reared back and stung my flank with the metal tab at the end of the belt, I fell into my tears with a howl.

When Patrick showed up, my eyes were still red, but I was ready with a new trick. Knowing he wasn't drunk enough yet to tell me he loved me, I opened a bottle of Mrs. H.'s Mumm's from the coat closet and set it in our pasta pot with three trays of ice cubes. We would spend hours kissing with our mouths full of champagne. We would let it spill onto our necks and chests, let it pool into our navels. We would lap it from our sex-mottled flesh. Later I would drag him out to the porch to help me find the moon.

YOU'VE REALLY LEARNED HOW
ELLIOTT

1982

I was taking an Italian class at the College of DuPage, because I needed to be good at something. I was no good at finding a job. I was no good at getting my sister to eat. While cutting the grass, a former area of expertise, I sheared the top of the water main in the tree box with the lawn mower blade. The grinding noise it made was so loud it pulled my stepfather away from his porn in the basement. He backed me into the garage door with the three scoops of his teats and stomach, his arm flung behind him toward the smoking motor. When he got angry, his features scrunched forward and center, like those faces carved into coconuts.

My stepfather was, as ever, a worthy adversary, but during morning complaints with my mother, which I heard from upstairs, he was choosing to revisit historic misdemeanors, rather than decimate me outright by naming the scarlet *F* branded on my forehead. That would be *F* for "Failure," *F* for "Freeloader": I had been home from Ithaca for five weeks, and everywhere I went my ears were pitched to hear "fancy school," "worthless degree," and "just desserts." On the rare occasions when my despair would leak into words, my mother would mention some branch of the armed forces. Was this the same woman who had proudly typed my college application essays? My brother, Frank, said a sales job at Penney's or Monkey Ward's could lead to rapid promotion, as long as I proved myself. Proved myself willing to memorize the brand differentials of kitchen appliances? Proved myself able to shoot the shit with managers in short sleeves? Because Frank had just bought a four-bedroom Dutch colonial on an accounting degree from a state school, I had to pretend his was sage advice. Compounding my humiliation, my new sister-in-law, Katie, a decent woman really, who taught typing and shorthand and other mysterious skills at a school in downtown Chicago, offered to lend me a Selectric and some manuals in case I wanted to learn how to touch-type; it was never too late to learn. These were my thanks for moving back home to usher at their wedding.

We were in the middle of the biggest recession since the thirties. Millions my age and above were unemployed, but the banality of our shared experience didn't dilute my shame. Two afternoons a week I'd jockey for space in the reference section of the public library to take notes from swollen paperback copies of the job-hunting and boost-your-resume books I was too proud to purchase. My arsenal for the future was a roll of twenty-cent stamps and a box of envelopes that didn't match the forty-seven remaining copies of the resume I'd ginned up at Cornell in a pregraduation panic.

Rob, my best friend from high school, took me out on my twenty-second birthday to a chain restaurant with fake Tiffany lamps and free baskets of ocher popcorn. Rob was also looking for a meaningful position—a term we mocked—but since his degree was in mechanical engineering, and his parents liked having him at home, I wasn't worried for his future. Rob was the kind of language nerd who teaches himself Esperanto, so over a second pitcher of Labatts, he made an interesting proposition: while we waited for those magical job offers to rain down upon us, we might continue our education by beginning another language at U of Du, which was the wisenheimer's name for the College of DuPage. In another alarming about-face, my mother was now in the habit of pointing out that C.O.D. was ranked one of the top community colleges in the country, so I should stop making fun and think about computer or business machine classes to enhance my marketability.

By the time Rob paid the check, he had picked Russian, and I, Italian. Our classrooms in the cement cracker boxes past the Yorktown Mall would look out over parking lots, the aluminum lamp poles and directional arrows would map their boundaries just as the founder's statues and spreading chestnuts had anchored the Georgian sites of our recent, yet irrefutably past-tense, triumphs.

Rob stopped at Poppin' Fresh on the way home. I weaved in and bought an entire French silk pie, two inches of chocolate chiffon topped with two inches of whipped cream, the richest pie in the larder. I was bloated from birthday sauerbraten, my mother's coconut cake, and the Labatts, but I knew my sister Tracy wouldn't accept an individual slice of French silk. The fiction was we might both like to have some pie.

She was watching horror movies in her bedroom. The plates and silverware under my arm chinked as I knocked on her door with my left hand. The French silk, dense and luxuriant, weighed down my right. I had learned not to bring food and utensils in separately—two trips gave her more time to defend herself. My greatest coup to date had been surprising her into half a cheeseburger and a small bouquet of French fries. She wasn't going to let that happen again.

Her lips tightened at the sight of the red Poppin' Fresh box. Tonight I noticed there was no meat on her temples or the sides of her brows.

"Oh, I'm full, Elliott," she said airily. I wasn't allowed to question how full she could be on six stalks of broccoli. Her food diary was for her therapist.

"It's my birthday."

"I know."

"You didn't have any of my cake."

"Coconut makes me choke, you know that."

"I want you to help me celebrate."

"Listen to this!" she said. Ignoring the chocolate and cream impasto glistening on the knife as I withdrew it from the core of the pie, she asked me what color was my parachute? I groaned, her cue to whip out my mother's treasonous birthday present—a copy of *What Color Is Your Parachute?* Being spotted at Cornell with *Parachute*, which purportedly transformed the job search into a fun-filled journey of self-exploration, was like being marked as a Jehovah's Witness.

Flipping through the pages of its heinously sensical fruitiness, Tracy began to read and riff: "Oh Elliott, what is the list of your internal furniture? Let's work on tools and instruments to help you: memories, feelings, and visions. What turns you on about seeing totalities of people? Making the familiar wondrous? The future is where we are going to spend the rest of our lives, so . . . any common denominators?"

One of the things I loved about my little sister was her sense of humor. From the time she was old enough to form a retort, she suffered nothing and no one, and now, starving herself seemed to have heightened her awareness of the absurd, as if ingesting next to nothing left her free to concentrate on the sham edges and false bottoms of every human gesture. Maybe she could *see* better on four hundred calories a day.

Tracy had dropped out of Illinois State midway through her first semester. She didn't belong in college, she reminded us, but Frank wouldn't let her apply to stewardess school. Ours was a family of graduates, Dad had wanted us all to go to college, the money was for education, and so on. At some point during my senior year at Cornell, she had stopped eating. Out of my father's Social Security, she paid room and board (boil-n-bag vegetables, Popsicles, and Swedish flatbread) and banked what she earned from Aladdin Cleaners. She was dating the night manager of a pizzeria in the same cheerful island of consumer conveniences across the street from our subdivision. My fantasy that she was secretly gorging on meatball subs behind his store on her breaks was put to rest when Dave, in over his head, called to ask me what Tracy's favorite foods were. More than anything, he said he wanted to watch her eat a meal.

Not that we knew any better than Dave what to do. My mother, somehow believing that anorexia was a more acceptable vocation than bulimia, prayed her head off and took weird comfort from the evidence that Tracy didn't make herself vomit. Things could always be worse was her attitude, and should it come down to hospitalization, she would be the first to give the signal to pump her daughter full of nutrition. Frank appealed to her vanity, told her how awful she looked, like a tropical disease, like a praying mantis, a fetus, no airline would take her now, and just wait until the fur came out on her arms. My stepfather, having clocked every forkful of food we'd eaten since the summer of '73, kept his counsel. Less of his money was going to groceries.

I brought home pies, cakes, doughnuts, ice cream, milk shakes, anything I could think of to draw the hunger behind her eyes down to her mouth. I made ratatouille and zucchini boats and lentil loaves, the dishes arty college kids love, but Tracy wouldn't taste them. I made up impossible stories of things I'd seen during the day, hoping to distract her hands into the bags of chips I laid like Persian pillows around her on my visits to her room.

That night, while we shot down my parachute, pausing to shriek at *The Mummy Returns*, I ate an emetic amount of French silk, but Tracy would only cut the tip off her piece, making a face as the little triangle shivered and fell away from the fork. When channel 26 had turned to static, she followed me downstairs to make sure I threw away the rest of the pie. I wasn't allowed to leave any for my stepfather. "Skull head!" I wanted to yell at her as I heard the foil plate sag against an empty bottle in the trash can.

I am going to night school to improve myself, I wrote on postcards to my college friends. To my cousin Tom Amelio, back living at home like me with an only-slightly-less-worthless degree in history, I added the phrase *and also for heritage reasons,* the joke being that he was the guinea wop fanook in the family, not I. I'd borrowed the heritage phrase from the girls in my class, but they were sincere when they told patient, beaming Mr. Penucci why they were taking Italian 101. With no heritage in my family except divorce and heart disease, I guess I had regarded it as an innate possession one couldn't enhance. How could learning the language make an Italian more Italian? And why were all these Italians-on-both-sides with ten pounds of perm so slow to accept the concept of masculine and feminine endings?

"Don't question, people, just memorize," I muttered, flipping ahead to chapter twelve, where, beneath the soft-focus picture of a flower stall in Verona, were the words *Il Congiuntivo.* I shuddered to think of their eventual, protracted mangle with the mood of doubt, desire, and contingence. By the time the class reached the subjunctive, I prayed that I would have found a meaningful position and bid *arrivederci à tutti.*

While Mr. Penucci led drills, I would sit in the back of class and pretend I was fluent by whispering paragraphs of text to myself as fast as I could. One evening in late September, fighting sleep while Mr. Penucci explained the placement of direct objects, a splay of my elbow knocked *Italian for Beginners* off my desk. I leaned over the aisle to retrieve it, but another hand had already grasped its spine. I glanced into the face of an older student with a carefully trimmed mustache and watery brown eyes.

He smiled and, holding out the book, said to me, winking, "O che sciagura d'essere senza coglioni."

Had I heard him right? A eunuch says this to the Old Lady in *Candide*; translated, it means "O, what a misfortune to be without testicles." I wasn't expecting to hear one of the great punch lines in French literature at U of Du. I gathered my wits and offered Pangloss's philosophy in return: "Tout est pour le mieux dans le meilleur des mondes possibles."

He smiled again. Then, sliding his fingers along an imaginary beard on the left side of his face, he rolled his eyes toward the front of the room. This was gestural French for "this is so boring."

"Ouais," I whispered back, "ça me barbe aussi."

During break, while Tina and Stella and Angelo smoked on modular seating units by the soda machines, Jerry Turner bought me a cup of coffee. He had been teaching French at U of Du for fifteen years. Having noticed that I spoke Italian with a French accent, he had taken a gamble with the Voltaire citation. That didn't explain why he would choose to disclose that he had no balls, even in jest, but it felt nice to be appreciated. He nodded his head past a bulletin board studded with magazine offers to indicate the location of his office. He suggested we might *pratiquer la langue* some evening before class.

When I got home, Tracy asked me what Mr. Frosting was wearing that night. She was sitting at the kitchen table with a fashion magazine. She liked my classroom recaps, especially loved to hear about Brenda, a morbidly obese woman who was a home radon inspector. Tracy wanted me to ask Brenda out to an all-you-can-eat Chinese buffet on Ogden Avenue. She would watch from another table and write everything down in her food diary.

"Who?"

"Mr. Frosting. God," she sighed.

"I don't know who you mean," I said, casing the sink for plates she might have dirtied.

"Mr. Penucci. As in penuche frosting."

I said nothing. I opened the dishwasher. The dishes were clean.

"Penuche, a fudge or frosting made from brown sugar, butter, cream or milk, and nuts," she continued. My mother said Tracy read cookbooks to torture herself, but I thought it was to torture us. I took out a glass and ran the tap. "Penuche frosting on yellow cake was Dad's favorite dessert, Elliott."

"I don't remember that," I said. I wondered how long she had been planning to ask me about Mr. Frosting. Self-starvers aren't spontaneous people.

"Mom!" she yelled to the den, where my mother and stepfather were watching the ten o'clock news.

Across the hall one heavy foot, then another, landed on the floor. Fee, fie, I thought. Foe and fum would be his freckled fists. It was my step-father's pleasure to say he could put me through a wall.

"Come in here if you have something to say," replied my mother.

"Didn't Dad love penuche frosting best of all?" she yelled again.

I began to pluck knives from the silverware basket. My mother came in, blinking at the light. The click of our ancient cocker spaniel's nails on the linoleum followed close behind her.

"Don't shout," she said. Her cheek was pebbled with the imprint of our couch. "Do you want me to fix you something to eat?"

Tracy yanked the ends of the belt on her robe in opposing vectors and folded her hands. "Your first husband's favorite frosting," she stated, as if this were "Desserts for $400" in a round of *Jeopardy*.

The imperative mode confused my mother, but Duffy moved to put her head in Tracy's lap to indicate she remembered my father better than anyone else. Tracy scratched her ears. I listened to a sportscaster flip out over an inside-the-park home run.

"Penuche icing, white cake," said my mother finally, shooting me a look of exasperation. Despite the working assumption that my mother was to be blamed for everything, she hadn't killed my father.

"Yellow cake," said Tracy, "yellow cake."

"Yellow cake, white cake, whatever box mix I had in the house, honey. It was the icing that counted."

Tracy, not satisfied with that answer, dismissed her. Then we argued about whether it was too late to call and weigh in with Frank about the frosting.

"Others perceive you as a Persuasive Leader, Mr. Biddler, but deep down you are an Assertive Leader," said Mr. Egert.

It was my turn to speak, but the dust-streaked paneling in Mr. Egert's office distracted me. Something else belonged on the walls, but I couldn't figure out what—a saber? A softball trophy? A Vargas drawing? Mr. Egert drummed a thick hand on my file as a prompt.

"Oh," I said. "I suppose that's good."

"It's excellent, Mr. Biddler. A Persuasive Leader exerts his will without alienating his peers and subordinates. It means you have an effective business personality."

"Subordinates?" I said doubtfully. "Mr. Egert," I remembered to add. Mr. Egert's first rule of communication was that the two words every person loved to hear most were his or her name. I could never repeat my interviewer's name too often.

"You are a leader. Mark my words, people will be working for Elliott Biddler sooner than he can even guess."

I wanted to point out that an Assertive Leader wouldn't need to pay for Mr. Egert's help. My $325 check to Allen & Associates, a job search firm in downtown Chicago, had already cleared. On this, my second visit, I was getting the results of my personality test and five hundred copies of a resume they'd revamped. At our first meeting, Mr. Egert had instantly gained my trust when, scanning my old resume, he had declared, "French literature? That sucks." Closing his pitch, which had invoked the firm's ability to tap *the hidden job market that everyone knows about and no one can enter,* he had also said, with obvious delight, "You don't know what you're doing, Mr. Biddler. Leave that all to us." Allen & Associates had guaranteed employment in six months. Only Tracy knew I'd spent all that money.

Mr. Egert's window was whorled with soot. I studied his walls again. An uneven row of certificates in cheap frames attested to his completion of several human skills workshops.

Mr. Egert hit a button on his phone. I loved that he loved his job. "Nancy," he said, "please bring in Mr. Biddler's materials."

Nancy twitched her way to the desk, her flats making oval depressions in the red industrial wall-to-wall. "Here you are, Mr. Egert," she said, showily placing a large stationery box between us.

"Thank you, Nancy."

"You're very welcome, Mr. Egert," she said.

"Yes, thank you, Nancy," I said to the ankle slipping through the door.

Mr. Egert lifted the lid like a blanket on the Christ child. I could smell fresh paper and ink. "Voilà," he said. "Go on, have a look, Mr. Biddler."

In bold block capital letters, beneath my address, was my Personal Summary:

ELLIOTT J. BIDDLER IS A DRAMATIC AND HIGHLY ARTICULATE INDIVIDUAL WITH MULTILINGUAL CAPABILITIES AND OUTSTANDING PERSONAL SKILLS.

I wondered whether I'd live long enough to ever find this funny.

"And here, Mr. Biddler, is a copy of your very own broadcast letter," said Mr. Egert proudly. With his middle finger, he slid a matching buff sheet toward me.

In addition to the resumes, I had purchased three hundred cover letters that began with *Bonjour* and closed with *Bien à vous.* Now all that stood between me and my life as an Assertive Leader was the arrival in the mail of my job leads, scientifically matched to my interests and aptitudes by the Allen & Associates research team.

Blushes don't begin in the feet, but I felt heat rushing north a great distance. I began to breathe through my mouth. Perhaps, on my way back to the train station, I could be hit by a truck on Dearborn Street, the *Bonjour–Bien à vous* boy cut down on the cusp of a brilliant career as a scholar of conversational Italian. I closed my eyes and saw what was missing from Mr. Egert's walls: a broad-mouthed bass. When I was able to speak, I asked Mr. Egert whether he fished.

"Pardon me?"

"Are you a fisherman?"

"No," he laughed, "I don't even swim."

"O coniglio mio, mio coniglio," murmured Jerry in my ear. I was squirming on his lap in a La-Z-Boy. The hand roaming inside my briefs was certainly making me tremble like a rabbit, and I considered hopping off for a pretend piss in his powder room. I wasn't comfortable with how hot Jerry Turner made me. Part of it—the discomfort, not the heat—had to do with his living in the next subdivision over from ours. From Jerry's living room window, I could see the football scoreboard of my old high school, almost count its lightbulbs. The idea that I could have walked two blocks to have sex with a man every lunch hour, then gone to trigonometry class, upset me. I was just as upset it hadn't happened.

"Coniglietto," he said. Baby rabbit.

"Coniglione," I moaned back, rubbing the nap of the pelt on his breasts. Big old possibly scary daddy rabbit.

Jerry and I were exploring the nuances of -ino and -inino and -etto and -acchio and -one. The French language, we both agreed, had precision, balance, clarity, and pomp, but Italian had the suffixes. This was only my third time at his house, but I knew that the brush of his penis against the bottom of my bare thigh was a signal we should head for the bedroom. I slid off and, kneeling on the fringe of a harvest gold shag rug, encouraged him further.

He would have liked, I knew, for me to call him mio coniglione (my big rabbit), but I wasn't going to give it all up. It would be too easy to disappear into Jerry Turner. The first time he pulled me to him in his little office before Italian class, I felt myself turning into a package to give him, a papoose he could strap to his chest instead of his back. My instant surrender was one big surprise. The other was his hairpiece.

I let Jerry take the stairs ahead of me. We both wanted me to make an entrance. I would leap onto him in the center of his king-size bed and feel him draw me in with his thick arms and legs. Big and little rabbit could roll and play for hours. The sight of a neat row of matched hand towels in the bathroom broke my stride. "Jerry," I asked him from the doorway, "how long have you had this house?"

He was naked now, the corals of his nipples and glans tipping out from his fur in the syrupy yellow light of a hanging lamp. "Since it was built," he said, "1974."

"Why did you pick Naperville?"

"It was a good buy, *coniglio mio.*"

"But you could live in the city."

"This is a great investment. Naperville has a solid tax base, it's convenient, close to work. It's already doubled in value."

"My brother Frank's new house has four bedrooms too," I said.

"Come here, baby," he growled.

I ran in and leaped. The puffy blocks of his down comforter tickled the edges of my legs as I landed.

It didn't matter so much to me that Jerry couldn't quite fuck me, since he'd transformed me into a grateful, gurgling cuddler, but he kept apologizing for it. A lot was going on. His father had been in and out of the hospital and he was going to have to spend more time with his demanding mother, who owned a small luxury hotel in Chicago. As he spoke of them, I looked respectfully in the direction of their photos on his dresser. I stayed pressed against his side for warmth but refused his offer of cocoa— again, giving half, keeping half. When Jerry floated the idea of taking a holiday trip to France together, I yawned that I was sleepy. While he pinned his toupee to its block on his dresser, pulling the ends out from under the edge of the mesh cap, I told him I thought he looked sexier without it. It was true.

At that, he strode toward me and stood at the edge of the bed. From the nightstand he picked up a foot-long candle, beige and as big around as a can of room freshener.

"I'd like to fuck you with this, you little shit," he choked out in a raspy voice. He slapped the end with the wick into his palm. "And then I'd like to tie you up and beat the shit out of you."

I rolled to the other side of the bed and felt for the floor with my right foot. "What did you say?" I asked, holding out an arm to defend myself.

Jerry began to giggle. He blew me a kiss and put the candle back on its wooden stand.

None of this, I tried to convince myself, would have happened if my endless love, Patrick Rowan Dulter, were any kind of correspondent. He could be sleeping with half of Magdalen College for all I knew, but given his history, it was more likely, and more alarming, that he was trying to go back to women. Later, drifting off in Jerry's arms, the hair of his stomach tickling my back with his breathing, I thought of my Cornell friend Lydie. Underemployed, depressed, weighing vegetables at an organic farm stand in Alexandria, Virginia, she had just written to say she was falling in crush with her forty-five-year-old boss. I figured I'd write and warn her that older men were jobs in themselves.

Tracy was getting thinner. Her boyfriend, Dave, thought so, my mother thought so but said nothing, I dared to say so, but she claimed the onset of cold weather only made her seem smaller. Her arms were jointed sticks. Her eyes had grown larger and had burrowed in tighter. On each side of her neck, the moats between the collarbone and scapula looked as if they could hold a cup of liquid apiece. I dreamed of ladling soup into them, again and again, and watching her skin soak it up.

She used to eat. We used to eat. Other teenagers raided the liquor cabinet; our rebellion was gustatory. When my mother and stepfather were out of the house for an evening or a Saturday afternoon, Tracy would get a gleam in her eye and say, "Let's eat something we're not supposed to!" The time he smacked us around for having a sheet of pizza rolls in the oven restricted us to things we could hide in a hurry, like a pecan ring or a bag of pull-apart cinnamon rolls. Our savory favorite was a pouch of the processed meat that my mother made creamed chipped beef with. It came out of the bag in a moist, smoky mound, and we'd peel off the slices, thin as linen handkerchiefs, and flutter them into our mouths as if we were guests at a state dinner. Or we'd crank the radio and whip up a batch of chocolate pudding. It would have hardly set before we'd be trading the bowl back and forth with serving spoons, gleefully getting away with it.

One October afternoon I was waiting for her in her therapist's parking lot. She never let me come in with her. On the way up Lombard's

LET ME SEE IT

commercial strip, she had pointed out every fast-food outlet. There's Denny's. There's Poppin' Fresh. There's Portillo's. I was about to get out of the car to find out whether her therapist even *existed* when I noticed a small pink sign three parking lots away. Sitting right out on Winfield Road was a branch of the Wilfred Academy of Beauty.

I couldn't believe it. This was like stumbling across the Alhambra on a trip to the drugstore. I say this because the Wilfred Academy ran a spot on local television that Tracy and I had made part of our lives that year.

The ad was ludicrously low budget, and although chipper, it preyed upon the fears generated by the recession. In its establishing shot, a new cohort of Wilfred trainees, young men and women of every size and color, stand at smiling attention in knee-length smocks. A professor in a lab coat looks at his watch. There is a sound of a bell and then a cut to an overhead shot of an enormous room. The trainees scurry over the checkerboard tile to their stations, and then begins a montage sequence accompanied by a soundtrack of violins plucking out a theme of busy fun: a black girl buffs the nails of a woman in a power suit; a white boy lowers a hair dryer onto a head lapped with squares of tin foil; another academician in a lab coat holds up a beaker of viscous gel for a circle of note-taking students; a man tilts a hand mirror, and a satisfied customer beams at the sight of the back of her head; an arm with bangle bracelets lifts a veined foot from a paraffin bath; and finally, a blunt-nosed nozzle attached to several feet of black hose slowly approaches a mysterious draped figure lying on a slab.

Then a voice cuts into the sound track—Tracy and I decided this was Mr. Wilfred himself, Mr. *Alfred* Wilfred—and begins to extol the values of a cosmetology degree in a cadence I can only describe as deadpan blandishment, as addresses and phone numbers and course offerings—Manicure Pedicure Makeup Perms Wrapping Coloring Highlights Waxing—scroll up the screen.

The violins begin climbing the scale during two final demonstrations. While a girl with stripped-to-straw blonde hair daubs liner on the upper lip of a fat black woman, Mr. Wilfred says, "Licensed and working." We'd stifle our laughter here, for fear of missing the true climax of the ad. Cut to a handsome Hispanic boy digging his fingers into the scalp of a wrinkled white lady. He stands behind her, and she seems bewildered by the

attention of the advancing camera; she winces when he squirts some liquid from a plastic squeeze bottle onto her wet crown and then, just at the
moment we are able to read the name José on his smock, he looks at us
and cocks an eyebrow. The camera loves José, eats him up, the violins go
crazy, he gives a thumbs-up gesture with his free hand, and Mr. Wilfred
says, "You've really learned how."

Cut to black. We'd laugh until we crashed into the walls from dizziness.
Tracy would keep the set running in her room all night long in the hopes
of catching this ad, and it was understood that I could be yanked out of
bed for it. When she caught me with the want ads at the kitchen table, she
would say, "licensed and working." When she left for her shift at Aladdin
Cleaners, I would say, "You've really learned how." It never palled.

A red parka loomed to my right, Tracy floating inside it. When she had
settled herself in next to me, I pinched two inches of loose fabric on the
side of her thigh.

"Cured yet?" I asked.

"Screw you," she said.

"Hungry?"

"Fuck you, Elliott." She whipped to the right, brushing her little spiral-
bound food journal onto the mud mat. The parka blotted the sun from
the passenger window. I decided to let it go.

"Hey bitch, did you know the Wilfred Academy is right there in front
of us?"

"The address is on the commercial," she said in a superior tone.

"Shouldn't it be like very far away?"

"Like where?"

"Like in the ghetto?"

"The suburbs crave beauty too, Elliott."

"Do you want to check it out?" I asked facetiously.

"*Wilfred?* What for?" she said.

"I dunno, I thought we could find José, kidnap him," I said. I knew she
thought he was cute. "Maybe he's on break."

"He's licensed and working."

"He's really learned how."

"I'd screw with him any day of the week," said Tracy.

"So would I."

Her parka whistled against the upholstery as she turned back to center. The scarlet *F* on my forehead stood for "Faggot" too, but I'd never told Tracy outright. I put the car into gear and drove while she ran the pull of her zipper up and down. She started to say something a couple of times, then stopped. I knew how her mind worked. If she asked me about being gay, I could ask her about starving herself. I pulled into the White Castle lot.

My sister wasn't eating, and I wasn't hungry enough for work. We were bad for each other now. I bought six sliders and an order of fries. I polluted the car with the smell of onions and cheap cheese. She rolled down her window. "That's right," I said. "Fill up on air."

When we got home, there was a package waiting for me on the porch milk can. My personalized Allen & Associates leads had arrived, two hundred sheets of green-and-white computer printout with names, addresses, and phone numbers. I was supposed to cold-call these companies and, applying my skills of persuasive leadership, book interviews with them. I took the stairs two at a time.

These were they: A-Aaa-Coast to Coast Bail Bonds. A Absolute Pressure Washers Inc. A Action Insurance Services. A Bauer & Co. A & A Candy & Tobacco Co. AAA Auto Glass. AeroStar Machine. Affiliated Title Management. Alkhan Construction. Allied Mortgage Capital Corp.

I stopped at Bohemian American Federal Savings and Loan. *Bonjour bien à vous.* Hello good-bye. I stuffed myself under the bed for the first time since I was twelve, the sentence *Che sciagura d'essere senza coglioni* repeating in my head like a measure of music while Tracy rattled the doorknob.

"What is the Russian for marsupial?"
Rob laughed at the other end of the line. "I don't know. Kangarooshki."
"The Italian is *marsupiale*," I said.
"I'm not surprised."
"Jerry didn't think it was so funny when I told him."
Jerry was getting harder to manage. Wig on, he was solicitude itself. Wig off, he was a hopeful sadist. It was as creepy, and as simple, as that. The crux was deciding which fashion I preferred. When I was at his house,

the potency issue tempered the violence. The nights I wasn't with him, he'd spin degrading scenarios over the phone that I couldn't laugh my way out of. They aroused me, but if I didn't stop him when he went too far, I was afraid I was assenting to their eventual performance.

Since I was the one who had orchestrated everything with and on Patrick, this about-face need to be taken care of generated greater fears. I balked when Jerry wanted to bathe me, powder me, feed me from his own plate, buy me fur-lined gloves and cashmere sweaters. He wanted us to be seen out together, drive me into Chicago for dinner, book seats for *The Nutcracker*, but I wasn't ready for that. The one time we went to the movies, I hurt his feelings when I brushed his hand away in the dark. In the parking lot afterward, facing each other as we leaned against our cars, I sarcastically asked him whether he had a pouch, since he made me think of a *marsupiale*. He cupped his hands at his waist, seemed to inspect them, then looked at me with his watery brown eyes. He reached over, traced a finger up the center of my chest, and said, "I really like you, Elliott."

In response, I pulled him into the back seat of my car and acted the compleat slut. The orgasm I spirited out of him made him crow with hope and washed me clean. And at that moment, if he had had a pouch, I'd have zipped myself in and told him to pull me out when we reached the Amalfi coast.

"He really likes you, Elliott," said Rob, recapping.

"Whose side are you on?" I said, smacking the phone cord against the washing machine. I opened the cabinet above the dryer. Next to the container of fluted cupcake papers were the boxes of pudding that had so tempted Tracy and me once upon a time.

"You can always stop seeing him," suggested Rob.

"I have underwear at his house," I said.

"Does that mean you're going steady?"

"I don't know what it means, but I've never been so horny in all my life."

Rob had had enough. He changed the subject. "Guess what?" he said.

"What?"

"I got a job."

"You what?"

"I got a job today."

"You didn't? *Today?*"

It hit my legs first. I felt like a bag of cement on bendable straws.

"With D & E Digital. Over in Lisle."

"Programming?" I said, trying to catch my breath. I knew French and a little bit of Italian, but he knew Fortran. Whatever its color, Rob's parachute had opened.

"Yep, I'm a junior programmer. I start the twenty-fourth of October."

Licensed and working. I collapsed against the dryer. My feet banged the metal door to the pantry, and my hand upset Duffy's water bowl.

"Rob, this is the best fucking news," I shouted. "I'm thrilled for you. I mean it. Je te prie d'accepter mes félicitations profondes."

"Il n'y a pas de quoi, mon vieux."

I told him we would celebrate as soon as humanly possible, but first I had another call to make.

It was the Friday before Thanksgiving. Rob's first weeks at D & E Digital had gone well; he'd shown me his ID tag on a chain, and I stuck one of his business cards in my mirror as inspiration and goad. We had begun the conditional tense in Italian class, I had contacted a grand total of six personnel departments from the Allen & Associates leads hidden in my closet, and gotten no word from Patrick besides a belated birthday postcard of the Admiralty Arch in Trafalgar Square.

Jerry, in the spirit of the season, had decorated. I sat in my car in the driveway and took in the bay window festooned with twists of brown and orange crepe paper, and the turkey-in-a-Pilgrim hat, musket, and Indian corn cut-outs taped around a plastic cornucopia glowing dead-center on a draped pedestal. Small pumpkins and gourds were scattered in the lava rocks around his hedges. I sighed. Gay men didn't belong in the suburbs. Finally he appeared behind the screen door and waved me in with a ladle.

I opened my bottle of wine and watched him light the candles. The timer dinged, and he covered the rooster table trivets with bowls and platters.

"My mother called me this afternoon," he said, dropping a roll onto my bread plate. I said nothing. "She said Elliott Biddler didn't show up for his interview yesterday for the assistant concierge position at her hotel."

I sprinkled pepper on my soup. "I didn't feel well."

"You couldn't call to reschedule?"

"I couldn't find the number."

"How old are you, Elliott?"

"How old are *you*?" I asked.

He cleared his throat. The anger had surprised me too. "You could have called me, you could have called information for the hotel number, you could have done something."

"I'm sorry. I didn't think I'd be right for the job."

"Are you kidding me? You're charming, you're handsome, you speak two foreign languages—"

"One," I muttered. I detached the au gratin scab from my serving of potatoes.

"One and a half! And God knows you're full of opinions. You'd love telling people which restaurants to eat in, which movies they should see."

"I don't know any restaurants in Chicago."

"That's why you're the *assistant* concierge! You learn these things."

I dropped my fork on the plate to stop him. I had deliberately muffed an actual job opportunity. In the days before the interview, I had polished my shoes, had Tracy dry-clean my suit, got my hair cut, and actively imagined myself dispensing advice from a desk in a paneled alcove of the Dunstan Hotel.

Jerry began again. "Did you think it wouldn't come up? Did you think that because it was a personal favor from my mother to me, Elliott, that there wouldn't be any follow-up to this, any repercussions when you decided not to show? That's not how it works."

"I don't want a job that you got for me," I mumbled.

"Why not? That's how jobs get found. People suggest their friends. I'm only getting you the interview—my mother does the hiring, she has an opening, and you're desperate for a job. At least that's what you've claimed."

He ladled some more soup into my bowl and clucked his tongue. "I just know she'd think you were terrific."

"I don't want your mother to think I'm terrific." It was bad enough that Jerry thought I was terrific.

Jerry started laughing. "Now you're just being silly. What am I going to do with you, *coniglio mio?*"

"I'm not your rabbit," I snapped. Jerry stopped buttering another roll. "Maybe we should stop seeing each other." I wiped my lips with my napkin, and watched with contempt as he turned on a dime.

"You could be right, you know," he finally said. "The job might not be right for you. Truthfully, my mother can be an absolute horror, and you'd have to move to Chicago. I think she's why I've settled in the suburbs."

"I'd like to move to Chicago," I said cruelly. I had been comparing rents that week in different North Side neighborhoods. With money coming in from the hotel, I could buy furniture and housewares with the last of my father's insurance. Tracy could stay over on weekends, and we'd sit in the bleachers at Wrigley Field when baseball started up again. Patrick would come back from England and go to law school at Northwestern. With my life fixed, we could start on hers. "I'm thinking Rogers Park, Morris Park, somewhere like—"

"Don't say that," Jerry interrupted. "I mean, what about Italian? Mr. Penucci would be devastated."

I rolled my eyes. "I can teach myself Italian."

"It's just that . . ."

"It's just what?"

"Shit!" he cried, having burned his fingers on the quiche pan. He moved to the sink to run water, so his back was turned to me when he said he thought I should think about coming to live with him. He wanted to take care of me while I figured out what I should do with my life.

That I had been expecting this moment made its arrival no less dire, but we still had to get through the meal and afterward. I was always planning for afterward: having the job, not getting the job, the sex, not the feeling. To get us through, I told him I would entertain his proposal, but that we wouldn't discuss it any more that night.

When we reached the bedroom, having been given a glimpse of my heritage, of my perverse, infantile worthlessness, I decided I needed punishment. So when Jerry, charged up from all the rolling around, began crooning nasty suggestions, I broke down and agreed to some restraints.

It was a major lapse in judgment. He dimmed the lights and stroked my back. I was placed on my stomach, so my vision was restricted. I heard the opening of a drawer, the opening of a jar. "You're going to take it all," he suddenly groaned. To my right, I saw his hand snatch up the candle from the nightstand.

My job was to be the baby, but even a baby has his limits, I thought, limits to respect should I cry out or beg Jerry to stop. He was merciless.

When it was over, and he had pulled it out of me, I lay there, choking, my face bubbling with snot. He released my ankles and wrists and turned me over. Then he kissed my forehead, brushed away tears with his fingertips, and thanked baby over and over. He had just the right cream for my tushie, he said, and in the morning, he'd make us a big big breakfast.

He went to clean up and start a bath with Epsom salts for me. Over the running water, I heard him talking again about my moving in. But first, we would take a Christmas trip to France and Italy, the first of many polyglot honeymoons. By the time he returned to the bedroom, a towel with which to swaddle me draped across his forearms, he was explaining the etymology of the word "honeymoon." I mumbled that I already knew that. I had managed to pull myself upright and was seated at the edge of the bed.

"Need some help, baby?"

I nodded, tightened my grip on the candle I had slid under the sheet, and looked into his hopeful eyes.

"Sit with me for a little while, Daddy," I said.

The intake of his breath at hearing me call him Daddy for the first time magnified the burn in my loins. He sat down, and I scooted left to give myself room. The light from the streetlamp in front of his house slanting through the blinds cast a glow about his meaty shoulders. I clubbed the back of his head with the candle and let go of it. I don't know whether it broke against his skull or the wall beyond him, but there was a loud crack and then the thud of his fall onto the carpet.

LET ME SEE IT

I stood up slowly. Deep breaths drew the pain up to my throat, so I took shallow ones. I listened to the running water. I noticed that steam had begun to pillow over the top of the shower curtain. It could continue to drift, I thought; it could pour into the bedroom, condense on the mirrors, moisten the wallpaper until it peeled down from the ceiling in butter-cream curls; it could mildew the furniture and the carpet and the leather soles of the shoes in the closet, rust the swags of chain on the overhead lamp, warp the photos in their frames; it could drench every board until the house collapsed in on itself like a sodden pumpkin, but it would never curl the toupee pinned to the block on the dresser.

As I hobbled down the stairs and into the den for my clothes, I heard Jerry moaning, "baby don't baby don't baby don't." Before anything else, I put my keys in my mouth for safekeeping. When I heard the sound of the water being shut off, I ran into the driveway in my bare feet. I had watched enough horror movies to know that the mummy always returns.

Somehow I made it home without having an accident. Turning onto our street, I saw that every light in the house was on. I fantasized that the electrical system, keyed to my distress, had become a beacon to draw me home but, knowing that my stepfather threatened us for leaving lights on, I realized that something was wrong. When I stood up again outside the car, the pain returned. Pushing away the image of my guts unspooling into my underwear, I held on to the decorative fence and, keeping my knees together, took small steps to the front door. Hearing me come in, Duffy trotted into the foyer from the living room and barked twice to say that it was time for me to take over.

Tracy was curled in a wingback chair, her feet drawn under her torso. She was shaking. Duffy resumed her watch from a distance.

"Trace?"

Her head dropped as if felled by an ax. I lurched in her direction with a cry.

"It's nothing," she said, springing a hand from the pocket of her robe to stop my approach.

"Tell me what happened."

"Dave forced me to eat something, that's all. No big deal. He said he wanted to see my jaws move on some food or he'd break up with me."

Tracy paused to blot her eyes with a wad of toilet paper. I was supposed to call Dave an asshole, so I did.

"I ate a fish sandwich and a large order of fries and an apple pie, and then *I* broke up with *him*. He called me an ugly freak."

She swung her feet down. She was ready to pack it in for the night, but I had something left to ask her, even if it meant hurting her again.

"How did it taste?" I asked softly. "The food."

"Far away," she said. "It tasted far away."

I wanted to laugh, but my insides were burning. I lowered myself very slowly into the couch, hoping the pain would ease in sitting.

"What's the matter with you? Where are your shoes?"

"I just got fucked by an Easter candle."

I told her the story and when I was finished, we stared at each other.

"What are we going to do?"

I don't know which one of us said it. I'm not certain whether either one of us actually asked the question, but it hung in the air, and we'd heard it.

Tracy moved first. She got up and headed toward the stairs.

"Turn some lights off," I called weakly. I stretched out on the couch, clutching my belly, and closed my eyes. I opened them again at the tickle of some fabric on my cheek.

Tracy was wearing a pearl-gray smock. It took me a moment to realize it was from the Wilfred Academy of Beauty.

"I bought these so we'd have somewhere to go," she said.

"I thought they'd be pink."

"Me too. Here," she said, holding out another one, a larger one in charcoal. She shook it a little to tease me into sitting up.

I took the bait. It was scratchy and smelled like packing peanuts. Something was missing.

"Where are our name tags?" I asked.

"We have to register first," she said sternly.

"I see."

"Tomorrow."

I nodded. She helped me to my feet and put my right arm into the smock. She went into the kitchen while I finished buttoning. This I could do. Learning the difference between a crème and a finishing rinse was

LET ME SEE IT

something I could do. I was practicing José's thumbs-up gesture to the camera when I thought I heard the refrigerator door open.

I stopped. If I turned around very slowly in my robe, I might catch her standing in the dining room archway with a bowl of pudding and two spoons. Beckoning. Instead, I hobbled into the kitchen and held my sister's hair back from her face as she threw up in the sink.

MISTRESS OF THE REVELS

TOM

1984

Shakespeare had brought them together, and Shakespeare would drive them apart.

Tom Amelio, a new hire at the Madison Stage Company, had spent his first weeks as Communications Assistant tracking down face painters and Chippewa storytellers for the theater's annual open house. Then came his first real challenge—writing a press release for the upcoming production of *Pericles*. Its hopscotching plot was difficult to summarize. His boss pointed him to Education Director Lucy Hax, who had paused halfway through her doctorate at the University of Wisconsin on women in Greek drama to, as she liked to say, bring the magic of live theater to the underserved. Lucy had been most helpful in their ad hoc meeting, providing him with the snappy technical term "prose romance" and insisting on the inclusion of "swashbuckling" in his lead paragraph, so Tom invited her to lunch.

Of the many intriguing notions she revealed to him in the noisy pub she chose at the edge of campus, perhaps the oddest was that a woman needed extra iron at a certain time every month. This, after she had appended a throaty "very rare" to her cheeseburger order. Like satin teddies and seed-pearl clips (Lucy wouldn't dream of piercing her ears), a platter of red meat she said was another way to celebrate her femininity.

Tom nodded sagely, although he knew that his mother and aunts didn't believe in womanly treats. He smiled to imagine them with him, listening to this East Coast career girl, blonde and very petite, but fluent in big ideas like "performance art" and "diaspora studies." As they waited for their food, Lucy interrupted the story of her life with racy assessments of select undergraduates at neighboring tables. The shoulders on this one meant swim team. This other, pulling snarls of onion rings out of a red webbed basket, had fingers she wanted to bite. The one in the take-out line with the lacrosse butt was definitely worth a nasty.

"A nasty?" asked Tom, new to the term.

"As in 'doing the nasty.'"

"Is that Shakespeare?"

"No, silly. It's black English. As in 'I love doin' the nasty.'" She giggled. "And I do." This was a voguish declaration, especially for a white girl from Connecticut with four younger siblings who lined up along the staircase on Christmas morning according to age, like the Five Little Peppers.

Lucy's interest in sex was stimulating, but Tom couldn't decide whether she was inviting him to second her taste in men, or more troubling, was flirting with him. In his mind, picking up and moving to arty, progressive Madison—his most daring act to date—meant he *was* out, but of course you had to say and do things to prove it. He didn't know how open he could be at Madison Stage; so far he had remained neutral about his sexuality. That meant, among other things, speeding past the queens in the costume shop on his way to the postage machine. They could waggle their wrist pincushions all they liked; he was part of the team crafting the public image of the theater and needed to be careful.

But that didn't mean Tom didn't yearn to be known. He was hoping that lunch with the worldly Lucy Hax would launch the kind of friendship gay men seemed to have with single women, but she hadn't asked him anything about himself.

"I think you're a cradle robber," he said in a pause, trying to match her jaunty tone.

"As long as they're legal."

"Is that sixteen, eighteen, or twenty-one?" Tom was twenty-three.

"Well, in Sparta these jocks would be over the hill—" And Lucy, who was twenty-seven, was off again: after college, but before grad school, she had taught Greek civ at a private school near Hartford. Barely five years older than her seniors, she had felt the need to establish some boundaries and had therefore adopted a somewhat antiquarian fashion silhouette. Tom was about to ask for an explanation, but their food had arrived.

"What about him, Lucy?" murmured Tom, reaching for the ketchup after the waiter had left.

"Small hands, weak chin."

"Not a swashbuckler?"

"Not at all."

"Not worth a nasty?"

"By George, I think you've got it," she exclaimed, rolling her silverware out of the paper napkin.

Tom laughed. That reference he knew—My *Fair Lady*.

A week later the final draft of his press release came back from the managing director with "Nice work, Tom," scrawled across the top. He stood at the copy machine and intoned "Pericles Pericles Pericles," inking a permanent good-bye to Kansas as it spat out eighty copies of his opus. He toyed with putting his parents on the mailing list, but a press release would be as foreign to the Amelios as a Tiffany's catalog.

With the economy in the toilet, Tom had had to move home after Purdue. He tutored at his high school, helped coach the wrestling team, and for extra money unloaded meat trucks with his father every other weekend at the Kroger. His former teachers failed to convince him that he was too intelligent to know what to do with himself just yet. His old boss Iulian tried to interest him in getting his own Zip'z ice cream franchise, but Tom thought doing so would be the equivalent of holding his diploma over one of the stove burners in the kitchen. Many of his college friends had ducked the recession by heading straight to law school, but they came from families who understood the concept of investment. There was no Amelio to convince Tom that a starting law salary would cancel his loan debt in a few short years. He'd spent some of his earnings on a Kaplan prep course, did well on the LSAT, but couldn't quite manage to send away for applications, or even look for paralegal work in a big firm across the river in Missouri.

One year in Overland Park turned into two. He began substitute teaching, but got no closer to any kind of career. The closet, and the onset of the gay cancer, kept him home most nights, but finally a Chianti spill at a piano bar in Kansas City freed him from purgatory. The pair of chinos Tom had stained belonged to Kyle Swern, an actor on a bus-and-truck tour of *42nd Street*. He wasn't Tom's first boyfriend (and "boyfriend," Tom knew, was stretching the term), but over the course of a five-show weekend, Kyle gave Tom his first lessons in pluck and abandon. Kyle wasn't furtive; he held Tom's hand in public and didn't stow him in the bathroom when room service knocked on the door with breakfast for two. During one drowsy interval at the Marriott, Kyle had spoken in glowing terms of the season he had tested his talent by doing a Shaw play at the Madison Stage Company; and finally, he asked Tom the million-dollar bootstraps question no one else would: why was such an attractive, personable graduate from a good school stuck living at home with his parents when there were jobs for sweet young things like him at every theater in the country, starting with the box office?

The approach of a handsome man might upset his wine, but Tom wasn't so green as to imagine that he could go on tour with him. Kyle had left for Topeka on Monday morning with encouraging phrases, but no forwarding address; Tom spent his drive home piecing together a riskier message. He made a call on Tuesday, and sent his resume and references to Wisconsin. The following week, driving his ancient Dodge the nine hours to Madison, Tom felt in his heart—an organ he seldom consulted—that the mention of Equity actor Kyle Swern in his cover letter had gotten him the face-to-face interview.

At the end of his first week on the job, Tom borrowed Kyle's head shot from the press archives. His side part, flared nostrils, and thin mustache made him look like a Danish pirate. Tom propped the photo on his nightstand against a resin Oscar statuette his cousin Karen had given him at the farewell potluck held by his puzzled relatives. *Madison? The theater? Really?*

In their good-bye embrace, Alphonse had slipped into his shirt pocket a surprise check for one-half of the room and board Tom had contributed all those months.

Tom fed the press release envelopes to the mail machine, which made as satisfying a rhythm as the photocopier, then he went to Lucy's office with a package of red licorice whips, her favorite, purchased in the convenience store across from his building in the hip Mansion Hill neighborhood.

Lucy wasn't alone. Vance, an African American actor from the *Pericles* cast, loomed over her desk, the better to read her finest tribute to date, a framed couplet to the beauty of her hair penned on a dinner napkin by America's leading black playwright, who had been part of a panel she had moderated on campus. At the sight of him, Lucy paddled the air with her tiny hands and exclaimed, "Oh Tom, Vance and I just wowed the kids at Johnnycake Middle School."

Vance, wary perhaps at a rival's approach, relaxed when Tom praised his recent appearance on a popular hospital drama. Tom looked forward to the day when he'd feel at ease around African Americans, a useful skill in public relations.

"You should have seen us get Shakespeare into their mouths," said Lucy.

"Say what? Whose mouths?" said Vance. But then he laughed. Even Tom could decode the message in Lucy's napkin: there was no color line to her affections. Vance left with a promise to go on more classroom visits—just not before eleven.

Lucy stood on a stool that she kept under her chair to prevent her legs from tiring. As she reached to rehang the frame, her left sleeve slid below a large, oval strawberry mark on her forearm. Tom averted his eyes. The mark reminded him of the tricky sequence at the theater open house when he had sensed that Lucy might be expecting him to make a pass. He had worn a tie to the staff after-party. Lucy, whom he knew only by name—this was before their pub lunch—had come over to the mezzanine bar where he sat nursing a beer. She tapped the knot of his tie, tugged at its tongue, and let her fingers linger on his abdomen. "Let's get you out of this lasso, farmer boy," she giggled.

Pretending he was ticklish, he stood and came up with the following whopper: "My girlfriend, Karen Masucci, gave me this tie. As a going-away present," he said.

"He's taken, everybody," said Lucy to no one in particular.

Tom had stood and chugged his already-empty bottle until Lucy joined a line dance, but today, buoyed by the press release in his hand, he said, "I think you want Vance's Johnnycake."

The picture wire hopped onto its hook with a little scraping sound.

Lucy braced her palms against the wall. "What did you say?"

"You want him, Lucy. You want him . . . *bad.*"

"Tom!" she shrieked, "Keep your voice down."

"And what's more—" he said, dangling the news until she'd stepped down from the stool and fluffed her hair—"Vance wants your Lucycake."

"No," she whispered. "No."

Lucy might fib otherwise to her family, but it was too early to settle down with a go-getter like her father. She confided that the banking sons and lawyering nephews of the theater's trustees didn't interest her. Lucy wanted to fuck actors—one per show, or six per season, in an ideal world.

They braided licorice whips and planned the Siege of Pericles Vance. Tom had never been on stage, or even seen many plays, but he found himself cuing her matrix of romantic strategies with an all-purpose, low-pitched "You must . . . *be.* . . with him." Lucy answered this directive with a gratifying fit of giggles every single time, giggles heard all over the admin bay.

Lucy revealed that one must never sit on a black person's bed without explicit invitation. Black men, moreover, weren't inclined to perform oral sex. Nipping a licorice braid, Tom recalled a wicked expression on Kyle Swern's face and attempted a reveal of his own, saying that he had heard that black men dug colored condoms. Instead of asking him where he had gotten his information, Lucy said that Tom must run right out and buy her a box.

"I'll go at lunch," he replied, concealing his disappointment. "They sell them across the street."

Lucy giggled again. "Look at me, corrupting an ephebe."

Alas, by the time *Pericles* finished its run, the number of times Lucy had managed to *be with* Vance in her Art Deco bedroom suite stood at two and a half, hardly enough to redeem the purchase of the almond-scented candles, the ribbed camisole, the purple teakettle, and the box of colored Trojans. Their *half* nasty was an elaborate champagne sleepover that had dwindled into a petting party. Confessing that he didn't want to get "jammed up," Vance was buttoning his peacoat by ten thirty.

Lucy and Tom decided at the postmortem that Vance was protecting himself from his growing feelings for her. The race taboo had been too strong. Tom cheered his mistress up by revisiting encounter number two: on a frigid Thursday morning, Tom had run to her office and convinced her to ditch her curriculum meeting at the Board of Ed and spirit her lover, presently smoking a cigarette in front of the theater, to her boudoir. She must make Vance pretend that he was degrading his English teacher, lay waste to her skirt, tear her woolly tights with a forceful swipe, and ravish her on the fainting couch in her entrance hall.

The improvisation was a triumph that made them feel like sexual spymasters, the Aphrodite and Eros of the NSA. Afterward, Lucy showed Tom the hairs that had rubbed off Vance's body. She had collected them onto a flap torn from a manila envelope. With a fingertip she swirled them into a tiny pile of coils, tinder for a fairy's campfire, folded the paper three times, and placed the memento into the lingerie drawer of her vanity table.

Kyle Swern's head shot was one thing, but human hair? "You're keeping *that?*" Tom had asked.

"I like evidence," she'd said, mysteriously.

"In case there's a trial?"

Lucy picked up one of the many crystal flacons on her vanity tray. "No," she said, "Greek and Roman women made *philtrons* in their everyday lives. The ingredients were very complex."

This time it was Tom who didn't take the bait. He guessed that a *philtron* was a love potion and let it go.

Their next campaign was launched mid-March at a coffee bar after the first read-through of *Hedda Gabler.* Wayne Thomas, playing Judge Brack in Ibsen's domestic tragedy, had sleepy brown eyes and a cleft chin, but he wouldn't see forty-five again, so what, Tom wondered aloud, was the attraction?

Lucy twined her fingers beneath her chin. "Oh Tom," she sighed, "a part of Lucy just wants her daddy."

"Wants her daddy *bad*," he replied, mechanically. Not willing to let her grab all the fun right off, Tom had been daydreaming that the actor playing Lövborg had Kyle Swern's exact, plush-pillow lips.

"All girls want their daddies," she said, secure in her position at the bottom step of the holiday staircase, the first and favorite little Hax. "My father spoiled me from the cradle. My mother says he cried like a baby on my first day of kindergarten."

Tom remembered his first day of kindergarten, when his brother Dan had yanked him out the front door. His mother had refused even to walk him to the bus stop, much less dry his tears. It occurred to him that he hadn't talked to her in weeks. That worked both ways, though.

He put them back on track. "What makes you think you can get Wayne?"

"Oh Tom," she clucked, sweeping the milk foam from her upper lip with a brush of her tongue. "I'm a gorgeous and sexy blonde."

This not infrequent assertion of Lucy's—categorical, but fishing—no longer made Tom anxious. Now it was something to swat aside, like a bottle fly.

"Sure," he replied, then did a little fishing of his own. "Are you sure Wayne's straight?"

Lucy made a face. "He's married, silly."

Didn't she even *wonder* whether he was queer? And why couldn't some of her confidence rub off on him? There were several bars near his building, but when it came to his own campaigns, little Eros couldn't join a support group or call a hotline, much less spill a drink on someone. One stocky older guy in the neighborhood, with round glasses and a sweet smile, brazenly cruised Tom on the streets. He was not a leading man like Kyle Swern, but Tom, dumbstruck with excitement anyway, would flee at the sight of him. His rationalization was that older men, especially *cruisy* older men, had a much greater chance of having the virus. So instead of sallying forth, Tom watched the nightly parade into the Cardinal Bar from Lucy's kitchen while she steeped pots of tea and served more helpings of her life story.

"I didn't see a wedding ring," said Tom.

"He was here in the Shaw, and I checked his status with the business office. Donna keeps the records."

"A Shaw play? Which one?"

"*Major Barbara*. Wayne's Undershaft was very subtle."

Kyle had been in *Misalliance* in the spring of '80, playing a character called Joey Percival. "Rather a toff," Kyle had said, his British accent polishing Tom's body like a chamois cloth. What Tom had needed that Monday in front of the *42nd Street* bus at the Kansas City Marriott was a friend to pluck the straw from his ears and push him onto the next Greyhound to Topeka to *be* with Kyle.

"The wife's name is Trina," said Lucy. "She's a television newscaster. They live in Connecticut."

"The business office keeps housing records?"

"No, I asked Wayne in the elevator."

"Fast work," said Tom. "Do they live near the Haxes?"

"They're farther north. They're restoring a farmhouse in Sturbridge County."

Tom bent his biscotto against the table until it snapped. A hazelnut half skittered toward Lucy. She slipped it in her mouth.

"I think I'd like to live in an old farmhouse someday. I'd read all day, bake bread and make stock, then wait for my man to come home and build a fire—"

Tom cut her off. "Don't be an idiot, Lucy. Farm wives are incredibly busy."

He looked at other customers, hunched into each other at the painted steel tables. Their long wool coats slung on the seat backs bled into connecting puddles of dirty water on the linoleum. March in Kansas was even grimmer than this: wind and snow, mud wallows and tire chains, red faces and cracked skin, and boots that never really dried. He felt lucky to be out of there.

"Did you just call me an idiot?"

He hadn't intended the cut, but hers was such an exasperating fantasy. And for all she cared to know about his family, he had been found under a cabbage leaf. "I'm sorry, Lucy, but the farmers I've met lead really tough lives."

"That's no reason to be rude."

"I know. It's just—"

"It's just what?"

Lucy wasn't going to pick up her cues unless he came out to her. He took a deep breath. "It's just that I got a letter yesterday . . ."

"Yes? And?"

"Karen broke up with me."

Her "Who's Karen?" expression was priceless to behold, but Tom was weirdly glad that she had manners enough to say she was sorry to hear it. She laid her hand on his, leaned in. A segue into bisexuality (at the least) might have ensued, but Tom lost his nerve and said it was a case of City Mouse, Country Mouse.

He accepted a refill from the waiter with almost comic gratitude. The chill would drag on for weeks yet, but he'd managed to kill Karen off and Kyle Swern's address was easy to find in Donna's drawer of W-2 forms. If he liked, Tom could send him a postcard of Capitol Square that read, "I took your advice. Here I am. Tom (Amelio)."

A gust of wind from the opening of the café door whiffled Lucy's curls. The sight of her fingers pressed for warmth against the porcelain cup made him smile. He could help spring happen for both of them.

"I think . . ." he began.

This cue was familiar. "Yes?" she said eagerly.

"You must . . . be. . . with Wayne."

All was forgiven.

Lucy made her educational pitch to the *Hedda Gabler* cast the very next day. In addition to classroom visits, she was going to need volunteer swordsmen for a stage combat workshop at the Shakespeare-in-the-Schools Festival. Tom, on deck outside the rehearsal hall with his program bio forms, was half listening to her with Phillip, the costume shop manager, who was waiting to ferry actors to the fitting room for measurements.

Phillip was older, with a goatee and earrings. His default pose was hauteur. That, and his ease with silence, unnerved Tom. With every passing second, he felt Phillip's gaydar whoop louder, like a Geiger counter approaching Three Mile Island.

"They seem like a talented group," Tom finally said.

Phillip accepted his feeble statement, then honed in on the challenges to come. "The Hedda is hippy, and Thea is going to be a nightmare. Theas are always a nightmare, because they want to be Heddas. Their corsets pinch, their shoes are too tight, they hate their wigs, what have you. This Thea looks especially bruising."

Phillip looked directly at Tom. It was his turn, put up or shut up.

"What about the Lövborg?" he said.

Phillip pounced. "Dreamy, dontcha think?"

"He reminds me of another actor I know," said Tom.

Phillip drew a finger down the length of Tom's nose. "Of course he does." The gesture was friendly, not aggressive, but Tom drew back and dropped the conversational ball.

They heard a familiar giggle.

"For Christ's sake, Lucy, get off the fucking stage," said Phillip.

Tom stiffened. "She's just doing her job," he said.

"I'll say. She's too short to be an actress."

"That's not very kind," said Tom.

His loyal remark sounded priggish and silly, and he knew he couldn't take it back. Phillip dismissed him for the time being with a tiny, sideward tilt of his chin.

When he wasn't called for rehearsal, Wayne Thomas built kitchen cabinets for his farmhouse restoration, manual labor that drew Lucy every day into the strange land of the scenic artists. Their first kisses were stolen in a dark corner behind the table saw. Out of the corner of her eye, she had spotted two stage carpenters in welding hoods and giant fireproof gloves pulling pipe from a metal hatch in the wall. They looked like astronauts, so Lucy told Tom that the touch of Wayne's lips had put her over the moon.

The next day Tom brought Lucy a first draft of the *Hedda Gabler* press release. He read out: "After appearing last season in *Major Barbara,* Wayne Thomas (Judge Brack) returns to the Madison Stage Company to explore Lucy Hax's crater."

Her eyes grew big and round.

" 'To *plug* Lucy Hax's crater?' " he said. "*Plug's* a stronger verb."

"You have to destroy this."

"How about, 'Get jammed up in her jam pot'?"

She kicked away the stool under her desk and stood.

"That's not funny. How could you write such filth?"

"Filth? It's all we talk about, Lucy."

"It is not!"

"Sex and mythology. The ephebe and the *didaskalos—*"

"The thing is, I like Wayne. I think I like him a lot."

Tom tried to catch up. "You mean you—like—*care* for him?"

She avoided his look. "Even more than that."

He pressed harder. "Like 'Three Little Words' stuff?" Lucy pinned her lower lip with her teeth. "After a little suck-face in the scene shop?"

Lucy balled her hands in the middle of her desk, as if she were trying to subdue the lacrosse jocks in one of her old Greek civ classes. The quantum leap in her statements so astounded Tom, so reminded him of forty-eight hours at the Marriott and an aftermath that included moving five hundred miles to Wisconsin, that he could do little else but persist with insolent questions—"Do married men kiss better than bachelors?" "Do middle-aged actors fuck better than Pulitzer Prize playwrights?" "Do you think when your father goes out of town that he cheats on your mother?"—until she began to cry.

"Why are you being mean to me?" she managed to gasp out.

Tom had never been so terrible to anyone in his life. He hadn't meant it, or so he told himself. More alarming than her tears, her purpling neck and cheeks, and the sight of such outsized misery in her tiny, shuddering body was the sense of how good it felt to punish her for their lopsided relationship.

Food and apologies were easier than an explanation, so he took her for pub grub and convinced her that the alienation of Wayne's affections from his wife would require a truly audacious first strike. Thus it was that a pair of Lucy's lace-trimmed panties, wrapped around an apartment key, slipped into an envelope of handmade paper and sealed with wax the golden yellow of her hair, was dropped into the *Hedda Gabler* mail slot.

Three weeks later Trina Thomas arrived for previews. Lucy, the other woman, took a page from Noël Coward and invited Mr. and Mrs. Thomas for tea. Tom played designated consort.

It was a gorgeous spring. All the windows of Mansion Hill were thrown open and the streets were lined with flowering Bradford pears. Tom drew deep breaths of their pungent odor as he walked to Lucy's with a box of scones. There was no delicate way to put it; Bradford pear trees in bloom smelled like semen. Pinckney Street in April smelled like cum.

Tom put it just that way to Trina, a beauty with silver hair, when she remarked on the unusual scent. Wayne coughed and Lucy sighed at the coarseness of men. Recalled to his role, Tom continued, "Lucy hates it when I say things like that. So very sorry." Then he swanned through one of the French doors into her bedroom and opened a dresser drawer. "Honey, where did I leave that—that thing?"

This improvisation put Lucy on edge. "What—thing? What?"

"Never mind, I found it," he answered. He picked up a bottle of perfume and returned to the dining table, making sure to keep the French doors open. No reason why Lucy's Deco bedroom suite shouldn't be part of the set.

"What are you doing with my L'Air du Temps?"

"Improving the atmosphere," he replied. Moving quickly, he touched the glass stopper to Wayne's hand, Trina's neck, Lucy's wrist, and finished with a dab on his upper lip. "That's better," he said, sitting down. The laughter was general, but strained. When he tickled a tulip in the center-piece, he knew the knock on his ankle under the table meant "settle down *now.*"

The conversation turned to Connecticut, and Tom's mind moved ahead to Monday, the culmination of their erotic plans. Many at Madison Stage thought that Lucy's Shakespeare Festival was irrelevant to the institutional mission, but it generated goodwill and funding dollars. As Mistress of the Revels, Lucy would be introducing the presentation of thirty-minute versions of Shakespeare put on by city schools. She would also preside over the scansion workshop and teach a simplified Morris dance to the seventh graders, all the while wearing a bejeweled period gown originally built for the theater's production of *Mary Stuart*. In addition to alerting the media that the governor's wife was handing out the prizes, Tom's chief festival duty was to ensure that Lucy got fucked in her farthingale in the actors' pass-through beneath the stage.

They had cased this eerie location the day before. Tom had never seen the inscriptions at Pompeii, so the crumbling plaster tunnel covered with years of autographs, quips, and scraps of dialogue set down in pen and marker and lipstick by actors waiting to make their entrances, spooked him. The neediest among them, loath to quit the safety of makeshift theater families, seemed to have commemorated themselves with the points of daggers. After some debate they had decided that Wayne should take Lucy against a wall, Elizabethan-sally-in-the-alley style, during La Follette High's *Julius Caesar*.

The sudden pressure of Lucy's head against his shoulder—not in the script—brought Tom's thoughts back to the table.

"What is it?" he asked.

"Nothing, honey," she purred. Her fingers were stroking his arm.

He saw instantly what it was. Trina, alert to something in the air besides the smell of pear trees, had set down her cup and circled her husband's elbow with both hands. Lucy, countering the move, was trying to make Wayne jealous.

Tom wondered if Lucy's pink toes were rubbing Wayne's khaki crotch under the table, a maneuver he'd used on Kyle with agreeable results. Would he ever start a plot to call his own? He shrugged off her hand and announced he required some ice water.

Lucy licked her lips. "Tom can get so thirsty."

Were he holding the water pitcher, he might have brained her with it. "Anyone else?" he asked.

LET ME SEE IT

"I'd like some," said Trina.

He went into the kitchen. "Lemon?" he called out.

"Yes, please," said Trina.

The rush of cool air when he opened the freezer door was a calming distraction. The bin was empty, so he removed a plastic ice tray, carried it to the counter, then stifled a shout at the array of used, party-colored condoms frozen in its compartments. He batted the tray into the sink; the little seed packages stayed put.

Tom covered his mouth and mulled the evidence: three Vances, five empties, six Waynes, for a total of nine—the Muses, a baseball team, or a small Trojan army of actors. Not only had Lucy been draining all the semen in the neighborhood, she was hoarding it. The score was nine to zero.

The refrigerator, tired of running with the freezer door open, started to buzz. Tom threw the tray back into the freezer and chucked in two tins of Twinings to let her know that he'd spotted more of her nasty, crazy-ass *philtron* ingredients.

Later, climbing back up the white marble steps after bidding good-bye to the Thomases, Lucy finally remarked on Tom's silence. Before he could craft a response, he spotted the stocky, bespectacled stranger who always cruised him. Carrying a gym bag, the kind with a racket compartment on the side, he was heading directly toward them. Ducking his gaze, Tom watched the muscles shift in the man's thighs. Not a leading man, but he looked great in shorts.

Tapping the side of her sandal on the step to release a pebble, Lucy straightened on the approach. The man slowed to a saunter. As he passed, his smile was as brazen and inviting as ever, but Tom also caught the lift of his eyebrow at the sight of Lucy.

Lucy stretched and offered her palms to the cum trees above. "Did you see the way he looked at me?" she murmured.

"Just now? With the gym bag?"

She giggled, fumbling with the brass doorknob to her building. It had a tendency to stick.

"One at a time, Lucy," he said sharply. "One at a time."

"He's too fat."

Maybe for you, he thought. He smacked iron dust from the railing off the front of his trousers.

Before rounding the corner onto Gilman Street, the stranger looked back. Tom called out a hello. Instead of returning Tom's wave, the man made a gun with his hand and pointed it at Tom as if to say "gotcha."

"Do you know him?" asked Lucy.

Next time there would be more than hello. Tom swept a line of sweat into his hair and opened the door for her.

On Monday, mid-festival, Tom entered the costume shop for the first time. A swag of pearls in Lucy's diadem had gotten knocked off during the photo shoot, Lucy having made the mistake of loaning the headpiece to a group of sixth graders desperate to share in its sparkle. Her grim expression—Lady Bountiful outwitted by the Natives—had been captured forever for the Wisconsin Foundation for the Arts photo archives.

"Oh, look," Phillip said. "It's Mr. Hax."

"Mr. Hax?" said Tom, in a voice that shut their laughter off like a faucet.

There were three of them, sibyls with long, lean bodies and cloth tape measures around their necks. They had been watching him all along.

"Don't mind us," said Phillip, pressing his hands onto a corset form. "We know we're terrible."

Tom crossed his arms to stop them from shaking, but found himself eager to answer some questions the costume shop had been pondering since his arrival in Madison. He began with the famous couplet to Lucy's hair. Canary had been the prize-winning playwright's simile, so Lucy was briefly christened "The Hairy Canary" until Tom's recitation of the Siege of Pericles Vance prompted a more satisfying (and permanent) nickname: Jam-Up Hax.

The drapers took their turn. Viperous and keen-sighted, they transformed her wardrobe, shoes, bags, voice, walk, hair, and all her harmless personal flourishes into hooting absurdities. Phillip aired the group opinion that Jam-Up was too short to go out in public, which led Tom to complete his performance by walking on his knees, arms outstretched, like a toddler asking "up."

The atmosphere was festive, and the diadem restored, by the time Rick, the stage manager of the festival, poked his head through the door. A fight had broken out in the mezzanine. He'd had to suspend *Julius Caesar*, and now Lucy was needed to calm her subjects and herd the next school on.

Tom checked his watch. He could have quit his supporting role as Mr. Hax on Saturday afternoon by choosing to chill Mrs. Thomas's glass of water with three coins of her husband's semen, but he had decided in Lucy's kitchen that that wasn't fair to the wronged, unsuspecting party. He chose instead a final, callous, shameful reveal: he told Rick that he could find the Mistress of the Revels under the stage. "Scepter in hand," he added with his own attempt at deadpan. The costume shop exploded with laughter.

As Rick was leaving, Tom noticed a flashlight clipped to his belt. He would ask for it later. There had to be a piece of Kyle Swern scratched in a corner of the pass-through. He'd go down there after all the school buses left. But if he was wrong, and there was no message for him on the walls, he knew he could come back to the costume shop. They had Kyle's measurements on file. They'd know how to track him down. Or maybe someone like him.

BUCCELLATI
TOM AND ELLIOTT

1985

One place to look for a suitable husband was the monthly dance at Columbia University. Suitable meant, among other things, *suited:* we were looking for a junior associate at a law firm, a thirtyish bond trader or ad writer or public relations exec with money to spend on above-ground transport, illegal stimulants, and surprise packages from the better department stores. We wanted a man at least two desks past entry level, preferably with a summer share. Or at least I did. My cousin Elliott was a different story.

It was late May, and I had been in Manhattan for less than a month. Contrary to my expectations, I had quickly found a job at R. R. Bowker, "the publisher's publisher." I worked for Zoltan Breslau, the man who had invented the ISBN number in 1957, but you can't eat prestige. My annual salary was $14,600. I needed nicer shoes. My sublet on Jane Street, brokered through a recent ex of my cousin's, would end in September.

Elliott knew where to look for a husband. He was shameless, fearless, and apart from the hours we'd spent in awkward proximity at his father's funeral when we were nineteen, I couldn't believe we'd lived a quarter of a century without ever meeting. Elliott had just done this thing called "Direct Centering," a human potential "course" that involved weekly sessions of ego reintegration. It wasn't a cult, he wrote to me in Madison—not that I had asked. Whatever it was, Direct Centering had given him the gumption to change jobs every six months, ask for better tables in restaurants, and pick up strangers, as well as the power to convince me to come to New York, where he said I belonged, plague be damned.

There was no physical resemblance between us, though Elliott, if bored in a restaurant or movie queue, sometimes asked people whether we looked like cousins. We rarely got more than a glance and a no, but an older woman once took her time before saying that there was something similar in the shape of our mouths. Elliott's delight at the news embarrassed me at the time. He called us Snow White and Rose Red, as he was fair and fine boned, and I was swarthy and strong featured. In the game of love and chance it was the other way around: I was the priss and he was the slut. I resisted the feminine implications of his nicknames; I was a working stiff in the big city with suits of my own and so I tried to rechristen ourselves Nord (short for Nordic) and Med (short for Mediterranean), but the names clunked out like cartoon barbells.

The name for what we were, archaic today, was Twinkie. We were Twinkies, moist and pliant confections to gulp in three bites, welcome sponges to soak in stronger flavors, with a faint, helpful grit in the aftertaste. Our freshness was hypothetically perpetual. At what point, after all, might a Twinkie, *could* a Twinkie, shrivel, sour, melt, or fester?

Owen Teeter called me a Twinkie, decently, hopefully, as he walked me to the 110th Street subway stop after we'd had enough of the Columbia dance. My phone number was folded into the small triangular pocket of his jeans, just in front of his right hip bone. It was two o'clock in the morning. At last sight, Snow White was striking hieratic poses in the center of the swarm, his hair swept into the improvised turban of his Cornell T-shirt.

My Purdue wifebeater had stayed put in my khakis. Elliott thought my legs were too thick for shorts and had talked me out of wearing them, a mistake. The combination of dried sweat and prickly heat from four hours of dancing made my thighs feel like they'd been rolled in cracker crumbs. I realized a train might take half an hour to show up, there would be no express stop until Seventy-second Street, and I had no air-conditioning.

Irritation flowed into the hand I offered Owen. "You can call me," I said. He smiled and shot his arms up in a sudden stretch of victory.

I wasn't so much of a priss, but Owen wouldn't find that out until the third date, should we get that far. We'd get that far, I grumbled to myself on the platform. Owen, thirty-one with thinning hair, had my phone number. Sticking to the first man who'd said hello wasn't effective husband hunting, and Elliott would chide me for it. It was like accepting the first job offered, which I had. It was like buying a madras shirt at Lord & Taylor, which I had. It's the Kansas in you, Elliott would say, shaking his head.

Kansas of me as well to have waltzed with Owen Teeter. Once the crowd discovered that the violin figure in three-quarter time wasn't a false start to the latest British import, the floor emptied with comic haste. Owen held out his arms. I placed my hand on his shoulder and said he should lead. His fingers tapped, then curled around my flank just below my ribs. The trick, Owen half shouted, was not to lean in. Don't look down, he said. Keep your back straight!

We weren't terribly terrific at it, but a waltz with a man was worth a try. Like cold sesame noodles, my culinary discovery that far-off summer of 1985. Peanut butter mixed with chili sauce, I wrote on a postcard to my parents, hard to imagine.

Elliott was working a plate of them the next day at a Szechuan restaurant off Abingdon Square that we liked.

"Did you go home with anyone?" I asked, launching the postmortem.

He grunted no and cut the glistening cable of noodles with his teeth before speaking. "First I mashed with a lawyer in a window seat. But I sent him off for drinks and ditched him when he started smelling like a hamster."

"A hamster?"

"I had hamsters when I was little, okay? He got excited, it *happens,* and the smell of Eau Sauvage mixed with his personal musk made him smell like a hamster. Or hamster shavings . . . perhaps," he finished daintily, a tone at odds with the sight of his chin gilded in swirls of peanut sauce. For all her pretensions, Snow White had terrible table manners.

"And then after the lawyer?" I asked.

"I let somebody do me in the bathroom."

I frowned. The first to take his shirt off on the dance floor, my cousin was also the kind of guy who managed to lay a groomsman at every wedding he went to. "Hand or mouth?" I asked.

"What do you think?" he said, his thumb bearing down on some egg roll filaments. Elliott didn't consider hand jobs sex. I did. Strike three for Kansas.

"What did this one smell like?"

"What's bugging you?" he asked.

"Did you wear a rubber?"

"They haven't proved that mumbo jumbo yet."

"You mean safe sex."

"Is that what they're calling it?"

"That's the gist of it," I said.

"The point to sex is danger, Tom, and I'm not talking about doing a baker's dozen in a row at the Saint. I just happen to believe that every intimate encounter should make room for the edge."

The arrival of our food tabled the discussion Elliott never wanted to have. Acknowledging the existence of the plague was the extent of his prophylaxis. On our side so far was the fact that neither of us knew anyone who was sick, or knew anyone who knew anyone who had died. Elliott forked a shrimp off my Triple Delight while I called the waitress back for chopsticks.

As expected, Owen Teeter's dossier horrified Elliott. Staten Island. SUNY Binghamton. Five years with the Peace Corps. In Ghana. Owen managed no accounts of any kind. Not even a paralegal, he taught English as a second language to refugees in the basement of St. Bartholomew's Church. His father was a trigonometry teacher, so a trust fund seemed the longest of shots. What was the attraction, Elliott wanted to know. Owen was a gentleman, I replied. The hand on my back as we threaded our way out of the waltz was courtly. "Very Edith Wharton," sighed Elliott, but I hadn't read her yet. Owen was cute, he was Irish Catholic, but, I quickly added, out and proud. My cousin and I had both fallen hard in college for Irish closet cases. That was the first of three oddball things we shared in common. The other two were an interest in foreign languages and a hyperactive Cowper's gland, which means we generated a lot of pre-cum, which was not the sort of detail we could have asked our older brothers about.

When I finished, Elliott tilted his head and went to the heart of the matter. I might not adhere to his rulings, but I respected the thinking behind them. "Tom," he said.

"Elliott."

"When are you going to learn how to take a compliment?"

"What do you mean?" I asked, flushing. I knew where he was headed.

"What I mean is, you're not under any obligation. A stranger comes up to you and says he thinks you're a sexy young man."

"I shouldn't have told you that," I hissed.

"I admit you were alone and vulnerable, I was off scoping—"

"Mashing."

"I apologize, but still."

"But still what?"

He sighed. "You can just accept the compliment. Say thank you and leave it at that. You don't have to sleep with him."

"I didn't sleep with him! I don't just sleep with people." I also didn't let people "do" me.

"You have to own your appeal, Tom."

Compliments were not part of an Amelio upbringing. I eyeballed the restaurant in a panic. Where was the hissing wok to slip and scar us with hot oil, the slosh of boiling water, the poisoned scallion hiding in a pancake, the thrown cleavers spinning toward our ears, the particle of virus in a chopstick splinter?

"We'll be trolls before you know it," I said.

Elliott dropped a heap of his empty sugar packets into my teacup. "Exactly my point, Rose Red."

"You don't even want to meet a man," I said with as much spite as I could muster. He laughed and suggested spumoni on Perry Street.

I worked in a building at Sixth and Forty-sixth, a couple of blocks from Rockefeller Center, where I would go and marvel at my right to eat lunch in the crowd. Sometimes I pretended that summer that I was retracing my uncle Henry's steps. In the early sixties, he had worked in Midtown as a comptroller for the Sealtest Dairy Company. Elliott, who saved absolutely everything, once showed me a scrapbook of company photos and news clippings from sales conferences and charity golf tournaments that his father had chaired. He had even loaned me one of his father's first briefcases. It was a simple zippered portfolio with frayed handles, his initials in gold long rubbed off the leather by his knuckles, and I fancied that Henry might be watching me as I bought fruit from street vendors, made bus transfers, carried home the dry cleaning, and signed chits for scotch and sodas.

As for what I did when the sun went down—well, better to have an uncle I'd never met watching from on high than my father, Alphonse, who only knew his way around a meat rack because he was a butcher. Elliott said he hoped the dead went to bed by ten, which was the hour he and I might begin to contemplate our plumage for the club crawl to come. Or perhaps Uncle Henry turned his gaze from our follies to revisit the haunts of his youth, the high-toned nightclubs and low-down bars where he had entertained clients during the June moon of Keynesian economics.

One thing was certain: both Henry and Alphonse would have been bored stiff to watch me at work. R. R. Bowker's most glamorous product was and remains *Publishers Weekly*. I was part of the team that compiled and maintained the database known as *Ulrich's Serials*, a comprehensive listing of all the magazines known to man. I was the German editor, hired to sort through the piles of new *Zeitschriften* sent to Bowker, classify them, and devise entries consisting of their title, their editors in chief, their frequencies, and, very occasionally, a one-sentence précis of their mission. *Advances in Metallurgical Spectography* said it all, while a fashion sheet titled *The Blink of an Eye* required my mindful explication. It was big news if a magazine changed its frequency: monthly to quarterly, or semiannual to annual. If an annual declined to the status of a biannual, it was expunged from the database. I myself would place the weekly list of German casualties on Zoltan Breslau's desk and nod in sympathy to his pained sighs.

These professional excitements were actually some weeks away. When I started at Bowker, the newest database feature was phone numbers for the American serials. The forthcoming *Ulrich's* had a hard June fifteenth deadline, so for my first month on the job, eight hours a day, I entered

LET ME SEE IT

thousands of ten-digit phone numbers. Nine strokes of the tab with my left pinkie took me to the area code field, the tenth to the exchange field. Hit enter and clear. The novelty of using a computer, not a feature of my theater job in Wisconsin, faded faster than a nosegay of violets. I took no pride from the fact that I could enter roughly twelve times more numbers in a day than my office mate, Joby Waldman, who had started at Bowker the week before me. I was simply the faster of two chimps.

After twenty-three years teaching high school Spanish in Bensonhurst, Joby said he was ready to make a mark in the field of publishing. Joby— and was that short for Joseph or Jacob?—made me nervous. He kept his briefcase between his feet at all times and gripped it with both hands whenever he stood up. On his desk he had placed a Ziggy statue that said "You're the Bestest," and he stored rubber bands in a red crystal apple. The slightest change in the routine—different colored printout, a new pass code, a blinking cursor—could derail him completely. For Joby, each magazine was a brand-new world. My attempts to help him log on, my suggestions that he count tabs instead of reading the screen were always met with a defiant "Yes, I know that." I got used to saying "Did you hit enter?" when I heard his fingers stop and his breathing get louder. If we ever finished with the phone numbers, Joby would be in charge of Mexico and Central America.

"Thomas Amelio," I said, picking up the phone one Monday morning. From the corner of my eye, I could see Joby leaning intently into his terminal, as if there were aliens within beckoning to make him their king.

"Good morning, Tom. This is Owen Teeter. From the dance." (Rose Red only gave out her office phone number.)

"Owen, I'm glad to hear from you," I said truthfully.

"Would you like to have dinner with me?"

I laughed. "You know how to surprise a girl, don't you?"

We decided to meet that Thursday at the Cupping Room Café. After hanging up, I tightened the knot on my tie and opened my weekly calendar. I loved filling up its rectangles.

"You're a gay guy, aren't you?"

I looked over at Joby. He was rubbing a spot on his screen with a putty-colored handkerchief.

"Yes I am, Joby," I said, amazed by his powers of detection. Elliott and I screeched at each other by phone at least twice a day. Elliott was working for an ad agency with more queers in it, he said, than a library school.

"You're fast with your fingers too." It was the first time Joby had acknowledged any difference in our ability to keystroke. I didn't know what to say.

"How many phone numbers did you enter last week, Tom?"

I shot out my cuffs. "They're not keeping track, Joby. They're really not," I lied. We were already known as the Tortoise and the Hare.

"Yes, I know that," he said. I flipped a page of my printout. He flipped a page of his printout. "I did seven hundred and thirty-seven last week," he continued, goading me. "So my productivity has increased."

"I should say so," I replied heartily. "Way to go, Joby."

"How many did you do, Tom?"

I halved my figure, then shaved off another hundred. "About thirteen hundred, give or take fifty."

I rolled backward in my chair to give us room. After a moment, as I pretended to locate something essential in my briefcase, I thought I heard him say, "I'm gaining on you, gay guy."

Working from an outdated Zagat's, Elliott had given me the wrong price range for the Cupping Room. Refusing an appetizer *and* a glass of wine *and* dessert would have been strange on a first date, so I wound up five dollars short on my half of the tab. As Owen's guest, I could duck it, but I felt bound to display some independence. The trouble was, my American Express account was all of three weeks old, so the options of splitting the bill with a card and cash, or paying with my card and pocketing Owen's share, exceeded my level of sophistication.

Owen drew first on his wallet; I said oh, let me put it on my card; thumbing bills, he said absolutely not, he'd asked me to dine; I said don't be silly, why don't I just give you these three tens and we'll figure it out later. At that, he struck the edge of the table with four fingers and said with unmistakable temper, "No half measures, Tom. If I'm buying you dinner, I'm buying you *all* of it."

I was a hick. Elliott and Uncle Henry and Edith Wharton could amen to that, but I got even by putting out that night on Jane Street, two dates ahead of schedule.

The next morning, when I opened my eyes, Owen was sitting cross-legged to my left, staring down at me. "What?" I said rather sharply.

He smiled as a little boy might. "I was just imagining what it would be like to wake up, go to the mirror, and have your face looking back at me."

I groaned and flung an arm over my eyes. He pulled it away, and I pulled him down to shut him up.

So that's how a courtly English-language instructor became my first New York, three-nights-a-week boyfriend. There was no other option for Rose Red. After a time, the flow of his compliments, supported by the movements of his body, ceased to embarrass me. Owen Teeter was great in bed, which was the trump I played whenever Snow White hooted to hear that I was turning down an investigation of Boy Bar in order to play bridge with Owen and his friends. Bridge, it was true, was as corny as Kansas in August, but I'd air enough gamy details about what else was going on to bring things to a draw over the sesame noodles at Sung Chu Mei.

Owen was the first man I'd slept with who let things occur, rather than made them happen. He was circumspectly, offhandedly collusive in a way I came to find irresistible. He brought dessert into bed. He brought me into the shower. He'd suggest I not wear underwear. I'd unzip and find him in a jockstrap. We'd stand. We'd stand in front of a mirror. He'd rut. Or he'd take his time. Or he'd really take his time. He'd talk about it when we weren't having it, then change the subject. His gift for making sex seem terribly dirty yet perfectly banal was liberating. I knew I had turned some kind of corner when, one day at Bowker, I reminded him over the phone to buy more condoms.

"Yes dear," he said dryly, letting me discover the moment.

"Wait. Did I just say that?"

"Yes, dear. Now, is there a particular lube you'd like to go with that?"

I hung up, amazed at my dirty, banal, sluttish, housewifely self. I resquared my haunches on my chair. I smiled to hear Joby jabbering in Spanish with Alicia, the coffee cart lady. The thought of Owen riding the subway down to Fourteenth Street with a drugstore bag on his lap made for a tumid afternoon with *Ulrich's Serials*, Deutsches division.

Owen would always be taking the subway. He wasn't a striver, didn't seem to care about money, a philosophy so at odds with Manhattan living as to be pre-Columbian. And this was back when it only cost twenty-five dollars to leave your apartment. As for his apartment, I ducked Elliott's every question. Owen had a room on the ninth floor of the Greystone Hotel, an SRO at the southeast corner of Ninety-first and Broadway. (Joseph Mitchell territory, but I hadn't read him either.) Even at high noon, light stopped at the glass entrance doors, so the yellowing mirror tiles on the walls reduced everyone in the lobby to lumbering ocher phantoms. The reception desk was covered with greasy, peeling contact paper. Taped inside the elevators were pictographs showing how to get the better of roaches, rats, and silverfish. The water-stained wallpaper in the ninth floor hallway, a repeating toile of the Woolworth Tower and the Statue of Liberty, barely kept truce with the quince-colored shag carpet that squished underfoot and gave off smells of dishrag and fumigant.

Owen wasn't embarrassed by his room, so neither was I. Housing in New York was always impossible, so I guess I assumed that like his job, the apartment was an improvisation until something better opened up. He must have had more than a hot plate, yet I don't recall taking any meals there beyond bagels with the paper. I remember running gear slung over the shower bar, and his track shoes hanging outside by their laces from a cup hook twisted into the grimy windowsill. The ironing board was out a lot, since he was fastidious about his shirts. It was something the Africans had expected of Peace Corps schoolmasters. I remember the bed frame was bolted down, the stress fractures and divots in the wall around the headboard attesting to decades of strong fucking. It was louche, but larky. Owen might look up from the board, meet my eyes, and swagger back for more. I liked that there was never more than two feet to cross to get to what needed to be done. Sex and ironing and reading and coffee and pissing and sleep were all of a piece.

At night, cradling me, rubbing my scalp with his chin, he would apologize for how much he talked. He said he had begun to store up new

LET ME SEE IT

thoughts for me. Most of the time I held my tongue—it is the Twinkie's prerogative to have nothing to say—but one muggy June night, Owen coaxed me into a historical discussion, meaning the five-week history of us.

I told him about Snow White and Rose Red, and how at first sight I had thought Owen was Greek and how that had made me nervous. I said I had enjoyed the waltz. I made him laugh when I recalled how a seven-dollar appetizer at the Cupping Room Café almost sank our relationship. Then, thinking to reassure him that I liked how things were, I voiced some of Elliott's milder misgivings about his material prospects.

Owen pulled away and flipped on the reading light. He bent over the nightstand and from its second drawer withdrew a bundle of green felt tied around the middle with a braided bow. He laid it out like a tiny shrouded body on his pillow, then adjusted the arc of the lamp. I sat up. He untied the ribbon, unrolled the cloth, and laid open a flap. There was a quick gleam of tines and crescents.

Six of the eight pockets in the cloth were tenanted. "Silver," I said. "Family?"

He shook his head. "It's Buccellati," he said. "As with everything else they make, fabric, music, painting, men"—here he looked at me, though my ancestors had tended goats in Umbria—"I believe the Italians make the most beautiful silver in the world."

He slid a dinner fork from its chamber and closed my hand around it.

"It's really heavy," I responded, idiotically.

"It's an Art Nouveau pattern, hand-cast and hand-chased, made to order. The craftsmanship is the same as it was generations ago."

"It's beautiful, Owen, no, no, it's absolutely gorgeous. It suits you."

He paused for a moment to stroke my knee and lay his head there. "This is all I have so far. I buy it piece by piece."

I looked down his back to the pair of hollows at the base of his spine where I liked to press my thumbs. The wheezing air conditioner in the window changed keys. I felt his jaw working against my knee as he raised his voice above it.

"If I wanted to, Tom, I could fly to Yemen next week. I could teach English to the royal children for an obscene amount of money. I could live in the palace. But right now I want to be in America."

"I know you do," I stuttered, cutting him off, "and I for one am glad you're here."

"Italians," he sighed, leaning back again to replace my fork with a soup spoon. He stayed in his crouch. "I can afford two pieces a year."

"A semiannual," I replied automatically.

I didn't get it, and he knew it. He placed each piece in my hand, hoping I'd get it. ("Very Helen Keller," Elliott would later say.)

"I do want things, Tom," he said, looking away now. "It's just that I'm able to wait for them one at a time."

"Happy Gringo Day," said Alicia, making change on her afternoon pass-through. The warp of her wish so tickled me, I tipped her a dollar for the coffee. My heart was light. I was going away for the Fourth of July weekend. Tucked behind my office door was a new burgundy leather duffel. Inside that was a black leather shaving case, a giveaway for opening a Macy's charge. My hostess gift was a slim 1948 edition of *Contract Bridge Made Easy*, filled with line drawings of women in hats.

Owen was poor, but his friend Jay Strickert, a Peace Corps alum with a trust fund, had a house on the Jersey Shore. Jay's apartment on Sutton Place, the most impressive I'd yet seen, was where we went for bridge. My first time there, something stopped me in the foyer. Beyond the hallway, across a drawing room, between two sets of French doors leading to a balcony, was a brooding, blocky painting, a portrait depicting the idea of a king. It was another New York first—textbook art in private hands.

"God, I love Chagall," I said recklessly. "He's one of my favorites."

"Thank you, it's a Rouault," said my host.

The rich were supposed to be sleek, and graceful about setting everyone at ease. Jay had a lumpy body and a spiny temperament.

Our fourth at bridge, Tony Neville, was my first link to the pre-Stonewall era. At seventeen he had hitched to New York from eastern Montana. A besotted agent got him into the Actors Studio and managed a nice stage career for him. In the late sixties, he'd had a lucrative second run in print ads, and now he sold space in a Jewish cemetery. I secretly regarded Tony as a template for what I'd hoped I could do with New York. I enjoyed playing the acolyte—the Merman vs. Martin stuff—with him, Owen smiling over the table at each question I posed. The Peace Corps queers seem to have skipped right to Sylvester.

From the moment my duffel jounced the bed in our guest room and I lifted Owen into the air, the weekend was my first taste of a different district in the gay community—the fresh-chervil side of the street. Friday night we grilled steaks as the sun set over Spring Beach. Jay, who could afford to be ironic about his setup, was hilarious on the topic of his family. He skewered each photo in a graveyard of silver frames on a Steinway until we were helpless with laughter. Collusive Owen lured me onto the dock about three in the morning, and we rocked with a view of the moon rippling on the waves.

After a few beach hours on Saturday, Tony and I went into town for lobsters and strawberries and farm eggs for homemade mayonnaise. We left Jay and Owen reading on the porch, *Contract Bridge Made Easy* riding the swell of Jay's sun-smudged belly.

Jay got mean at dinner. He started by mocking the way Owen shared his claw meat with me. Then he ridiculed Owen's bed-sit at the Greystone until Tony shushed him. When I started to clear the dishes for dessert, Jay put his fist on his plate and said that Twinkies didn't have to do anything.

"I'd like to do my part," I mumbled to the discard bowl of artichoke leaves.

"Twinkies don't have a part," he scoffed. "They don't have to clean or cook or drive. They don't clear dishes. Twinkies have one part, and it better be stiff."

"Enough, Jay," said Owen.

Jay set a napkin ring spinning on his forefinger. The lobster juice from his plate dribbled down his arm. "They only have to put out," he insisted, cracking himself up with his visual.

"I might be a Twinkie," I said, "but I'm not a gold digger."

"No shit," he snickered. Owen, at the sink, bit a nail. "Now if this were Africa, Tommy Titmouse, it would be different." Jay eyed the wine, but Tony was quicker on the draw. He shrugged and wedged the napkin ring like a monocle between his brow and doughy cheek. "If this were Africa, I'd be your bwana, and you'd be my houseboy. You'd have to beat my clothes on a rock. Cook for me, repair my netting, brush my hair, boil my drinking water. You'd brush bwana's teeth if he asked."

"Why don't we get some air?" said Owen. Jay waved his arm to nix the suggestion. His monocle fell and dinged against the lobster hull on his plate.

"And you'd be so grateful for those nine stinking American dollars *a month,* you would service bwana in every way. Of course, you're too old to be a houseboy. You're past it. Isn't that right, Owen? Don't you think Tommy Titmouse here is a couple of harvests older than Bata was?"

"This isn't the place for this, Jay," said Owen. He shut off the tap.

Jay turned back to me. "We never knew exactly how old Bata was." He swept his plate to the floor; some silver went with it.

Owen was leaning, face-out against the counter, his fingers pushed into his temples, as if a mesmerist's pose could will Jay to silence.

"I don't know," Jay continued, "I suppose we should have split the tab, Owen. Each of us could have paid him four fifty. A dollar twelve a week for services rendered. Bata didn't mind double duty, did he? Young and smooth as he was."

At that, Owen whipped past me and dragged Jay out of his chair. Despite the fifty-pound difference, he pushed him out the kitchen door. Their shouts trailed to pips, and then it was just the roll of the waves again.

Tony and I did the dishes, then repaired to the music room for brandy. Drawing upon what he had learned from Harold Clurman, Tony began to play solitaire, a trivial activity that masked his serious intention, which was to tell me that Owen had come back to the United States to find himself a husband. My crew cut from the Astor Place Barber Shop was two days old, so my trivial activity was to take delight in rubbing the back of my head against the nap of the velvet couch. "Owen's a great guy," was all I would allow.

"He's aces, Tom. I don't want him to go back to Africa."

I thought of a young black man standing forlornly outside a grass hut. Holding Uncle Henry's briefcase. "If he can't find Bata," I said, "he could go to Yemen and make a fortune."

Tony chuckled, another feint. "They put queers to death over there."

I followed the skitter of a daddy longlegs along the picture rail behind his head. "Wow," I said, "that's insane."

I picked up the other bridge deck and suggested double solitaire, which I hadn't played since I was a kid. Then I got him started on Mabel Mercer. When Jay and Owen got back, we ate shortcake in silence. That night, the next morning, and twice the next day—Gringo Day—I made certain, since Jay's room was next to ours, that the sex we had was almost comically noisy.

"What suit are you wearing today?"

"The seersucker."

"God, I love you in that. The pink tie?"

"I prefer to think of it as 'dusty rose.'"

"Of course, lover," said Owen lightly.

I bared my teeth. Since our weekend in Jersey, he had begun slipping that word in, and I'd been letting it pass. I scribbled "lover" on my blotter to remind myself to ask Elliott how to finesse my way out of it.

"Can you knock off at four?" he asked.

"Sure," I said, with the breeze of Zoltan Breslau. "What's up?"

"Meet me at 46 East Fifty-seventh Street, between Madison and Park. That's the south side of the street," he added—unnecessarily. I knew my odds and evens.

Before I left to meet him, there was a crisis at work. The office manager, a retired Fosse dancer with a two-foot braid, brought in a plastic bin and set it down directly in front of me, rather than next to my terminal. Atop a fresh pile of German periodicals was my nameplate. Thomas Amelio, twelve white letters against a black wood-grain finish.

Given the brain-blanching level of the work I did, it hadn't occurred to me that a nameplate was on its way. This was a milestone, Alphonse would get such a kick out of it, something grave was in order, but the moment felt silly to me, ridiculous even. "Where did this come from?" was the best I could do. To cover my awkwardness I picked the thing up and slowly traced the grooves with a reverent forefinger.

Joby Waldman stood up; for the first time, he forgot to pick up his briefcase and so he half tripped over it as he went to block the open door with his body. According to the office manager, Joby's nameplate had been delayed for "explainable" reasons she wouldn't explain. Joby kept repeating that he had been an employee of R. R. Bowker forty hours longer than Thomas Amelio, so where was his nameplate?

The tension was so awful, I weakly offered that A came before W in the alphabet. Joby stamped his foot and snarled, "Yes, I know that," but wouldn't let the office manager out of the room. As he grew more strident, the other members of the Ulrich's group gathered a couple of yards beyond the door. When things became too gruesome, after Joby revealed how much he had spent the previous summer on a publishing skills course, how much he had spent on his business wardrobe, how hard he had looked for a job, how involved his commute was, and how proud he felt to be part of the Bowker family, they ducked their heads and peeled away. Joby wasn't short for Joseph or Jacob. It was long for Job.

Owen was waiting for me in his one suit, an olive worsted from Tripler's, custom-made, and his best tie, Hermès. He was bobbing with happiness at my approach. I wished, and not for the first time, I could be what he saw.

"We make such a handsome couple," he said, kissing me on East Fifty-seventh.

"This isn't the Village," I said.

"I don't care, beautiful. They know me here," he said, tilting his head toward the vitrine of the Buccellati boutique.

They did know him at Buccellati. He was too excited to notice the quick play of eyes around the horseshoe of cases as he bid the staff good afternoon. He stated his intention to purchase his first dinner knife, his voice beating against the cushioned quiet. "And what pattern have you?" asked a face tightened with surgeries. "I should be in the register," he replied airily. She pretended for several minutes that he was not in the register. When Owen gave the name of his pattern, she pretended not to understand his pronunciation.

I thought of that small green roll in his nightstand drawer, and decided to defend my boyfriend against these Continental closet cases, gray about the temples, and bottle-black spinsters from the Dalmatian coast. I wanted to remind them that the root word for service is "servant," so I pretended to be my cousin. Keeping my mouth sealed, I dropped my jaw, let my

eyelids droop, and placed them all, as Elliott would, in the middle distance. I ignored offers of assistance and picked up their catalog as if it
were coated in motor oil. I glanced at two pages and sniffed "*zu Barockstil*"
to no one in particular. I recall sneering at an arrangement of sauceboats.

Seated on the couch, I carefully twitched my crossed left foot. Owen
buzzed about the cases looking for a piece of his pattern until he recognized it, then drew the mocking attention of the man who had handled
his most recent transaction.

"Ah, of course, *signor*, the cream soup spoon," the salesman finally said,
tilting a palm upward.

"Yes, the cream soup spoon of November last."

"You are ordering à la carte, no?"

"À la carte all the way," grinned Owen.

I could have smacked them both for that exchange.

Rose Red as Snow White couldn't be budged from her throne, so at
Owen's urging, the salesman laid a square of green cloth and the knife
before me on a mahogany tea table. I picked it up. It was superb; it was
exquisitely heavy, timelessly weighty. It could pay for two months of my
sublet. I made some calculations: sometime in the early years of the
twenty-first century, Owen would own enough Buccellati flatware to host
a dinner for six in his room on the ninth floor of the Greystone Hotel,
provided the salad forks could double for dessert.

"It's quite lovely," I said in a bored fashion to the middle distance. I
placed my hand on Owen's forearm to signal my approval, but the excitement in his eyes had gone.

Why was I acting like that, he wanted to know when we were outside
again.

"Acting like what?" I said. The reaction of the Buccellati sales staff to
his nine one-hundred-dollar bills had beggared description. I had wanted
to spear their eyes with lemon forks.

"Like you were beyond it all. You were horrible to those people, Tom."

"*I* was horrible?"

"I was embarrassed for you," he said.

I was so stunned, I walked into a parking meter. "You were embarrassed? *You* were embarrassed? For me?"

To this day I don't know whether Owen was aware of their misconduct, or knew and chose to ignore it. At the time, the rage I felt for having my behavior misinterpreted eclipsed my shame for having spoiled his rarest—and dearest—pleasure.

To pretend that we could travel through a quarrel, we went for brunch the next day at the Hungarian coffeehouse up by Columbia. It was miserably hot. They were out of the babka, and it was the day I learned I hated *kasha varnishkes*. Owen didn't understand my ambivalence surrounding the arrival of my nameplate or my confused feelings about Joby Waldman and his mark in the field of publishing. He said this was because I never talked about work, I never talked in general, which was my cue to be sarcastic about everything. Finally, rather than pin it all on him, kasha included, *his* suggestion, I shut down.

On the walk back down Broadway, Owen made up for my silence with cheery, dispassionate anecdotes about African heat, thereby releasing me to contemplate why I had gone to Jay Strickert's apartment the night before. Why had I taken a cab to Sutton Place at nine forty-five? Why had I given my name to the desk attendant? Why had I expected Jay to be home? Why, after he'd shut the door behind me, did I unzip my fly in the foyer and give him my stiff part to suck, locking eyes with the Rouault monarch on the faraway wall?

Having reached the southeast corner of Ninety-first Street, I slumped against the Greystone Hotel and stared at the traffic island until my vision blurred. Owen asked me if I wanted to go upstairs. I shook my head. Did I want to walk in the park? Nap in the park? Catch a movie? Go to a museum? Nap at home? Meet up later? So many things to do in New York.

I shook my head against all his suggestions and squinted into the sun. The light burned tangents along the tops of my eyeballs and into my brain. All my information could leach out along the edges of these flaming arrows and sizzle to ash and vapor on the sidewalk if I so chose, but the heat and the light and the smell and his gaze—and maybe even the noise, I prayed—stopped three feet to my right.

Owen spoke again.

"Sometimes, Tom, I think you've got a life going on inside that I know nothing about."

If I stretched out my arm, I could cool my fingertips in the shade. And if I stood perfectly still for another ninety minutes, I could disappear into it altogether.

ELBOW AND LEGS
ELLIOTT

1989

Elliott Biddler peels the lid off a tall cup of convenience store coffee and prepares for his day with a bit of philosophy. It would seem nearly axiomatic that if his older brother has the money to purchase a new six-bedroom house, he wouldn't, or shouldn't, need to rely on relatives to help him move into it. Sitting on a bottom stair in a slightly used five-bedroom house, Elliott can hear Frank shouting tape gun instructions to their mother, Ruth, who is building boxes in a faraway room.

Elliott doesn't know how a twenty-one-hundred-dollar mortgage payment can leave Frank without the funds for a commercial mover. The brothers don't discuss finances. They don't discuss much of anything, but Elliott can be counted on to be a groomsman at Frank's weddings and provide a pair of wobbly arms for his moves. Elliott works at a frame shop and, apart from collectors' items he would never part with, has nothing to be financial about, while Frank is an accountant like their father was.

Henry Biddler made big moves. He stag-leaped from Washington, D.C., to Philadelphia to Detroit to Houston to Chicago and then landed in Cincinnati with a new wife and two stepsons, only to die six weeks later on the same November day in 1979 that the sixty-six American hostages were seized in Iran. Frank, as Elliott sees it, piddles around the Chicago suburbs, adding another unused bedroom and bath as he goes. This time he isn't even leaving town. He and Kristy are moving to the far side of St. Charles Road, to a newer Winfield subdivision where aluminum dovecote mailboxes stand at the end of culs-de-sac whose names sound like candle scents.

Frank turns up, kicks Elliott's sneaker, and says let's load. He looks tired already. The brothers go into the living room and eye a striped sofa.

"Shouldn't we start with the really heavy pieces?" asks Elliott.

"Nah." Frank rotates his hands out and back, like he's getting ready to dive. There are scratches on his forearm. They lift. Frank is taller and stronger. Elliott's end slips in the motion and pulls at a mat of hair above his knee.

"You should have worn long pants," says Frank. He cannot get over how hairy his little brother has gotten. The last time he saw Elliott without a shirt, he thought of the Cro-Magnon men in the diorama at the Field Museum. If the Cro-Magnons had been blond.

Out on the driveway Frank jerks his head at the contents of their mother's linen closet—blankets, sheets, towels, bedspreads—stacked neatly, like wax-papered sandwiches, alongside the retractable truck ramp. "Jesus," he groans.

"They're buffer for the corners. She said."

"She's insane."

The brothers are in the truck now, a twelve-foot can that will clang under their feet until it fills with floor-sample furniture and snap-top tubs of sports equipment. Frank keeps fit by playing on intramural teams three out of any seven nights of the week. He doesn't plan on checking out at forty-eight like Henry did.

They stand the sofa on one end. Elliott knows the day will feel ten times longer if he starts defending their mother this early. On a whim almost, he decides instead to top Frank. "You know what she said to me?"

"What?"

"She said I kissed like Dad."

"No fucking way." Frank's real laugh is like a goat. This one is fake. "You kissed her on the mouth?"

"Her cheek. I leaned over in the car, went for the cheek, and she said, 'You kiss just like your father.'"

"What does that *mean*, though?" asks Frank. Could you remember how someone kissed after, how long was it, eighteen years?

"Beats me. Quick. Dry." Powdery, Elliott adds to himself—her cheek, his lips, and the texture of Ruth's comment. He looks forward to telling their sister about it. Tracy is away at a hair convention in Florida.

"Jesus. Don't kiss her then," says Frank. His little brother's capacity for affection embarrasses him still. Until he was nearly ten, Elliott would wait just inside the door to be picked up when Henry came home. He would lay his head against his neck and rest his hand inside his father's shirt pocket. Frank, at the end of the front hall, would catch his father's eye. Henry's expression in these moments was the same he gave Frank in batting practice. It said watch the ball, not the pitcher.

Elliott shrugs and says, "I'll bet you kiss like him, too."

"Shut up, idiot," says Frank.

The air is cooler outside of the truck. Elliott, aware that the events of the day derive from the effectiveness of Frank's kisses, tightens his belt by one loop. There is a new mistress—a new "Cookie-Do" from the office, thinks Ruth, who has been parsing the signs with Elliott all summer. Kristy nervously agreed to an even bigger house. His mother would love Elliott to intervene, to say something, anything, to halt or narrow the focus of Frank's spray, but sex, unlike square footage, is not a Biddler topic.

As the morning goes, a few of Frank's sports buddies show up for small sections of time. To Elliott, they are iterations of Frank, earners in cutoff sweatshirts, with emergent potbellies and confident eyes. The brothers intersect randomly, catch glimpses of each other through doorways, step around each other on the shiny aluminum ramp. Frank is sweating, moving fast. Once he gets going, he wants to be gone.

After the furniture has been loaded, Elliott, the family puzzler, remains in the truck to find safe pockets for lampshades and shafts of air for bundled hockey sticks. Handling three taped boxes, gritty with crawl space dust, depresses him. Unopened through two previous moves, they contain years of his wedding and birthday and housewarming gifts to

Frank: lithographed World Series programs, a many-drawered carpenter's chest, baseball banks, a *Lost in Space* lunch box, bar ware from Paris, a game of Clue from the 1940s, hopeful heirlooms all. Personal effects, to be worthy of the name, crave air and light, fingers and eyes upon them, but his brother won't affix any kind of a signature to his walls or tables or shelves. Elliott had asked an early wife about it once, and she had said, in a clearly borrowed phrase, that she and Frank preferred "neutral public spaces."

Shortly after eleven, Frank initiates the lunch argument. He wants pizza, but Ruth has packed egg salad and deviled ham sandwiches. Their bickering thins the ranks of the fair-weather movers.

"Elbow, come on out of there a second," Ruth hollers from the porch.

Hearing the ancient nickname makes him shiver; Elliott le Beau, the Handsome Prince of Somewhere French, was the boy he didn't turn out to be.

"What?" he asks, hopping from the truck.

"Are you thinking you want sandwiches or pizza?"

"I'm thinking I just ate breakfast. Can't we get this first load to the new house and then eat?"

"You need protein throughout the day," says Ruth.

Elliott hears a goat laugh.

"What does *Legs* think?" Elliott asks. Frank was an expert base stealer, so Henry, who coached his Little League teams, started calling him Legs. Unlike Elbow, he fulfilled his early promise and went on to be a champion miler in college.

"Pizza," barks Frank.

Eventually Elliott casts his expected vote. "I don't care," he says. "You know I'll eat whatever."

The four of them picnic in the living room, their shoulders sagging away from the smudged white walls. The balance of egg and celery in the salad is palatable to Frank, and Elliott, to please his brother, is careful to eat a piece of each of the three kinds of pizza he ordered. Kristy picks the cheese off her piece until Frank tells her to stop it.

After a toilet break, Frank backs down onto a card chair and wipes his mouth. "When is the phone going to be hooked up?"

Elliott and his mother exchange a glance. Frank without a phone is a trapped animal, and Kristy, possibly, is ovulating. Like the previous wives, Kristy imagines a baby will be a way to hang on to Frank, but she doesn't know much. Tracy's name for her is "The Idiot."

"Tuesday?" says Kristy, with the plaintive intonation that irritates them all. She tests a bruise on her thigh. The fiction is she's a klutz.

Frank rests an ankle on the opposite knee. "God*damm*it," he says.

The timbre of his curse, the hammer blow of the second syllable, combined with the pose on the chair rolls the boulder from the entrance to the tomb and Henry Biddler steps forth in welcome visitation to his second son. This is why, no matter how tense moving days can get, Elliott helps Frank scuttle between his suburban shells. Elliott presses down his eyelids to peer into the past.

When his boys were small, Henry Biddler, with a highball and shoes off, would sometimes sit at the edge of his easy chair, then cross an ankle on top of his opposite knee. The triangle of space between his legs was an invitation to play a version of billy goat's gruff. Kneeling at his feet, Frank and Elliott would take turns pulling on a trouser leg. "Who's that?" their father would growl. "It's me, Mr. Troll." "Who's me?" "It's Elbow. Can I cross your bridge?" At this point Elliott would have poked his head through the opening. With the lamp glowing from behind, his father's face would be dark and scary. "If you pay the toll," he'd say. "What's the toll, Mr. Troll?" Elliott answered, giggling at the rhyme. "Push the button and give me a kiss." Elliott would press the side of his father's knee. The legs would shake and tighten, threaten to squeeze him to death as he pushed up. At times they would trap him until Elliott screamed and pushed a dozen buttons on the drawbridge of his chest. Then his father would lean down to kiss him. Elliott would wrap his arms around his neck and Henry would slide him up his trunk to a rye and tobacco heaven.

Elliott opens his eyes and watches Frank sink a basket with a pizza crust into the trash can. He has doubtless forgotten the troll game. The enemy of patience, he used to kick Elbow's feet to get him to finish his turn.

Frank peels off his sweatshirt. Thumbs of pale hair fringe the edge of his underarms. Elliott can never get over that Frank lacks the body hair to match his physique. The spin Elliott used to put on the statement "I've got one older brother" could sometimes make his sexual contacts roll in from the edge of his futon for additional information.

Ruth sniffs the air, makes a face. "You boys smell like two woods pussies," she says, her down-home term for skunks. Elbow and Legs hightail it out of the living room, leaving the women to rebox the pizzas. How they smell to their mother is too close to how they kiss, and Frank, after all, is stripped to the waist.

Six miles away, Frank's new house has Tudor timbering, yet peculiar brick turrets shoulder either end of its length. A domed atrium escapes like a gas bubble over a pair of grand oak doors. All it lacks, Elliott decides, is a waterslide. Yard-poor, it shares Barberry Court with a structure that resembles an Art Deco handbag, a bottle-green Moorish fantasia with a widow's walk, and a cement hole in the ground waiting to flourish into something equally singular and exclusive and starting at seven hundred thousand dollars.

They take in the beautiful afternoon, sunny and crisp, football weather. There are worse months to move than September. The new sidewalk ties everything together like a magic ribbon. Elliott imagines chipmunks and squirrels and voles emerging single file from the woods to lay tithes of nuts at Frank's feet.

Frank seems reluctant to release the scimitar bolt on the hatch. Elliott shoots him a look. "I think I ate too fast," says Frank.

"Are the toilets hooked up?"

Just raising the question roils Frank's guts. "They better be." Biddler men do not, as a policy, throw up.

"Sam and Larry said they'd meet us here."

"We can start though, can't we?"

A blue-and-white truck halts at the honeycomb of mailboxes. Frank, mouth-breathing to distract his stomach, suddenly needs a person to step down from it, a mailman to wave to on Saturdays to come, but only a left arm slides out the window. Elliott expects outlandish parcels to match the homes—sombreros, moose heads—but today's catch is unexceptional. "Whatever you do, don't run to get the mail," he says to Frank.

The hatch slides up with one quick jerk.

Even without a postal truck to cue them, one or the other will have to make the reference. It's as much a part of moving Frank as sandwiches vs. pizza for lunch. Henry Biddler died of a heart attack while running after two kids who had blown up his mailbox. Early one Saturday morning in November, he had dug a hole at the bottom of the driveway to his new house, poured cement, and put in a mailbox. It blew up during dinner. Henry spent his final afternoon, the Sunday when the hostages were taken at the embassy in Teheran, installing a second mailbox. There was a second explosion, again at dinner, and off he went through the back door to catch the culprits. When he didn't come back, their stepmother, Yvonne, sent their stepbrothers, Duane and Matt, eight and ten years old, out to look. His dinner napkin was caught on a branch of a new boxwood tree. They found him face up in a cornfield.

What Frank remembers most about Henry's wake is the spectacle of Elliott's collapse before the corpse and the sound of his unstoppable, luxuriant sobs. Month after month after month, the anchormen began their broadcasts with "Today is day number such and such of the Iran Hostage Crisis." One hundred, then two hundred, then three hundred daily cc's, the loss of his father was an ever-lengthening hypodermic of numbing agent. Frank's first wife disappeared circa day one hundred and seventy-six. Because he couldn't imprison and torture the boys who'd blown up the mailboxes, he directed his fury against the Iranians. Frank considered enlisting in the Marines until the Cookie-Do who became his second wife talked him off the ledge.

He would have voted for Reagan anyway, but the release of the hostages in '81 was still a trump to play whenever Elliott got shrill about politics. Elliott, his impossible little brother with a life-size cutout of the Romper Room Lady next to his front door and an apartment packed tighter than a pawnshop. Ruth has been hinting all summer that Frank and Kristy should take Elliott into this new house, cut some spare keys, and give him a bedroom and bath in the empty wallboard harem upstairs. He could be their child, or, in case of a misfire, their child care. That he knows Elliott would refuse an offer is both relief and affront, Elliott whose congenital refusal to compete can make Frank white with rage.

Sam and Larry show up, cheery and interchangeable. The furniture pieces move to their familiar stalls like farm animals. The sunburns the men sustain on their arms and noses make them feel athletic.

"The woods behind us are protected," says Frank at one point. "They can't be developed."

"Terrific," says Elliott, guessing.

Elliott carries a box of bathroom stuff into the master bedroom. He hears a flush. "In here?" he calls out.

Frank appears and leans on a built-in vanity. "Put them there." He wipes water from his face, blots his hands awkwardly on his sweat pants. "I wouldn't go in there if I were you."

"Don't worry," says Elliott.

"It was that fucking egg salad," Frank says. "Or the deviled ham. She lets the mayonnaise sit out."

"What's wrong?"

"The runs. I'm achy. Maybe chills."

"What were you doing last night?"

Frank ignores this.

Elliott, scrabbling in the box, retrieves something more historical than Maalox. He holds up a milk glass bottle in an ogival shape. "You don't use this, do you?" he asks.

"Nah."

"It's so sixties. Where did you get it? Woolworth's?"

"Beats me," says Frank, sheepish. They used to take turns giving Henry Old Spice gift sets for Christmas. Sensing what's coming, he shifts his gaze to the warren of freshly milled doors radiating from his center.

Elliott tenderly rotates the bottle, as if it were genuine whalebone. He pauses before twisting off the top. The unmistakable, one-of-a-kind fragrance releases a second payment from the vault of memory—not from Henry this time, but Frank.

"Hey," Elliott says. His scalp is tingling.

Frank braces his heels against the floor to resist the undertow in his brother's voice. "What?"

"You gave me a stick of Old Spice for my birthday. I was in fifth grade. Remember?"

Frank isn't supposed to remember the way Elliott isn't supposed to be sexual. He shakes his head and says that deodorant is a dumb gift. He flips a light switch, but mere electricity won't stop Elliott when he gets like this.

"Are you kidding? It was a fabulous gift because I so completely didn't need it. I didn't have hair under my arms, I hadn't started sweating, puberty was years away. I remember you were lying on your bed in the Ginger Creek house, the room with the ladder shelves, reading *Sports Illustrated* and I told you, I mean I basically *announced*, that I wanted a stick of Old Spice deodorant for my birthday and you laughed and said 'What for?' "

Frank rubs his nose, not risking a look. "Yeah, well. You said you wanted it." This he says loudly, curtly, instead of, "Don't cry on me."

He tries to take the bottle out of his brother's hand. "Fifth grade, huh?" he says. "Then I was in ninth. The year before the divorce."

Elliott nods. "Near the end of the separation. I used to roll that Old Spice under my arms thinking that maybe that was the way to make the hair grow."

"It must have worked, bush man," says Frank, relaxing just a bit.

"It was maybe the nicest present I ever got," says Elliott.

"Shut up," says Frank.

"I mean it. I was just a kid. You knew that I needed it more than I needed it."

"I said shut . . ." Frank clutches his stomach. "Jesus."

"Run," says Elliott.

The bathroom door closes, and Elliott takes another whiff of Old Spice. The dry pull of the stick rolling against his empty armpit was the one pitch of manhood he'd eventually caught. Now Elliott is careful to put the word "hairy" in his ads and wonders whether this late-blooming carpet on his body—tumbleweeds on shoulders, wisteria down his flanks—is an unreported symptom of the virus.

Frank, sick on the toilet, remembers the two years in the Ginger Creek house, remembers the start of his puberty, two years playing ice hockey on the pond, two years jerking off under the ladder shelves. Masturbating to the idea of Madeleine, his father's first and only Cookie-Do. Her exotic name wafted like incense up through the air ducts while Ruth and Henry scrapped over her in the kitchen. Frank wonders whether his father intended to lose his family when he went back a second time to that cocktail lounge on Kedzie Avenue. Frank, the champion base stealer, has learned—or has he?—when a man can safely order another Manhattan and when a man had better totter back to his car by his lonesome. He raises his right hand and grips a brass towel rack above his head. He doesn't like to think about these things.

The brothers park and wait in the rented van at the train station. Elliott refused any version of dinner. Ruth has gone home with leftover pizza. Kristy has scared up sheets for the king-sized bed. As they soldiered on, Frank's grouchy mood kept the women at bay, so only Elliott has noticed the citreous stain gathering force in his eyes. He knows that Frank's arms and hands will be jaundiced in the morning.

Frank coughs. "So . . . do you think this house is bigger than Dad's last house?"

He must ask this, and Elliott must answer. This new six-bedroom on Barberry Court is very big, but Henry Biddler had built his final house for Yvonne and Duane and Matt and Elbow and Legs and Tracy, loving the image of himself as a man who could almost double his paternal holdings overnight.

"No," says Elliott truthfully.

"The Cincinnati house had only five bedrooms."

"There was a screened-in back porch and a separate library."

"I have a game room, plus the library."

"With no books."

"That's not the point. I think this has more overall footage."

Elliott, afraid for his brother, who will turn yellow in the night, snaps. "Look, if I said your house was bigger," he says, "would you stop moving?"

"What's that supposed to mean?"

"Obviously you make more than he ever did; can't you leave it at that? You only saw the Cincinnati house once. After the funeral, the pictures were stacked against the walls, remember? Waiting to go up. Waiting for him to put them up."

Elliott pushes down the memory of Henry's walls crying out for their provider while Frank quietly says he does too remember and then suddenly, after ten years and five houses, they both know why Frank's walls are always bare. The knowledge cuts the truck in two.

Through the windshield they watch a man daintily spread a plastic bag on a bench and lie down until Elliott breaks the silence.

"Tracy and I have visited his grave, Frank, but not you. Why have you never gone to visit him? He's all alone there."

Frank doesn't say that he would rather have been airlifted into Teheran and been blown to bits freeing the hostages than ever see that hole in the ground again, than ever hurt that way again. His gorge rises; he breathes through his mouth again. Moths beat at his window. His right hand moves from the steering wheel to his hip pocket.

"I don't want any," says Elliott. At the end of any day together, they have become fluent in each other.

"You could use it."

"No, I couldn't. I could definitely not use it."

"Buy a bed frame, for God's sake." Frank has a fantasy that elevating Elliott's futon will leave all the men he imagines exploit his brother's sweetness stranded on the floor.

"My bed suits me fine."

"Then rent a bigger place for all your junk."

"It's memorabilia, asshole. My *Lolita* poster is worth more than your entire living room set."

"Just take it," insists Frank, wallet out.

"To make you feel better?"

Frank's eyes are throbbing, and his bowels are twisting again. "No," he says, finally too exhausted and sick to prevaricate, "because Dad said I should look after you."

"What?" says Elliott. He repeats it once, and once more.

Frank tilts his left wrist. They have six minutes. "He said I should always take care of you." Elliott, lost in the nuance of "always," doesn't hear the rare catch in his brother's voice. To still the waves of sadness breaking inside him, Frank says, "Look, Dad knew what you were."

Elliott slams himself sideways, as if force alone might open the passenger door.

"Knew what?"

"He knew," repeats Frank, wiping his forehead with a pizza napkin.

"No, he didn't," says Elliott, who might have also grown fur to protect himself from the fact of nobody ever caring to know.

"He did."

"You don't know that, Frank."

"I do. We talked about it my freshman year."

Elliott pushes his hands against the glove compartment. "No you didn't!"

"He visited me at school one time, he took me to dinner, and we talked about everything."

"I was still in high school! There was nothing to know." Elliott is pleading now.

"Come on, Elliott." Frank's voice is lower now, sexy in a way, ten cc's of his famously effective Cookie-Do lulling agent. "He always knew. We always knew you were different that way."

"There was nothing to know," says Elliott, about to be sick himself.

"It's okay."

"It's not," wails Elliott.

"He knew and that was that. For God's sake, Elliott, calm down."

An old switch is flicked, and this time it's Frank who recalls something useful. He begins to hum, then sing, "I'm a lonely little petunia in an onion patch. An onion patch. An onion patch. I'm a lonely little petunia in an onion patch. And all I do is cry all day," while Elliott's archives burn to ash on the gearshift between them: the jewelry box for Christmas, his grandmother's beaded purse, the beautiful queens on his mother's fancy bridge decks, the jaguar bracelet from a neighbor boy, the china he washed, the silver he polished, the napkins he pressed, the tulips he planted, the enthusiasms he hid, the enthusiasms he faked, the miniature tea sets and men's underwear pages in the Sears catalog, the grounders he missed, the catches he dropped, the bats he was afraid to swing, and the innocent safety of Henry's lap.

A teenager across the street hoists bags into a Dumpster. Elliott can do nothing with Frank's counterclaim except slide the truck rental agreement along the top of the dashboard and rest his head against the glove compartment.

"Your house *is* bigger, Frank. You win, you win for all time," he says between his legs, "and I want you to stop hitting Kristy and I want you to stop screwing around. You'll get sick and die—you'll get more than hepatitis, asshole."

"Hepatitis? What are you talking about?"

"Look in the mirror, Legs."

Frank takes a moment.

"So what?" The voice is proud, shrewd.

"Promise me you'll call a doctor first thing in the morning."

"The phone's not hooked up."

"Call from work, call from the street, call from a neighbor's."

The crickets are now louder than any phone.

"I don't hit Kristy," says Frank.

"Oh please," says Elliott, "Maybe not her face, but look at her thighs. Look at your arms."

"What about them?"

"Aren't the scratches hers? Or are those the latest Cookie-Do's love marks?"

The force of Frank's punch to the ceiling shivers along the metal cage of the cab. Elliott rights himself.

"It's a crime to pretend anymore. Whatever you do, don't give hepatitis to Kristy. If it's the wrong kind, it's a terrible, horrible thing to have."

"I guess you know all about it. You're the one who's going to get sick and die," yells Frank. He batters the ceiling with his fists until they hear the train whistle.

Both short of breath, they eye the pay phone under the eaves of the old brick station. Without a trunk to connect them, neither the elbow nor the legs can express the wish that the other not get sick and die. The crossing alarm sounds, the bar drops, and there is nothing Elliott can do except press his lips to his brother's smeary, febrile cheek.

In Chicago, Elliott checks his mail as he climbs three flights of stairs. A catalog of antique toys has arrived from Connecticut. He listens to a phone message from his sister, takes a long shower, and steps over to the sink.

In Winfield Frank takes a tumbler of whiskey into the living room. The phone, a beige island in a sea of dark carpet, is plugged in, but there is no tone.

Elliott blinks in the mirror. What he remembers most about Henry's wake is the salmon paint, two coats on the face, one coat on the neck and hands. He opens the medicine cabinet with wet fingers. He and Frank, not his stepbrothers, should have been the ones to find Henry in the cornfield.

Frank sits in a chrome-and-leather armchair that swivels. He thinks again of tracking down Madeleine, the Cookie-Do who wrecked everything.

Elliott picks up his razor, examines the blade. He sets it down, leans his arms against the edge of the sink. Veins appear. He lets the water run.

Frank hears Kristy calling from a faraway room. She has freshened up, she says.

Elliott wets a bar of soap.

Frank stares into the cave of his gas fireplace. Cold weather will come, and he will turn a brass butterfly in the wall, and a double row of blue jets will burn pretend wood, and warmth will seem to occur. But Frank does know better, he really does. He takes a swallow of his drink.

Elliott wonders at the bar of soap in his hand. Will he always be five years old, held tight inside his father's legs? The hot water from the tap generates fresh steam.

Frank sits in the dark, wanting to spin in the chair all the way to the telephone. He sets his right ankle on his left knee. He does in fact remember (and wouldn't Elliott be surprised?) the troll game. When Frank came through Henry's lap, however, the point was not to get caught. They were building Frank for speed, not kisses.

Water droplets glitter in the hair on Elliott's chest. He closes the cabinet, hunts for his eyes in the condensation on the mirror. They are clear. Frank's eyes, he thinks, must be yellow as a cat's by now. He will be flat on his back for a week. Kristy will have to unpack everything in what will be known henceforth as "Hepatitis House."

Frank swallows, tastes sour. The brackish taste and smell of himself, plus the smell of fresh wall-to-wall carpeting, nauseates him. His bowels rumble. He will not throw up.

Elliott closes his eyes. He is crouching in the cold by his father's shoulder. Dead cornstalks scratch his ankles. He rests one hand on the packed earth to steady himself. The other hand is curled in the shirt pocket, holding Henry's still-beating heart. From the bottom of the right edge of the frame, Frank's left foot is springing after the other for help.

Frank's cheek is hot, wet. He tests where his brother's lips have been. Their taste, their rage, their loss, all is immiscible. Which one will die of it first?

Elliott carefully soaps his right armpit, picks up the razor. The hair bends, falls under the blade like a curtain.

LET ME SEE IT
ELLIOTT AND TOM

1992

Wynken, Blynken, and Nod. Dixie, Trixie, Buster, Sonny, and Polly. Kukla, Fran, and Ollie. At last count, Elliott Biddler had eleven T-cells, and these were the names he'd given them. His cousin Tom, on his first trip to Paris, recognized the lullaby fishermen and the TV puppets, but Elliott had to explain on the RER back from Charles de Gaulle—in the mock-bristly tone Tom remembered from their New York summer of '85—that Dixie, Trixie, Buster, Sonny, and Polly were the five no-neck monsters of Gooper and Mae Pollitt in *Cat on a Hot Tin Roof*. One of them had hit Maggie with a hot buttered biscuit so she had to change.

Tom, ever the acolyte and now the houseguest, said, "Elizabeth Taylor and Paul Newman."

"Well, yes. There's the *movie*. On stage it was Ben Gazzara and, if you can believe it, Barbara Bel Geddes." Tom shrugged. "From *Dallas*."

Elliott stopped talking long enough to drag Tom's duffel back under their seat. His forearm seemed no thicker than the grip of a golf club. Tom was glad to sit side by side in the train car; it allowed him to take in the changes in his cousin at his own pace. They'd not seen each other in four years. In the terminal, Elliott's head had looked at first glance like a dead beige balloon stretched over a frame of Popsicle sticks, or a battered wasps' nest.

"And if you get more T-cells?"

"Effie, Deena, and Lorelle. Tinker, Evers, and Chance are too butch."

"Absolutely."

"Bullshit, Tom. You don't know who they were."

"A double-play combination for the Chicago Cubs in the early part of this century."

"Right," said Elliott. "I forgot you have one of *those* fathers. How is Alphonse?"

"He's good. He sends his best."

"And Aunt Janet?"

"No change there," said Tom, making a tiny face.

"I was hoping I'd get to meet them one day."

"You might still could, cousin."

"Do they have passports?"

"Alphonse?"

Tom, smiling at the image of his father boarding a transatlantic jet, missed this first declaration that Elliott wasn't coming back.

Tom was in Paris at Elliott's invitation. In February, out of the blue, he'd gotten a phone call from Elliott asking him to go to the May wedding of his college obsession, Patrick Rowan Dulter, to a Franco-Brit hand model named Nicole Braithwaite. (Tom suspected the hand model business was a joke.) Tom hadn't known he'd left the country, so Elliott explained that he had had to stop working in 1990, when the facial wasting had begun making the customers at the frame shop nervous. How like him, Tom thought, to drop the bomb that way, pretending he already knew and allotting no time for questions or sympathy. He'd just barreled on, saying that when it looked as if the cost of AZT, which wasn't working for him anyway, was going to bankrupt him into moving in with family, he'd chucked Chicago rather than be beholden to those people. Health care was free in France, and the pipeline moved faster. He was living in a fourth-floor studio on the Île Saint-Louis off the proceeds of his movie poster collection—his sister, Tracy, was selling them and wiring the money.

Elliott had also gotten ten grand in a bequest from his old friend Mrs. Hagopian, who had died of cancer. When he'd left the States, he'd flown out of Boston in order to say good-bye to her, and she'd been the yellow of the damask fabric on her Chippendale sofa. They feted the grim reaper all weekend with pinot grigio and lurid remembrance, leaving the lobster salad to the cats. Before hanging up, Elliott had sniffed, but only a little, at Tom's newish life as a pension lawyer in Colorado.

A month later Tom heard from Tracy, who had gotten wind of the upcoming Dulter wedding; and although they had never met, she managed in one call to make Tom promise to bring her brother back alive. Some new clinical trials were starting, and she would walk through fire, blow her senators, even move up to Washington from Norfolk to get him those drugs, it couldn't be too late, he'd always been there for her, now he was going to have to accept help for once in his goddamned life.

The stone steps were so steep and narrow in the building on the Rue Saint-Louis-en-l'Île, the men had to grip a rope strung through rings sunk into the wall. Elliott stopped at the landings to describe the neighbors he knew, and Tom listened behind his words to gauge any shortness in his breath.

Elliott had been a lifetime pack rat, so the bare walls and stretches of empty floor in the studio were a surprise. There wasn't even a coffee table. A boom box and a couple dozen CDs on the bottom shelf of a built-in bookcase had replaced Elliott's massive, multifarious record collection. Other shelves held photographs and books and, most curiously, a small jade bodhisattva flanked by incense holders. Tom knew the mortally ill sometimes got religion, but Elliott had always been aggressively antispiritual. A diagonal wooden truss, two feet thick and black with age, bisected the space. Elliott stepped under and around it to point out the kitchenette and bathroom. Through the French windows they could hear the muffled noise of tourists lining up on the street for Berthillon ice cream.

Tom tensed when Elliott pulled out a queen-sized Murphy bed and insisted he try a nap for his jet lag. He hadn't visualized—though he should have—their sleeping arrangements. "I could have gotten a hotel room," he said.

"In May?" said Elliott. "In this quarter? Forget it."

"I can afford it."

"Really? How did that happen?"

"The law. I practice in Denver, remember?" Tom didn't really expect Elliott to remember this.

Elliott jumped five questions. "Are you out at work?"

"Absolutely. We don't, however, make a show of my religion."

There was little for Tom to show beyond charity bike rides and switchboard shifts with the Colorado AIDS Project. As for sex, he had relied on 800 numbers through law school. Insane hours at the firm made it easy to retreat even further from live-action giving and getting.

"And your parents know?"

"About you? No."

"No, darling, about *you*."

"Yes. Years ago."

"Right," said Elliott, visibly annoyed. Tom wondered whether the forgetfulness might be a sign of dementia, but then he recalled Elliott's need to always go first. Tom had come out to his parents before Elliott confirmed his own mother's suspicions, but Elliott insisted he'd upped the ante by telling Ruth he was gay *and* positive in the same phone call.

"If you won't nap—"

"I didn't say I wouldn't." Tom would sleep, or feign it, if it meant delaying the introduction of discomfiting topics. It could be that Elliott was tired and just wouldn't admit it. "What will you do?"

"Read my *Picture Book of Saints*. Whip up a mouthwatering spirulina frappé."

"I hope you're doing more than spirulina."

"Relax, Tom. I'm doing the mumbo jumbo *and* the nucleosides. On Tuesdays and Thursdays I take bread to the poor, like Saint Elizabeth of Hungary."

The smell of incense woke Tom up. Elliott was sitting forward in an easy chair between the windows, with Tom's suit jacket spread across his lap. The plumes of smoke spiraling behind his shrunken head made him look like an idol with bamboo arms, and the jacket, a sacrificial offering.

"It's a beauty," Elliott said, stroking the lapel of the jacket.

Tom was annoyed that Elliott had gone into his luggage until he noticed the tears on his cheeks. "Are you okay?"

Elliott shook his head. "I get weepy about clothes. Clothes and that's *it*. My friend Galt says that's not a good thing—the not crying. The one time I've ever really broken down, sobs *plus* snot, was when I put away my summer clothes back home. I hated the idea of never wearing them again. I love my sweaters, but I adored my shorts."

"I remember. I remember you that summer in a pair with tiny colored stripes."

"Lilac, orange, and teal," said Elliott, inspecting a sleeve. "Saks, deeply discounted. This was before gay men shut the door to pleats. Hey. These cuff buttons actually unbutton."

The sartorial approval spurred Tom's memory. "You were wearing them that day we almost picked up that man together at the pier. You wouldn't sit on a piling for fear of getting them dirty."

"They were brand new, girleen."

"What did we think we were going to do with him?"

"We were just jazzed on the day. Anything was possible. He wasn't my type."

"He was even less my type," said Tom. "Your type was all types."

"Not quite. They couldn't be stupid, and that guy was dumb as a box of hair." Elliott stood to slip the suit jacket onto a hanger. "And then you left me there."

"No, we left *him* there and went for Chinese at Sung Chu Mei."

Elliott pulled the window open wider and set the hanger on its knob. The crowd below for Berthillon sounded noisier, closer, as if a tumbrel were making its way to the Place Notre Dame. "Moving to Paris has been a blessing."

"How so?"

"Men in shorts are *absolument défendu*. Are you hungry?"

"I can always eat," fibbed Tom, who, having just caught up to a different meaning to one of Elliott's remarks, felt a surge of nerves in his stomach. He had not left him in New York, or to New York. How could Elliott think that?

"Excellent. We're going on an All-the-Fats-of-France Tour."

"No ice cream though, okay?" said Tom. His job making soft-serve as a teenager had killed his taste for all versions of the stuff.

"Berthillon makes the best ice cream in France."

"We'll see."

Before swinging his legs to the floor to get up, Tom studied the ceiling for a moment. He calculated that at least sixteen generations of Parisians, anonymous and indigent, had lived out their time under these beams, had worn hollows into the stone steps descending to the street. Some must have helped build Notre Dame with no more than axes and faith. History was the point of Europe, he thought, happy with the cliché of it. He ought to have come over sooner, and under less dire circumstances. Tom guessed that Elliott had a year and half left. No trial, even for a miracle drug, would save him.

Elliott thought his landlocked prairie cousin would enjoy some fruits of the sea, so they dined that night at Chez Jenny, a bistro off the Place de la République. Joining them was Galt Hiler, who, Tom decided before they were through with the appetizers, made an odd sidekick for Elliott. Short, bald, thickset, and red-bearded, Galt was Hardy to Elliott's Laurel. His speech and gestures were deliberate, he didn't sparkle in the ways that Elliott had historically required and that Tom had always felt he himself had fallen short of. Then there was his Buddhism, made manifest in the prayer and the slow reverence before their three-tiered tower of seafood, which was as richly festooned as a showgirl's headdress. Galt had grown up on Long Island, the son of a garage owner, and if his high baritone hadn't announced itself while he was prepping for his bar mitzvah, he knew he would have been content fixing cars in Hempstead for the rest of his life. Now he sang in the chorus of the Opéra and volunteered at a clinic for patients with le sida, which was how he'd met Elliott. They bickered like an old couple, or rather, Elliott sniped and Galt laughed, a resonant rumble like a ball bouncing in a barrel.

Galt was also blunt: wiping his stubby fingers with the lemon from the finger bowl, he asked them if they had ever slept together.

The cousins were equally aghast.

"I told you, no," said Elliott.

"I know," said Galt. "I wanted to hear what Tom had to say."

"Absolutely not," said Tom.

"It happens."

"It didn't happen to us," said Elliott.

"Not even close?"

"NO!" Tom looked for help, as if the maître d' might eject Galt for broaching the topic of incest.

"You're talking like you know something about it," said Elliott.

"I diddled some of my cousins in the sixth grade. Doesn't everybody?"

"No," said Tom.

"Diddling isn't sleeping together," said Elliott.

"We didn't meet each other until we were twenty-five," said Tom.

Galt slowly looked from one to the other. Tom noticed hairs cresting his ears, like a flower bed of tiny crooked lightning rods. "Both of you must have been very beautiful."

"I suppose we were—in a strictly contrasting fashion," said Elliott.

Hoping to halt the discussion, Tom refrained from mentioning the salad days of Snow White and Rose Red, but Elliott was warming to the idea of family play. "You know," he said, opening a mussel, "I've never even seen Tom's cock."

"Elliott—"

"Not even in a bathroom, at one of those open troughs that were all the rage."

"Don't call it that," said Tom. "Call it a penis, if you have to."

"Why?"

"Because I'm your cousin. Boyfriends have cocks. Relatives have penises. If they have them at all."

"That's interesting," said Galt.

"No," said Elliott. "Midwestern."

Tom had known better than to follow his cousin into any bathroom back in the day. Handicapping his adventures was one thing, but seeing Elliott's equipment, or watching him work it, was not to be—what—borne? Endorsed? Encouraged? Look where it had gotten him. Tom changed the subject, asking how it could be nearly nine o'clock and still light out.

Galt laughed. "It's the latitude. We're parallel to northern Québec."

The rest of the conversation was given over to the wedding, to be held three days hence in Neuilly-sur-Seine. Elliott began by second-guessing the length of a black veil appropriate to an afternoon wedding. He seemed not to realize that his physical appearance, with a man at his side, might be drama enough at the Dulter-Braithwaite nuptials. He spun scenarios for disrupting the ceremony with historical truths, or thought he might steer the bride to a quiet corner of the reception to debrief her on the special needs of her husband's hindquarters. He would hate for her to break a nail on one of her famously remunerative hands.

Bitchery aside, Tom knew Elliott was pleased that Patrick respected their past enough to invite him to the ceremony. Elliott's ability to stay in contact with ex-boyfriends impressed Tom, who only thought of *his* college swain, Boyd McIlhenny, and those reluctant Hoosier hand jobs he'd mistaken for love, with anger. Over dessert, Elliott reaffirmed that all that he had ever required from Patrick Rowan Dulter was for him to call out Elliott's name on his deathbed. No more, no less. Tom, woozy with champagne, five courses, and jet lag, decided he would settle for Boyd turning up at his office in Denver and kissing him back of his own volition, just once, for real.

After leaving the restaurant, Tom looked for a taxi stand, but Elliott had already veered to the right.

"Where are you going?" Tom called out.

"I'm taking you on my personal trail of tears. Its primal stop is a few blocks away. Does Boulevard Richard Lenoir, or the surname Sirjean, ring any bells?"

Tom shrugged. It was always his job to shrug, so Elliott explained they were heading to the apartment building of his host family from his junior year abroad. As they walked, Tom remembered the acid tissue-paper letters Elliott sent him from Paris about the Sirjeans and his drippy Christian roommate. He also remembered Elliott's coming-out letter. At the time, Tom had found it extraordinary, and maybe even a bit hot, to have a first cousin his age who had also turned out to be gay.

Elliott ducked into a courtyard and motioned not to follow him. Tom and Galt listened to him empty the contents of his stomach.

"I was worried that might happen," said Tom. "He overdid it."

"He loves food," said Galt. "And he wants to keep up."

The simple truth, plainly stated, brought tears to Tom's eyes. "It's good you're here," he said.

"He's glad you made the trip," said Galt.

"We had just the one summer. We lost touch while I was in law school. Elliott always had gypsy feet."

"I know."

Tom risked the truth. "I'm supposed to bring him back."

Galt didn't seem surprised. In response, he blew out his breath and pressed the heels of his hands into his sternum, as if he were coaxing his heart to do something.

Elliott returned and wiped his face with the handkerchief Tom offered.

"My cousin is the last man in America to have a hankie on his person."

The lights were on in the third-floor windows of the Sirjean apartment. To get a better angle on the past, they crossed to a fenced-in park in the median. It was the hour for dog walking, and a group of old men were attempting a last game of *boules* in the near darkness. It was the height of lilac season; the scent overpowered all sound except the tinkle of leashes and the thunk of the balls in the dirt. The men focused on the light until Tom's eyes began to blur, but no spectral silhouettes rippled across the sheers.

Elliott broke their silence. "They're glued to their variety shows. One wonders if they still take in Sweet Briar *bébés*. I worry that Bruce Teakel and I might have killed the franchise."

"Do you know what happened to Bruce?" asked Tom.

"He's teaching in Singapore. Jesus remains satisfied with him."

"Elliott was a hilarious correspondent," Tom said to Galt.

"Misery is the wellspring of comedy," said Elliott. "Not that you wrote me back."

"I was too afraid to. You were so *out*."

Elliott gestured to the corner opposite. "I bought my aerogrammes at the *tabac* right there. They knew me. I was the pizza-faced Huck Finn."

"You might pay the Sirjeans a visit," said Tom, hoping to press into his cousin some of the cheer he felt to be standing at this end of history.

Elliott shook his head.

"I don't mean tonight. If you want, I'll go with."

"They wouldn't recognize me. *Mes décombres*, that is."

Tom looked to Galt. "His ruins," said Galt.

"I also killed their son."

"You can't know that, Elliott," said Galt sharply.

"He's dead, I do know that." Elliott turned to Tom. "Jean-Christophe died in '89, on the twelfth of March, at the age of thirty-six. He left behind a son and a daughter. They might be up there with their grandparents right now, living in my old room. Also infected."

"Exact routes of infection are impossible to trace," said Tom, wishing he believed it.

Galt cleared his throat. "Elliott. Darling . . ."

Elliott struggled briefly against the arm Galt had put around his shoulders. "Yes, sister songbird?"

"Where are your tigers?"

"Sid and Nancy? Nancy and Sluggo?"

Galt said to Tom that Elliott needed to carry a tiger for peace and carry a tiger for forgiveness. The high lamas in ages past would meditate for hours on tiger skins to symbolize their conquest of fear and desire. The Elliott of yore would have hooted with laughter. Late-stage Elliott pulled from his pants pocket a pair of pink school erasers with cat faces stamped on them.

"Peace and forgiveness are the two tigers of my apocalypse."

Out of his depth, Tom wondered aloud about the impermanence of an eraser and got two different responses. Elliott said that Van Cleef & Arpels didn't make affordable portable tigers. Galt, stopping a taxi, said that impermanence was the whole point.

Elliott was so spindly now, there was plenty of room in the Murphy bed. He went right to sleep, swimming in a ribbed gray singlet that buttoned from scrotum to sternum. There were no lesions on his body, a relief to Tom, but the hair on his shoulders, like patches of lichen—when had that happened? Once upon a time Elliott would have lasered, tweezed, or blow-torched that away.

As Tom drifted off, he listened to the soft bubble of his cousin's breathing and thought about Galt's tigers. They kept turning into panthers with orange neon eyes, like the light that sat on top of the television set when he was a boy, put there, Alphonse used to say, to prevent boob tube blindness. It was a vacated superstition, like his grandmother Amelio's habit of taking out her bobby pins in a thunderstorm for fear of being struck by lightning. The panthers were carrying the cousins, though, not the other way around. He and Elliott were riding them out of a jungle, sidesaddle, on blinking mirrored cushions, arguing about who had which. Tom reached to look for a name tag on his big cat, but its sleek black neck was bare.

Thursday was reserved for the Left Bank leg of the Biddler Trail of Tears. It was the province of Gérard Dupont, the *dragueur* who had given Elliott more than the clap in 1981. He had perished in the first great wave, before the virus was identified. Elliott kept a copy of his obituary too, and although he might not have courage enough to renew an acquaintance with the Sirjeans, it was somehow no problem for him to buzz the bell to Gérard's old lair off the Rue Dauphine.

A sallow woman, whose ears divided the strings of her stick-straight hair, answered the door, a violin bow in her hand. She backed up at the sight of Elliott. Without French, Tom couldn't follow their conversation, but Elliott had her laughing straightaway, then she invited them in.

"Tom, this is Isabelle. Isabelle, voilà mon cousin Thomas."

They shook hands. Tom held his smile as preemptive apology for anything that might go awry in their visit.

A music stand was the centerpiece to the tiny room, which was half the size of Elliott's studio. "Gérard lived *here?*"

"No," said Elliott. "This was for writing and fucking." Elliott addressed each corner of the room. "The desk. The chair. The bed. The sink." Then, to a door: "The toilet." He repeated it all in French for Isabelle, then asked her a question, which she answered with another giggle.

"She cooks with a hot plate," said Elliott.

That was a fat strike two for Tom. Mention of a hot plate, plus the ironing board set against the wall—presumably Isabelle pressed that black skirt hanging from the picture rail for performances—took him to a discard from his own past, to another tiny bed-sit stiff with sex and history, with running shoes strung out the window from a cup hook. Tom didn't know whether Owen Teeter, the ESL teacher who had liked him too much for his own good, was alive or dead.

It was funny how, at thirty-two, Tom had had as many sexual contacts as Elliott had T-cells. Eleven. He had not always been safe. Owen's friend Jay Strickert, whom Tom had perversely slept with a few times that same summer of '85, had died of lymphoma. Jay was dead and Owen was missing, but Tom—and here was the shaming, medieval fact of him—wouldn't get tested. He preferred to live believing he had it, believing he deserved it, believing he might have infected Owen; but he also believed that believing this worst was what kept him clean. His life in Colorado was a celibate clock watch, and his history, eleven beads to worry in an abacus; here, in the locus of his cousin's infection, the beads took to the air and became a vortex of atoms spinning off orbit and pinging the walls.

It was getting hard for Tom to breathe. He told Elliott the pollen count was murder, so they left Isabelle's chamber with a promise to attend her next concert. Fresh air and street life helped him recover from the pressure of his oppositional superstitions. Owen, he convinced himself, as he had a thousand times before, had gone to the Middle East to teach English for princely sums, and was happily partnered with someone who appreciated him.

Elliott needed a prescription refill, so their next stop was the same clinic on the Rue d'Assas where he'd been diagnosed with gonorrhea eleven years before. Elliott greeted the receptionist like an old friend. Posters about le sida had pushed the lesser STDs into a far corner of the waiting room, which was crowded with wasting men and women of all ages and colors. They found seats under a gold-framed lithograph of Louis Pasteur, whose old eyes had seen it all and missed nothing.

Tom fetched Elliott some water and watched the shuttle of his Adam's apple caught in the straw of his shrunken neck.

"I'm glad you're here," said Elliott, wiping his mouth. "I promise you'll have sightseeing time tomorrow."

"France isn't going away," said Tom. "I'm here for you."

"I couldn't have managed going to Gérard's walk-up without you."

"You could have taken Galt."

"No. I wanted somebody with me who knew the old me."

"Is that why I'm going to the wedding?"

"Partly," said Elliott with a smile. "Galt's not attractive enough to be my date."

Tom was shocked. "I'm your cousin, not your date."

"You know that, and I know that," said Elliott. "But we look nothing alike."

"So my title is . . . ?"

Elliott bent the paper cone between his fingers. "Intimate what-have-you," he said airily.

Tom stood to help steer a patient into his seat, an action that put room between his anger and Elliott's preposterous plan.

"I wouldn't have come if I thought I'd be posing as your boyfriend," he said. "That is too fucked up."

"Lover. Long-term companion."

"It's a bad movie. I won't do it."

Elliott gave Tom the crumpled cup, then drew from the inside pocket of his blazer three sheets torn from magazines. He unfolded them and held them out.

They were Van Cleef & Arpels ads. All featured a ravishing woman with porcelain skin and heavy-lidded, oversized green eyes. Her hair and her jewels differed in every pose, but the bemused smolder of her expression was constant. Most appealing was a shot of her head framed by the crook of an upstretched arm. How many secrets might those bedroom eyes conceal, and how many bracelets had they sold?

"With a face like that, who needs hands?" murmured Tom.

"Exactement, mon cousin."

"Would it help if you rubbed out her teeth and eyes with a tiger eraser?"

"Funny," said Elliott. "But bad karma."

"Those have to be colored contact lenses."

"We'll see."

"*You'll* see. I'm not going under false pretenses."

Elliott took out exhibit B, a half strip of photo-booth photos Tom had seen years before. He held them closer to the glass-brick window. Elliott and Patrick, spring of their senior year, the daisies drooping in their hair plucked on a walk downhill to the Ithaca Commons. Walking just to walk, love past compass, rapt, unsundered, unguarded, April.

"Patrick picked those flowers," said Elliott. "It was a very rich hour. Maybe my richest hour of all."

Tom understood that Elliott didn't want Patrick to think he was dying alone. For all concerned he hoped that the other two photos in the strip were also held in safety somewhere, maybe zipped into the waterproof compartment of a Dopp kit in Neuilly-sur-Seine. Tom also understood that it didn't have to be Patrick in the photos. Like a deathbed appeal, there just needed to be *a* photo, proof of Elliott's loving and having been loved in return.

What Tom didn't understand was whether love was the only thing that mattered in the end, really. If so, he was in trouble. No images like that existed of him, and the way things were going, he thought, none ever would. He crouched down to place the photos in Elliott's palm. He cupped both of his cousin's knees and said that he would go to the wedding if Elliott came back to America with him. He'd pay for his flight, set him up with Tracy, or near Tracy, or wherever. They both wanted him back in the States.

Elliott refolded the ads with the care once taken with identity papers at the East German border. "That's your best offer?"

"For today," replied Tom.

"Very Lambert Strether," drawled Elliott. Tom shrugged. It was always his job to be a beat behind, a year late, a continent away. "Lambert Strether is the unpersuasive and unlikely hero of *The Ambassadors*, Henry James's penultimate novel. Sent to Paris to rescue his nephew Chad from a wicked woman. In my case, at least according to my mother, Paris is the wicked woman . . ."

Tom didn't want to know how the book turned out. To the end of his own days, he'd confuse Lambert Strether with Louis Pasteur, who was the first person he saw when Elliott's number was called and they got up to claim his prescription at the reception desk.

With the subject now on the table, they made a game of it on Friday. For every reason Tom thought Elliott should come back—the Mall of America was opening in August—Elliott would counter with something like raw milk camembert. After lunch, with rabbit *rillettes* and *blanquette de veau* trumping the Grand Canyon and the Costume Institute at the Met, they went to the Marais. The Place des Vosges, Tom had to agree, clearly bested every Broadway musical since *Sweeney Todd*. The Place des Vosges was the most glorious spot he had ever seen.

But weren't there stateside discoveries still to be made? Elliott could trade off between Denver, with Tom, and Norfolk, where Tracy owned hair salons and bred Dobermans. He could get into the new trials and ACT-UP all he liked on the Washington Mall, during an election year no less. They could solve the mystery of the Amelio-Biddler family rift. Tom had always fantasized that if Elliott met his aunt Janet for even five minutes, he'd be able to charm her into spilling everything.

As they strolled the quarter, Elliott allowed Tom these humorous hopes, while he kept tapping the windows of his past: the bakery with the best meringues, the men's store with the most advanced undergarments, the dive bar where Jean-Christophe Sirjean had followed him into the stall. His favorite photo booth on the Rue de Turenne had vanished, but the kitchen store where he'd once bought a hot-chocolate bowl for his mother was still doing a good business. And what of *his* mother, Tom wanted to know. Didn't he want to spend more time with her?

"I lost them," replied Elliott, pausing in front of a fruit stall. "By the time I got here junior year, I'd lost both Henry and Ruth. I know those aerogrammes made me out to be miserable, Tom, but Paris was a peak time. Once things started to look terminal, I decided I wanted to return and gutter out here like a Zola heroine, stinking under a staircase like Gervaise Coupeau in *L'Assommoir,* or like her daughter Nana, my face a pestilent Jell-O of blood and pus on a pillow, while the crowds below scream, 'To Berlin! To Berlin!'" He laughed. "Now, that's what's called using your major. My nineteenth-century novel prof would be impressed."

Elliott talked Tom into a mocha *religieuse*—the list of pastries he had to sample before he flew home on Monday grew hourly—then took him into a *brocante*, the kind of tatty jumble shop that was disappearing in the rapidly gentrifying Marais.

"What happened here?"

"Nothing," said Elliott, missing Tom's dig.

Elliott greeted the *patronne* and made her smile with some observation. By now Tom had figured out that Elliott had to disarm strangers with his wit before they had a chance to shut the door to contagion.

"Have you gotten a wedding present?"

"I have a year, technically. Or not," he added, rolling his eyes. "No, I thought it was time you got serious about souvenirs."

Tom didn't have his cousin's eye for fine things. He had supposed he'd get his parents a pricey scotch and a Chanel something in duty-free. "You were supposed to be the souvenir," he said.

They gravitated to what dealers call "smalls," the items generally heaped in glass cases under or near the payment counter. What drew Tom to a one-button linen purse about the size of a cigarette pack was the red farmhouse embroidered on its front. The structure wasn't particularly French; it looked more like a one-room school in New England, the kind of thing stitched on a colonial sampler, which was about as old as America got. The ancient silk knots on the inside of the purse remained a brilliant red and gold and black, while the walls and windows and the trapezoidal roof outside had faded to pink and straw and gray. It smelled of ancient sachets.

"What do you think?"

"I like it," said Elliott. "Madame says it's from the 1840s."

But Tom balked at the price and settled instead on a pair of identical cast-iron men, maybe two inches tall, wearing business suits and briefcases, the kind of figure who, judging from their fellow citizens in the wooden box—ice skaters and nurses and chefs and policemen and farmers—had originally populated a train set village.

Elliott was less than enthusiastic. "These you could buy back home."

"Don't you see," said Tom. "They're us. In 1985."

"We didn't match."

"No, but we both wore suits."

"We didn't wear hats."

"But still," said Tom, his voice almost a plea, "we had briefcases. I carried your father's briefcase, remember?" He needed Elliott to indicate in some way that their five months in New York together was another peak time.

"Do you have it still?" Elliott's tone was acid.

Elliott said he needed to rest up for the wedding, so that night the cousins took a break from each other. Tom knew that people facing mortality weren't overly invested in the tribulations of the living, but as Galt Hiler drew him out through dinner, and hours of walking, and pausing in the middle of what seemed like every bridge that spanned the Seine, he realized he was hurt that Elliott hadn't asked him any genuine questions. Whether Tom would answer them was beside the point. He wanted to be asked.

Galt asked and listened, and Tom asked back. They swapped stories about growing up gay and working class. Unlike the Amelios, who had put no expectations on Tom, the Hilers looked to the miracle of Galt's voice as revenue potential. In his late twenties, after nearly going insane trying to work the levers of a classical music career in Manhattan, Galt had discovered Buddhism and walked away from money and ego striving by following a guru/lover to Paris. When that ended, he'd stayed and found the Opéra chorus job. It was a nice paycheck, but his idea of earthly paradise was losing himself in a Bach cantata in the small church choir where he sang on Sundays. Singing and helping people like Elliott take action in the face of death had become his purpose.

The distractions of Paris, the indisputable Frenchness of the people seated in cafés, and the buskers and the glide of the bateaux-mouches made it easier for Tom to unburden himself of everything that had gone wrong, or was still wrong. He began with his embittered mother and his embarrassing father, whom he did love, then went on to Boyd McIlhenny and the Purdue closet, the missing Owen Teeter, the dead Jay Strickert, the boredom of his work, his fear of getting tested, the guilt that drove him to offer money and time to the afflicted, but not, like Galt, his physical presence, the guilt he'd feel with the passing of his cousin, whose recklessness had always terrified him, the lack of love and purpose and direction and abandon in his life, everything.

Finally Tom was talked out, and thirsty, and had no idea where they were, except on a bench facing the river.

"What are those?" he asked, pointing across the water to a series of great iron rings set into the stones of the retaining walls. To him they looked like the door-knockers to heaven.

"They use those to tie river barges to the docks."

"I could have guessed that. I'm a little drunk," said Tom. Then as if to prove the statement, he said that Galt would make a great monk. He had the build and the bald and a lot more, too.

Galt gave one of his wonderful, rumbling laughs. "Here's what I think we should do, Tom."

"Now?"

"No, it's too late for that tonight."

"Oh." Tom was a little disappointed. "What?"

Galt laid Tom's left arm across his stomach. "You should get tested, and I should be the one to draw your blood."

"Really? You?"

"I can do it so softly you won't even feel it."

Galt slowly drew his fingers from the crook of the elbow down to the wrist and complimented Tom on his veins. That Tom should be so pleased to hear of their quality was testament to the calvados and to Galt's inability to speak with a forked tongue.

"I pick this one," said Galt, brushing skin with his thumb.

"I wouldn't feel it?"

"No," said Galt, smiling up at Tom. "You'd only feel me."

Tom felt a lot of things just then, starting with the cobblestones pushing back against the sole of his loafer. They might have kissed, but Tom retreated at the last second. Instead, he reached his other hand around to pet the wiry whiskers on top of Galt's right ear.

"I don't shave them," said Galt. "They're a tribute to my grandfather."

Tom regretted his hesitation all the way home, but was too self-conscious to attempt rerouting things with words. On their good-bye hug at the north end of the Pont Marie, however, his crotch spoke for him—it lunged forward, as if following a dotted line into Galt's center.

Elliott was dozing in the chair. A glass with the green dregs of a spirulina shake was set beside him on the floor. Air from a fan was whiffling his chest hair and the pages of a book in his lap. Tom picked up the glass and rinsed it in the sink. He took two aspirin to fend off hangover. Coming back for the book, he saw that Elliott had woken up. In his palm was the embroidered purse from the bric-à-brac shop.

"You went back for it?"

"The shop was on my way. You can put your little businessmen in it. Give them a safe home."

"On your way to what? You were supposed to rest up."

Elliott smirked. "On the way to tea dance."

"*Tea dance?* Where?"

Tom was incredulous that Elliott would still haunt the bars. In America the moribund would sooner run amok in the streets than face the censure of their healthy brothers. "You're impossible."

"No. I am a woman of Paris, and like any woman of Paris, nineteen to ninety, I wish to be thought of as still in the game. And so, I see, do you."

Tom wasn't sure what Elliott meant by that, then remembered the pressure of Galt's fingers on his wrist.

The phone rang early, ahead of the alarm. Tom heard voices, then silence. He cocked open an eye. Elliott was glaring down at him.

"You haven't gotten tested? What is that about?"

Tom groaned. "Galt wasn't supposed to tell you that."

"Of course he is. We've been triangulating this whole trip."

"Well, guess what? Galt told me you were blind in one eye. Why didn't you tell me that?"

"Don't change the subject. Why haven't you gotten tested?"

Tom, not up to a fight, said to the depression in Elliott's pillow that it was easier to proceed feeling as if he were positive.

"You call *celibacy* proceeding? This is 1992, you idiot. Find the fuck out. They're making new discoveries every other month."

"What if I can't shake the feeling that I deserve to have it?"

Elliott kicked Tom in the side. "Shame and science are different disciplines. Look at me."

Tom turned. Elliott, backlit in the morning sun, was a talking clothespin.

"Who raised you, Tom? *No one* deserves to have it. Do you think I deserve to have it?"

"No," Tom groaned again. "I don't." He hopped up and ducked under the wooden truss to get to the bathroom.

Elliott, giving him no peace through the closed door, raised his voice. "I know when you're lying. No one deserves to have it, not even me. Why did you leave New York that summer?"

"Can we not have this conversation while I'm pissing?"

"You're not pissing."

Tom wasn't, but he had to, which required getting rid of his morning erection. He kneeled on the floor, pressed his penis against the cold toilet bowl, and told Elliott that he had hated his publishing job, that his sublet was ending, and that there was no future for him in New York.

"Every future there is, is right there in New York. And don't hand me that about your sublet. You left a month ahead of time. You went AWOL. For a while I thought maybe some sugar daddy had flown you down to Rio. Or Morocco."

No chance of that, thought Tom. He stood up and began talking over his stream. "There was no future that matched where I thought I needed to be."

When he emerged from the toilet, Elliott served him coffee and mourned that horse pisses like Tom's were another thing of the past. He lived a constant dribble. The alarm rang. Tom switched it off and sat back on the bed, hoping the discussion was over, but Elliott started the next round.

"You don't plan your future at that age. You let it happen."

Tom scoffed at that; one fable Alphonse had dinged into his children was the Grasshopper and the Ant. "Do you like the future that happened to you? Checking out fifty years ahead of time?"

"No one could plan for the plague."

"But you could have planned against it! You ignored the signs, the warnings, did whatever you wanted, Elliott, you did whoever you wanted, consequences be damned." Tom took a sip of coffee, felt its heat sink to his stomach.

"And now I'm paying the price, right? You can say it, Tom. Shame has no way in with me now, and you—tu seras le cousin dont le cousin est mort."

"I don't speak French."

"You'll be the cousin whose cousin has died."

Elliott had used the word at last. Afraid he might cry, Tom balled the hem of his T-shirt into his eyes, but found he was furious instead.

"I didn't leave you in New York," he shouted into his hands. "It was your town. You were cock of the walk. You and your fast behind didn't need me there."

"You left in July, midweek, for Christ's sake, who does that? Without any warning or provocation. You took off with my father's briefcase and left me with tickets for Arms and the Man! I called your office, and they said you'd given your notice. Now dry it up—"

"I'm not crying, asshole," said Tom.

"—and tell me what the fuck happened to you."

Elliott sat on the bed, directly across from Tom, pulled the T-shirt away from his face, and forced him to hold his gaze. Tom took in the paper skin, the lost gum tissue, the divots torn from his cheeks and temples, the cracked lips, the sunken eyes, one glassy and useless, the extra-long eyelashes, the straw hair, the short, sour breaths.

Tom told Elliott about Owen and Jay: the silver pattern, the Rouault painting, the Jersey weekend, the terrifying ease of just doing someone in the middle of a plague. He had fled New York because he didn't want the power of sex to turn him into a heedless slut eyeing the goods of strangers at a trough. The potential had always been there; acting on it had scared him too much. He decided to leave before he fell down Elliott's rabbit hole.

Tom had to do something to relieve the misery in his guts, something heedless, as it turned out. He went for more coffee and cracked his head full force against the truss. He saw stars—it does happen—and hit the floor with cartoon force.

Elliott brought him to with a bag of ice and plenty to say.

"Well, girleen," he said. "Look where it got you. KO'd by caution. You need some movement. Get tested. Let Galt draw your blood tomorrow, then tear his clothes off and fuck him in the examining room. Live to tell. Live to tell me about it. I'll bet he's got a beer can down there. I've always wanted to know."

"Tell me something I don't know."

"Did it never occur to you that that's why I'm still here? Fuck peace and forgiveness, I carry a tiger for curiosity. I plan to study every last second of that wedding and dine out on it until it's all over. I'd write you a letter about it, Tom, except you are going to be watching for what my glaucous left eye misses and we are going to compare notes later, and—"

Elliott stopped, a horrified expression on his face.

"What is it? What's wrong?"

"Fuck me, I sound like Auntie Mame. You should run from any man who says it's his favorite movie. It's labored, labored beyond all redress."

"I promise."

"Okay, then. Now get up and walk, Lazarus. You've really learned how."

A tailor had taken in Elliott's finest suit, a double-breasted gift from Tennessee Williams's last agent. (Obituary on file.) They iced Tom's bruise some more, tried concealer and changing the part in his hair, to little avail, then cuff-linked and pocket-squared and lint-brushed each other into presentability. They shared the cat erasers and the metal men. Their taxi started to honk, but Elliott was hesitating about whether to bring along a silver-topped cane.

"You're going to need the cane," said Tom. "To hack your way through the mob at Berthillon."

"Not to mention Nicole Sylvie Braithwaite-Dulter. You take the cane."

"I don't need a cane."

"Take the cane. It goes with your pocket square."

"Handkerchief."

"*Mouchoir.*"

"*Taschentuch.*"

"Snot rag."

"Blowrag."

"Cum catcher . . ."

They might have gone all the way down the stone stairs like this, but as they neared the second landing, Tom stopped Elliott with a gentle pull on his linen collar, so loose around his neck.

Elliott startled. "Did I forget something?"

"No."

"Did you?"

"No," said Tom. His other hand tightened its grip on the stair rope. "I want you to promise me that when it's really getting to be . . . all over, that you give me time to come back. And help see you off."

Elliott's neck rose with his breath and met Tom's fingers.

"To Berlin," he assented. "To Berlin."

The French have a saying, "*C'est le samedi; les cons se marient.*" It refers to the street charivari expected at village weddings. Roughly translated it means "Idiots get married on Saturday." Neuilly-sur-Seine is the sort of French village, however, where money buys quiet and the occasional string quartet for three hundred guests. In a beautiful private garden, with an ornamental pond and topiaries to rival those he'd sat under in the Place des Vosges, Tom played the part of Elliott's stoically-supportive-yet-ever-hopeful butch lover. More than a few Americans—certainly no Brit or Frenchman would reference the obvious—mentioned their bravery.

Salvers of *kirs royals* enlivened the receiving line. When they reached the happy couple, Elliott rather rushed through Patrick in order to spin a cloud of amusing French with the bride. This left the groom, who, Tom noticed with satisfaction, no longer had hair enough to tuck a daisy in, to say to him that he was glad, mighty glad, that Elliott had a special friend.

There were many potential replies, all forked, but in homage to Galt, Tom paused, then blew out his breath and pressed the heels of his hands into his sternum. If this was the start of his own Buddhist practice, it felt good.

"You lucked out, Patrick," was what he said.

Then it was time to eat. A waiter pointed them to their table, which was just around the pond, in front of a large willow tree. Elliott, needing to lead, shrugged Tom's hand off his elbow. Tom squinted into the sunlight and saw not a tree, but a brown canvas tepee with a circle of tomahawks around its middle. He looked down and saw not lilies floating in a pond, but plastic squirt guns bobbing in a wading pool.

He looked ahead at Elliott, and the chips really fell. Thomas Amelio had not read *The Ambassadors*, and might never, but the sorceries of Paris, and the cranky valor of his impossible, impermanent cousin, and a bruise from an unyielding truss, and the apéritif bubbles, and the luxury of light shining through the poplars and people in the Braithwaite garden, combusted all at once into a recollection that would do Lambert Strether proud, and would, for once, give Tom the upper hand and—maybe just this once—the final word.

Tom reached and took his cousin's elbow again. "You have seen my penis," he said.

Elliott stopped. "What?"

"You have seen my penis. And I've seen yours. I've touched your penis, in fact."

Hungrier guests began stepping around them, off the flagstones, the women careful of their heels in the grass.

"Shush, Tom. We are at a *wedding*."

"In fact, yours was the first penis I ever touched that wasn't my own."

"Will you behave?"

"And you touched mine."

Elliott turned around. He took off his sunglasses. "You're drunk. Now stop it."

He was not amused, but Tom was giddy with the memory. "You and I met one time before your father's funeral. We were just kids, little boys. It was summer, because our tepee was up in the backyard. Your parents had dropped you all off at our house in Kansas and gone somewhere for the weekend. The tepee, Elliott, remember the tepee?"

Elliott nearly clipped a bridesmaid with the sudden flail of his arm.

"We'd been in the kiddie pool," Tom continued, "then we had Popsicles. Your tongue was orange. Mine was purple."

"We were wearing bathing trunks, and you said, 'Let's go inside the tepee.'"

"It was boiling in there, a thousand degrees."

"Our suits were wet, and you said—"

"No, *you* said—"

"No, Tom, you said—out of the blue—"

"Nothing is ever out of the blue," crowed Tom, and it was true. "And you said—"

And then, either from surprise, or to stop his ears, Elliott pitched into the pond. Had he lost control of the cane and stumbled, or did he dive? Some of the flagstones were uneven, and others were mossy. Tom followed. To those left on shore, his reaction looked closer to a leap.

ACKNOWLEDGMENTS

Baltimore is a fine village for writers. In the years when I couldn't get arrested in the third person, I was fortunate to have Jane Delury, Kathy Flann, Christine Grillo, and Jean McGarry on hand to stiffen the spines of my wobbly narrators. Also in the vicinity are the inspiring, gregarious, and equally necessary Elizabeth Hazen, Laura Wexler, Betsy Boyd, Elizabeth Dahl, John Rowell, Michael Downs, Ron Tanner, Geoffrey Becker, David Bergman, Mary Jo Salter, Marion Winik, and Jessica Anya Blau.

I'm grateful to the readers and editors who pulled my stories from the slush and then improved them with their careful attentions: Thomas Long, Wesley Gibson, Charles Flowers, Mark Drew, Peter Stitt, Richard Labonte, David Leavitt, Magdalen Powers, Kristofer Whited, Sophie Beck, William Johnson, Jason Lee Brown, the late Jay Prefontaine, Carolyn Kuebler, and Stephen Donadio.

Thanks to Center Stage, for many years my host organism and copy center, the Maryland State Arts Council, the Ucross Foundation, and to life- and book-sustainers Chuck Graham, Janet Horn, Michael Checknoff, Ellen Bintz Meuch, David Grossbach, Allen Kuharski, Merrill Feitell, Joe Lazzaro, Michael Brady, Sanford Sylvan, Kathy Shapiro, and David Nolta.

Thanks as well to Raphael Kadushin, Don Weise, Gina Frangello, and my agent, Katherine Fausset, who were early advocates for linking the stories.

I am deeply indebted to Mike Levine and his entire team at Northwestern University Press for taking on the collection, and for taking such profound care with it.

I started my first story in 2001 during a playwriting residency at the MacDowell Colony. Much of this book was begun or worked over or finished during subsequent stays. I can think of no safer spot to try something new than a studio in those woods.